PRAISE FOR

SENATOR'S SON

"Luke Larson has provided an outstanding—if thinly-veiled—personal account of the decisive event in the successful turnaround for U.S. forces in Iraq, the Sunni Awakening. He also provides an unflinching and unromanticized account of the costs paid by the junior Marines and Soldiers who made that turnaround possible often only by their sheer force of will." – Major Adam Ake, Iraq War veteran, former Rhodes Scholar

"As a future officer I will ensure every man under my charge reads this book before crossing the line of departure. Any civilian who wants to know combat should read at their own risk as this is not some Hallmark depiction!" – Sergeant Link, USMC three Iraq combat tour veteran and MECEP officer candidate

"Larson's novel rings with the gritty street cred of a man whose scenes and prose have been grounded by the investment of his own blood and sweat. The first authentic work of fiction to emerge from the cauldron of the Iraq war." –David J. Danelo, author of *Blood Stripes* and *The Border*

"Slashing… an unsurpassed compelling narrative thread that pulls you in close to a vital subject rarely examined in a war novel." – Jeff Buck, Chairman Eternal Valor Foundation

"An epic novel that screams of truth. You know the truth lies deep in this story because Larson shows not only the heroics but also highlights the blunders." – Sergeant Yeast, USMC two Iraq combat tour veteran

"Larson, a Marine combat veteran, vividly captures the challenges facing our men and women in uniform today. Although fiction, it is very evident the story is full of truths learned the hard way through real life tragic sacrifices. The lessons are surprising paradoxes: The more you protect yourself with firepower the less secure you become. If you kill an insurgent or create collateral damage the action could end up creating 50 more insurgents. After reading Senator's Son I could not shake the thought that sometimes not shooting is the best action." – Rick Smith, CEO and founder TASER International

SENATOR'S SON

AN IRAQ WAR NOVEL

LUKE S LARSON

K.E., INC.
Phoenix

SENATOR'S SON

Printed in the United States of America
K.E., INC.
Phoenix, Arizona
Edited by Judy Fraker

Library of Congress Cataloguing-in-Publication Data
Larson, Luke S
Senator's Son: An Iraq War Novel/Luke S Larson.– 1st ed.

p. cm.

ISBN: 0615353797
EAN-13: 9780615353791

Cover Photo courtesy Major Rory B Quinn, USMC
Cover Design and Artwork by Sarah Decker– Forks, Washington

WWW.LUKESLARSON.COM

This book is dedicated to-

Shaun Blue
First Lieutenant
United States Marine Corps
December 28, 1981
April 16, 2007

and to-

James Cathey Jr.

Who will never know his father-

James Cathey Sr.
Second Lieutenant
United States Marine Corps
October 8, 1980
August 21, 2005

FOREWORD

Sitting on a couch after returning from my first tour in Ramadi, Iraq, as a Marine Corps infantry officer, I was angry and confused. How could the finest military force the world has ever seen be struggling in Iraq? We certainly were not losing in 2005 2006, but I personally did not return home to the states with the sense of accomplishment that we had all wished for. It was not the death of my comrades that frustrated me; it was the inability for me to rationalize what their sacrifices had produced. It was on this couch that I can remember a change occurring within me. Over and over in my head I repeated to myself, "There must be a better way." My experience overseas gave me the knowledge to determine which tactics could be practicably applied and which were only theoretical frameworks, but it was the months away from combat which afforded me the perspective to understand that if we as a military were to win this war, we had to change everything. To reach an acceptable outcome in Iraq I believed, as I still do, that we had to realize that the Iraqi people came first and that the destruction of our common enemy was not the priority. Our weapons were a tool, but they were not the answer to the complex situation that remained abroad.

That was my personal transformation, but all across the military there was a general understanding that there had to be strategic, operational and tactical shifts. There is a false perception among many that change can simply be implemented with a swift order from a superior. Those who have served know that this belief couldn't be further from the truth. These changes place our men and women serving in uniform in a dangerous situation. A far more dangerous situation than continuing on with the status quo ever would. To be successful in counter insurgency operations, the outside force and the local population must be one, in almost every sense of the word. Military forces can no longer shield themselves in bases and armored vehicles. It is

I

the personal touch of a hand shake and the trust garnered by looking another in the eye that simply cannot be faked. These are the lessons that were learned by Luke and others in Iraq. These are the lessons which forced Luke to write this novel. I use the word "forced" purposefully, because he did not have an option. The blood that remains on both our hands will never wash off. The best we could do is to ensure that other leaders who faced similar complexities learned these lessons without wasting lives.

This novel is about a fight within the military that continues to rage to this day. It is a piece that every young officer and new non-commissioned officer must read as they will surely find themselves in a similar predicament, placed in a world where the easiest action is to pull the trigger. Yet that action seldom leads to the outcome desired. Combat today is significantly more complex as the goal of battle is to win the support of those caught in the middle. The novel was a medium that allowed Luke to best portray the chaos that surrounded us during our time in the Corps, but much of it is fact. For the casual reader, you will be afforded a gripping story undoubtedly. This story is written for the young man or woman deciding how he or she will lead. It is written to avoid unnecessary loss. We had to learn the hard way, but I hope this novel will make your transformation into an effective warrior that much easier.

Mauro Mujica
Washington D.C. 2009

ACT I- Denial

ACT II- Learning Curve

ACT III- Understanding

ACT IV- Execution

Note: Glossary of Marine & Iraqi terms appended at the end of the book

ACT I
DENIAL

The real war will never get in the books. — *Walt Whitman*

Current Date: September 21, 2047

The United States, after enjoying decades of naval dominance, was visibly challenged by China in the face of the world. Over the last forty years the Asian Empire had invested billions into their submarine force and their underwater fleet now secured the South China Sea in the Pacific. Their control of the sea had become very clear when a U.S. Navy Carrier Strike Group sailed through the Straits of Malacca.

It was common for the U.S. Navy to patrol the main shipping channel between the Indian Ocean and the Pacific Ocean. This strip of water remained one of the most economically important shipping lanes in the world. During the Carrier Strike Group's exercise, a Chinese Submarine snuck into the middle of the formation unannounced and surfaced, surprising the ships. Three other Chinese Submarines surfaced surrounding one of the U.S. Navy ships. The message was clear. Our technology was good— theirs was better.

The incident in itself would be alarming but not war worthy. The issue was further complicated by Malaysia's creeping occupation into the small country of Brunei. The countries of Malaysia, Indonesia and Brunei all shared the world's third largest island, Borneo, located in the South China Sea.

Off the coast of Borneo in the Spratly Islands, Malaysia claimed stake to a recently found oil reserve that lay within Brunei's sovereignty. Brunei resisted the claim and Malaysia responded by invading their neighbor's country under the protection of their Asian big brother.

The Senate would vote in a few days on a joint resolution that could launch the U.S. into a major military action that would either secure peace or be the igniter of the next world war. The House was overwhelmingly in support of the President's joint resolution and the Senate favored it but would need the only undecided senator's vote to secure the majority needed. In Washington, all were experts and the man whose state only accounted for nine electoral votes now became the focus.

When thinking about the consequences, the senator continually thought of what had been asked of his generation. He recalled the last time when a decision that he had made carried such weight. It had been forty years ago in the Al Anbar Province of Iraq as a green lieutenant on the streets of Ramadi.

1

1

Sweat poured down John Magruder's forehead. He squinted trying to see through his protective glasses. The lenses fogged up from the heat of his sweat. He took off the glasses and wiped them with a handkerchief he kept tucked in his gear. *Why do I have to wear these damn glasses?*

His helmet pressed down on his head trapping the heat. Inside the humvee it hovered around 120 degrees and it was hotter inside John's gear. He tilted the helmet up and put his glasses back on. The vehicle drove west down Route Michigan, the main road in Ramadi.

The mobile section approached checkpoint 295, notorious for improvised explosive devices, and he braced himself for impact. John took a deep breath and held it in as the vehicles rolled through the checkpoint.

He winced in anticipation. Nothing happened. He continued to hold his breath and slowly turned to look out the window. *Holy shit, no explosion!* His muscles slowly relaxed.

"What do you know?" said John to the driver, "Today might be a good day after all."

The convoy rolled another 150 meters.

BOOM!

His reflexes jumped as he instinctively tightened his grip on the door handle. Dust and debris rained onto the windshield from the explosion. From his previous IED encounters he knew by the blast that the bomb failed to cause damage to his vehicle. *Barely missed it!* The explosions still startled him, they always did, and his mind ran through the endless possibilities that could occur in the explosion's aftermath.

"Sir, that IED almost hit us!" yelled the driver.

"What about the other vehicles?"

The radio squawked that the other three humvees in the mobile section remained undamaged. The lieutenant relayed the report to the command post and breathed a sigh of relief.

After their near miss, the mobile section pulled into the Snake Pit. The heavily fortified Marine firm base was John's surrogate home.

When all of his vehicles were inside the base and accounted for, John stepped out of his humvee. The Marine lieutenant's twenty-three year old face looked fatigued. Permanent bags had appeared under his eyes since his arrival to Iraq. Despite his tired demeanor, the lieutenant carried himself like a Marine officer— his stance suggested a constant readiness.

John sighed and commenced his post patrol ritual. He removed his helmet and clipped it on his flak jacket. He ran his fingers through his sopping wet hair and walked over to the clearing barrels. John took the magazine out of his weapon and cleared the rifle. He turned off his radio and unstrapped the throat protector that routinely scraped his neck.

The latest explosion brought John's total near miss count to fifteen. The earlier explosions inflicted severe damage to his vehicles, but his unit had yet to take a serious casualty. He prayed for his unit's safety to endure the quest. He knew— even with the help— he would have to will his platoon through the deployment's chaos. Their journey's success would rest upon his leadership.

* * *

He opened the door and heard arguing. John looked at the other two lieutenants, the three of them crammed in the tiny room.

"I reckon you wouldn't," said one lieutenant in a southern drawl.

John dropped his gear, intrigued by the conversation.

"You most certainly would!" yelled back another lieutenant, sitting across the cluttered room.

An unlit cigarette dangled out of Cash's mouth. The lieutenant's black hair contrasted against his pale blue eyes.

Cash stood five feet eight inches and barely weighed 160 pounds. The other lieutenant, Bama, looked like a linebacker and had at least a foot and 75 pounds on him.

"What are you homos talking about?" asked John.

Hearing them talk, it would sound as if Cash was the bigger of the two.

"Eleven Army bubbas burned up last week south of the river."

4

John nodded his head and looked at the southerner. Bama's bottom lip protruded from an enormous dip of smokeless chewing tobacco. The large lieutenant spit a slew of brown fluid into a styrofoam cup.

"Bama thinks if he gets hit with a fuel enhanced IED he won't go into shock before he burns alive. I disagree," explained Cash, "I think you would."

As he finished the sentence explosions rattled in the distance, shaking the small room.

"We've only been here 25 days," said Cash, "A unit normally takes half their casualties within the first 30 days..."

John shook his head. *Eleven soldiers burned alive. I know the Marines are having this same discussion right now. We need to focus, it is only a matter of time before a Marine gets killed or injured.*

He thought about the statistic. *Thirty days. The first thirty days is when a unit takes half of their casualties. We have to keep paying attention and push through these next five days. Maybe we'll make it without a single casualty.*

* * *

In the short time before they deployed, John became close friends with the other lieutenants.

A month earlier, on the morning of their deployment, John picked up Bama and drove to Cash's house.

Cash's wife, Jill, stood in the driveway with her blonde hair blowing sideways. Cash grabbed his pack and sea bag and threw them in the back of the truck. Jill walked to the door and tapped on the window.

She looked in at Bama and John.

"Be safe!" shouted Jill over the sound of the diesel engine.

"And please take care of Cash!"

Her lip quivered as she finished her sentence.

"We'll be all right hun," replied Bama.

"Cash will be taking care of us," yelled John.

Jill gave her husband one last hug and kiss. They held each other tight for the final moment as wind blew around them. He whispered something in her ear and jumped in the truck.

Cash looked out the window at his young wife waving. As they drove away, she disappeared into the night. Cash felt guilty about leaving her. The guilt was made worse by his own eagerness to deploy. The truck remained silent.

"Put some music on," said Bama.

Cash rummaged through the glove box and found a Celine Dion CD.

"What the fuck is this?"

"I took Amy to go see a Celine Dion concert in Las Vegas last weekend," said John, wincing in anticipation of the ball busting about to occur.

"We sat front row and it cost me $1,500, so I bought the CD."

"Right," said Bama as he nursed an enormous dip.

"Well we should at least listen to it I guess," joked Cash.

John fully expected one of the other lieutenants to change the CD after the song started. No one did and the song played on. As the music started to build, John burst out the words—

"I drove all ni'ght, to get to you. Is that all ri'ght I drove all night..."

Cash and Bama looked at each other and smiled. In no time the truck filled with the sound of three infantry lieutenants singing Celine Dion at the top of their lungs.

"I drove all ni'ght, to get to you. Is that all ri'ght I drove all night..."

* * *

Heath walked into the briefing room aboard the Snake Pit. The former wrestler wore his cauliflower ears with the same pride as he did his Marine Corps' high and tight haircut.

He stared at the forty Marines waiting to receive his operations order. Cash and John held their note taking gear in the front row. Any time forty men crammed in the room, the smell of sweat and Iraqi dust created an atmosphere of slight claustrophobia.

Heath looked at the map. *It is pointless to go down there with all of this ass if we do not intend to leave stay behind elements and hold the ground.* His gut told him something might happen on this mission.

He voiced his objection to higher but was told the mission must be done. Despite his reservations, the company commander decided that if higher mandated the mission then their reasoning must be justified. He intended to carry out the mission and do everything in his power to accomplish the sweep.

In the dark room, a projector displayed a glowing map of Ramadi on a white screen. Heath, in a calm but authoritative voice, started his operations order:

"Orientation— we've been here thirty days. Although we've experienced a significant amount of contact, Golf Company has not had a Marine killed or seriously injured. We are still on the steep side of the learning curve.

Situation— we are a few weeks from the elections for the national referendum of Iraq. This is big news for the country. Currently the *Sunni*s are holding out from participating in any of the political processes. We have reports that indicate the *Sunni Sheiks* realize if they do not get involved in the political process in Iraq, they will miss having any say in the government. This may be a huge tipping point for Ramadi and all of Iraq. To disrupt attacks during the referendum, we are going into the worst part of the city. We have reports that all of the dirt roads are rigged to blow with fuel enhanced IEDs. These areas have been declared black— no travel allowed off paved roads, dirt roads are a no go.

Mission— Golf Company conducts a sweeping mission in southern Ramadi in order to clear out enemy strongholds and disrupt any enemy attacks that may be in preparation phases for the elections.

Execution— Golf Mobile, John, you will take your vehicles and send in a lead element as a screen. Cash, you will conduct the dismounted portion of the sweep to phase line purple. John, remember your main goal will be to satellite around the dismounts providing a mounted screening element. The guiding feature will be big power lines. If you get into trouble go to the power lines, they all lead to a paved road.

Admin and Logistics— Gunny, ensure everyone has plenty of chow and water. Also, have an ammunition resupply plan to push ammo to the dismounts from the trucks if needed.

Command and Signal— I, the company commander, will be with Golf mobile two. Isaac, the executive officer, will roll with John in Golf mobile one.

Any questions?"

* * *

John and Cash linked up outside of their room after the brief. John looked at his watch which indi-glowed 2359. He lit a cigarette.

"So what do you think?" asked Cash.

"I don't know the boys are shook up about all of these IEDs. Sooner or later something's going to happen."

Cash inhaled the smoke and exhaled into the night.

"I think you're wrong. We are going to go down there and all of those shitheads are going to hole up. The people will see them run away and we'll accomplish our mission, easy day."

"We're moving down there with 500 Marines, soldiers, and tanks. There are probably a handful of actual enemy down there and when we roll in with a Patton force they've got to know to go to ground," said John, "We'll gain nothing."

He looked at Cash. *He doesn't understand.*

"You know what my dad told me before I left, Cash?"

"What?"

"He told me don't be in a hurry to get your Marines killed."

"Well I'd hope somebody is thinking the same thing about Golf."

Three and a half hours later, John's watch beeped and flashed 0330. He kicked Cash.

"Get up man."

"Yeah," mumbled Cash, still asleep.

"No, get the fuck up, dude, we've got a mission."

"Yeah, I'm up."

* * *

In his truck, John conducted pre-combat checks. On his headset he gave a countdown to his vehicles, "3, 2, 1, go." All of the humvees fired up simultaneously. They used the technique in order to throw off the enemy of how many vehicles were leaving the firm base.

John called all of his vehicle commanders into the center of the staging area to go over the mission one last time.

"All right gents remember if things get crazy, push to the power lines. Do you have anything for me?"

"No sir."

8

At 0521, Golf Company pushed from their protected firm base into the city to conduct the mission.

* * *

"Gents, let's use bounding overwatch," ordered Cash.

Third platoon started to move throughout the city in a methodical fashion. One squad set up an overwatch position. After hearing they were covered, the other squads moved through the ville searching houses while one squad continually remained in overwatch.

Cash climbed up on an adobe roof. He heard explosions. Black plumes of smoke rose throughout the city. Random spurts of gunfire echoed in the distance. The contact in the ville excited the lieutenant. He enjoyed the adrenaline rush.

He remembered going through training as a black and white memory. The exercises of conducting raids and patrols were physically difficult. The events required strong leaders to get through the friction of the complex events. Despite the difficulty, they lacked the excitement of the unknown, which was impossible to re-create.

This was different. The explosions were real. The thought of a catastrophic event and the consequences of life threatening situations wrapped around the lieutenant's mind. The pressure weighing on him may have caused others to fall apart, but it caused Cash to focus. His senses were more aware. His actions were more clear and forceful. This was intense. This was in color.

His first squad leader ran over to him and yelled.

"Sir, what do you think is going on?"

"I think we're in their backyard and they don't like it," replied Cash in a bravado tone as the radio chirped.

This is fun like a game. A loud explosion interrupted the lieutenant as a large plume of smoke rose above the adobe buildings four city blocks to the south.

"Golf Three, Go Firm, Golf Three, Go Firm!!!" barked the radio.

Fuck that's right where Golf Mobile's lead element should be! Cash's stomach dropped. Suddenly his worries about John's mobile section replaced any feeling of excitement.

2

"Shit," yelled the driver.

An IED exploded, tossing rocks and fragmentation onto the windshield, creating a dust bowl. The vehicle remained undamaged and continued to drive on the road.

"Sir, I'm going to push towards the power lines," said the driver.

"Go for it," said John coolly, as he tried to reach Heath over the radio to report the IED.

After the near miss, the five men in the up-armored humvee began to tense up. Isaac, the company executive officer, held a map of southern Ramadi spread over his lap. He yelled to the turret gunner sitting in the top of the vehicle.

"Which way are the power lines?"

The corpsman yelled back, cutting off the private in the turret, "Sir, I see them to our east."

The driver turned west off of the paved road. He saw a set of telephone lines.

John looked out the window. He glanced to the east to see the large power lines that resembled something running along an interstate highway in the states. *Something isn't right.* He looked to the west and saw the small third-world country telephone poles with a mess of wires tangled from pole to pole. Out the window he saw a stray dog run off the dirt road.

BOOM!

BLACK. Darkness. Smoke. Dust. Confusion. The smoke and dust were too thick to see anything. His eyes widened as he lay pinned underneath the mangled humvee. Everyone gasped for air. Upside down, John tried to regain the rest of his senses.

He smelled diesel. The pinging sound in his ears put him in a relative coma state. The intense high pitch sound faded to a low ring and he began to hear something that grabbed him with horror.

Drip, splash … Drip, splash … Drip, splash…

Diesel dripped upon him. As the smoke and dust lifted, he saw the fuel spilling into a puddle underneath his head.

"We need to get out of here!"

He crawled out of the passenger side, the door torn off from the explosion. *This vehicle is going to blow!*

John tried to stand up and immediately fell to the ground. *I need to get up. Calm down. Get the men out.*

He tried to stand again and fell. He reached back and felt a chunk of his right leg missing. He looked at his hand covered in blood. The red fluid dripped off his trembling hand.

John wiped the blood on his cammies and looked to the vehicle. The driver was still inside. Sparks bounced off the puddle of diesel. He looked behind him and saw a Marine convoy on the paved road a hundred meters away. He crawled back to the door of the wrecked humvee.

"Flynn, Flynn, we have to get you out of there."

No reply.

"God damn it, Flynn!"

John lay in the dirt, drenched in blood and diesel. He looked back at the paved road. He climbed inside the vehicle. Diesel dripped on his neck as he crawled through the passenger door.

The majority of force from the explosion impacted the driver's side of the vehicle. Flynn's limp body lay pinned in the smashed humvee.

"Flynn, we gotta get you out of here!"

He pulled on the driver's arm trying to get him released from the vehicle's grip. John pulled unsuccessfully. More sparks bounced off the puddle of diesel and the vehicle started to smoke.

Suddenly John felt his leg being pulled.

"John, we gotta get you out of there!" yelled Isaac.

Shots echoed in the distance.

"No, we have to get Flynn!"

"John, they're moving in on us!"

Isaac pulled on the lieutenant's good leg. The shots stopped echoing and started to ping as they hit the wrecked humvee.

John clenched Flynn's arm and his grip only became tighter as the executive officer pulled on his leg.

"He's dead, John. He's dead."

Isaac grabbed John's leg with both arms. He crouched down and gave a tremendous tug, pulling the injured lieutenant out of the vehicle.

The executive officer threw John over his shoulder, struggling to lift the injured lieutenant wearing 80 pounds of protective gear.

Isaac drew his pistol with his left hand. Over his right shoulder, he held John and ran to the casualty vehicle.

John looked back at the wrecked humvee. A blurry object screamed as it flew through the air. The rocket exploded on the humvee, igniting the wrecked vehicle into flames.

John watched the flames, mesmerized by their glow, and started to get light-headed.

"Stay with me," said the corpsman.

Despite missing a leg, the corpsman administered first aid to the wounded officer. John became sleepy and weak. His right leg was drenched in blood. The corpsman slapped him across the face.

"Sir...sir."

John slipped into unconsciousness.

The corpsman's leg burned in the wreckage as he treated the other wounded individuals. Isaac was the only Marine to walk away from the IED blast. He pulled the corpsman minus his leg, the turret gunner, and the other lieutenant out of the vehicle.

The corpsman immediately tied a tourniquet on his stub and did the same to the private turret gunner who lost his left arm. The corpsman took off his own shirt and shoved it in John's leg to stop the bleeding.

Two days later, John would awake in a clean sterile hospital in Landstuhl, Germany, thousands of miles from the horrors that existed on the streets of Ramadi. Flynn's body never made it out of the fiery ball.

* * *

Three blocks to the north of John's burning humvee hulk, Cash crouched down as explosions went off around the city. Two Black Hawk helicopters circled the area above.

"Golf three actual, this is Golf six," came across the radio.

"Golf six, send it."

He leaned against his radioman, white knuckling the handset, waiting for Heath's response.

"We took a KIA and have three WIA. I need you to go firm while we conduct the CASEVAC. Set up security on your rooftops and cover our northern flank. Do not continue movement until I give you the green light."

Heath's voice sounded unemotional, very logical and precise, as if he ordered an iced latte from Starbucks.

"Roger," said Cash.

His mind raced. *KIA. Killed in Action.* All of a sudden, the high-stakes game was no longer fun. Up until that point, nobody had been injured or killed. The near misses were exciting and only stoked the adrenaline rushes. *Holy shit, somebody died. This is real.* The excitement was replaced by a choking tension.

Over the radio Cash heard one of John's corporals giving orders to Golf mobile. He knew if the corporal was calling out over the radio John might be one of the casualties. He wondered if John was dead.

From the street no Iraqis could tell that Marines filled the three houses, but the people knew the Marines were in them. They always knew.

Cash looked at his watch. *Man, we've got to get moving. This is suicide staying in the same area for more than a half an hour.* In forty minutes a lifetime passed as third platoon roasted in their gear and watched their momentum slip away. Cash cursed the enemy under his breath; he feared his squad leaders were doing the same.

* * *

Forty minutes later the handset chirped, "Resume the sweep."

All three squads from the platoon exited out of their houses and continued the sweep. Fireteams bounded across the dirt road to set up far side security as the rest of their respective squad followed in trace.

Cash bounded across the road when, for a moment, time stood still. Everything ceased. The world stopped rotating and in that moment, Cash was completely aware of the situation. His body, anticipating that something was about to happen, enhanced his parasynthetic nervous system to the point where he processed information at a rate where everything appeared be in slow motion.

He turned to the left. Three Marines from first squad bounded across the street. Each figure had stopped in his moment of clarity. The Marines staged as statues for his revelation. He turned to the right. Four Marines from third squad were equally frozen for his epiphany.

He gulped. *I've made a tremendous mistake.* He feared his error might cost a Marine's life. He had forgotten to assign one of the squads to stay back in overwatch.

At that point, all three squads from third platoon were moving at the same time with no overwatch. As the frozen statues registered in his mind, rounds began to penetrate the ground only a few feet in front of him.

The impacts sliced the dirt, causing dust to splash in the air. Suddenly the moment was no longer in slow motion and the world crashed down upon Cash.

"Get to cover!"

He grabbed a smoke grenade and threw it over his point man's head. Two machine gun bursts danced around the Marines as they ran to cover. The yellow smoke billowed up, cloaking them from the incoming rounds.

Cash got his bearing and led the squad into a house. He ran to the roof to assess the situation. He received a report that no Marines were injured.

On the roof, he tried to assess the situation. He had made his first mistake and the platoon knew it. The sergeant looked at him.

"Sir, what do you want to do next?"

Cash looked back at him. *You're asking me what to do? I almost got us all killed.* His confidence wavered. *The sergeant is good; he can get his squad out of this.*

"Sir?"

What about the other squads? I'm the lieutenant; I need to get the whole platoon out of this.

"Sir?"

I need to get my platoon through this mission. He looked back at the sergeant and shook off his doubts, regaining his confidence.

"Second squad will stay in overwatch," said Cash in a solid tone. "We'll move out and continue to sweep. After we set up, third will be in overwatch. Keep me up to date on who is covering while the rest of us move."

* * *

Back at the command post the intelligence report said Golf three broke the ambush and continued to sweep the rest of the day to phase line purple with no additional contact.

Cash saw his squad leaders walk over to the smoke pit. He looked at them. *They know I fucked up. I should have assigned a squad in overwatch.* He thought about going back to his room. *We'll learn from our mistakes, they don't need me to tell them.* He started to walk towards his room. *Don't be a pussy. You have to go confront them now or they will think you're too arrogant to admit when you made a mistake.*

He started to walk towards the smoke pit, and then stopped. *They already know. You'll look like a bigger idiot if you go over and admit you messed up.* He thought about what his father would do in the situation.

"Gents, I fucked up. I take full responsibility for today's actions. We are damn lucky no one got killed in that abortion."

The squad leaders looked at the lieutenant surprised by his statement.

"Give me a smoke, damn it. In the future, in a situation like that, if you know I fucked up let me know."

* * *

Higher forbade Heath from leaving stay behind elements in the city. After entering into every home in southern Ramadi, the Marines went back to the security of their big bases.

Golf Company, outside of having the mobile platoon badly bruised, having one Marine dead and several injured, had nothing to show for the mission in southern Ramadi. The people still supported the enemy, not the Marines. Cash smoked his cigarette and thought about John's prediction. *He was right— we gained nothing. If anything— we made the situation worse.*

3

In their room, the lieutenants staged their gear against an open wall. Their flak jacket vests, Kevlar helmets and other kit took up a significant amount of space. On a plywood wall, above the gear, in black Sharpie marker ink their names were written.

The wall read:

CASH   BAMA   JOHN

Bama looked at the empty space reserved for John's gear. *There is no way I thought he'd get hit.* He picked up the Sharpie and crossed off John's name. He wrote something above the space.

Cash opened the door and caught Bama vandalizing John's name.

"Good one. Have you started getting all of his shit together yet? Isaac says we need to have it packed up and shipped to his parents."

The mood was awkward between Cash and Bama. They both felt some additional pressure after the company's first casualty. No one wanted to acknowledge it. Bama broke the ice.

"I can't believe he's hit. It's surreal that he was here shooting the shit with us a few days ago and now he's gone."

Cash looked away and said nothing. The two lieutenants rifled through John's items as they packed them up.

"Look what I found," said Bama.

He grinned ear-to-ear and held up a Celine Dion CD. They both laughed.

"We have to get over to the chow hall for Flynn's memorial," said Cash interrupting the moment. He pointed to his watch.

As they walked out of the room Cash looked back at what Bama wrote above John's gear.

"NEXT LT."

* * *

Flynn's memorial became a highly public event for the battalion.

Bama and Cash walked up to the chow hall overflowing with Marines.

"Who are all these folks?" asked Bama.

"I guess they're all from battalion."

The two lieutenants crowded toward the back of the chow hall and Golf Company's senior enlisted Marine, Skinner, walked by in a hurry. He pushed his way through the crowd. Bama reached out and grabbed him.

"Hey first sergeant, what are all these tourists doing here? There's Marines from Golf that can't get in."

"Well lieutenant, if there's no room, I suggest you leave to make room— the people from battalion are staying."

At the front of the chow hall a makeshift memorial stood in honor of Flynn. Desert camouflage netting covered a box. On top sat a brand new pair of tan Marine boots with a shiny black M16A4 rifle pointed upside down. Flynn's Kevlar with a desert digital cover rested upon the butt-stuck of the rifle. His dog tags hung around the pistol grip.

Behind the rifle and boots, an American flag hung 45 degrees to the left, and a bright red Marine Corps flag hung 45 degrees to the right. In front of the boots sat a color photo of the eighteen-year-old, smiling in his utilities.

The Navy Chaplain, a grotesque fat man who barely fit into his uniform, asked the Marines to bow their heads for prayer.

"I'd like to think that Flynn was a Christian," preached the overweight sailor. He quickly turned the memorial into an unwanted sermon.

"You know a lot of people say they believe in Jesus, but you really don't know. Today I pray that Flynn made it to heaven."

Next the sergeant major spoke about how he personally knew Flynn and that it was a tragedy such a good Marine died. The ceremony ended with the Marine Corps hymn.

Bama and Cash snapped to attention. The boom box sounded off, *"From the Halls of Montezuma...If the Ar'my and the Na'vy, ever look on*

Hea'ven's scenes, they will find the gates are gua'rded by United States Marines."

"Who the fuck does that guy think he is— Tom Cruise?"

Cash nodded toward a lieutenant wearing a tan flight suit with his collar popped. The new lieutenant wore black Oakley Sunglasses and gel spiked up his blonde hair.

"That's lieutenant Greg Parodi," replied Bama, "I reckon he's coming to Golf to take John's platoon in a few days."

They stared at the odd-looking newcomer.

"He went to IOC with me. To be honest, I think he's a douche. He drives a Porsche or some shit, real stuck up and I think he went to Georgetown."

Cash studied the replacement.

"The colonel assigned him to headquarters' company cause he's such a kiss ass. Yeah, he looks like a neophyte."

Bama nodded.

"I even think he's a vegetarian."

* * *

Bama and Cash walked to the smoke pit and stood on the back side of a plywood shade lean-to. They lit up a pair of Marlboro Lights. As they inhaled their nicotine fixes, a group of Marines discussed the memorial service on the inside of the plywood shack, unaware the two lieutenants were listening in.

"You know, that's utterly wrong, what the chaplain said. One, how the fuck does he know if Flynn was a Christian, and two, who the fuck is he to say that shit at the dude's memorial? What the fuck."

"What about that bullshit the sergeant major said," replied a lance corporal. "Okay— say he was a good Marine, but to say you knew him personally— what a crock of bullshit. I bet you old sergeant major couldn't even name all of the platoon sergeants in Golf, let alone a driver."

"I saw the sergeant major yoke some dudes up for wearing white socks," said the corporal, "He asked a sergeant why he was wearing white socks and the sergeant told him, sergeant major because it's 130 degrees out here and we don't get fresh laundry but once a week. So the white socks are the best way to keep your feet in good shape."

"What did the sergeant major say?"

"He said, 'Well devil dog, in this battalion we wear black socks because white socks are a sign of being undisciplined.' Isn't that the stupidest shit you've ever heard, this arrogant fuck is telling a sergeant he can't keep his feet in good shape over some admin bullshit rule? He obviously doesn't appreciate that dudes are dying out here. If I got a 50-50 chance of getting burned alive, the least they could let me do is wear white fucking socks."

"He's not even a grunt," replied the lance corporal, "I think he is a truck mechanic or some shit. Meritoriously promoted to every rank, you might think that means he is good to go. He couldn't even tell you the max effective range of my machine gun."

"If he wants to instill discipline, he should ensure all of the weapons are clean, make sure guys know how to operate their weapons systems and shit like that; not worry about white socks and holes in cammies.

"And first sergeant, that pogue ass bitch is no better; he's an air-winger too. He's all about the rules, the wrong rules, rules that don't mean shit out here in the ville, and sure as hell aren't keeping anybody alive. Last time I checked Iraq's dangerous. You got snipers, RPG teams, IEDs, suicide IEDS, fuel enhanced IEDS, pressure plate IEDS, and the people motherfuckin' hate us. I heard the battalion commander tell Heath the battalion was getting in contact an average of nine times per day! Nine times!"

The two lieutenants crushed out their smokes and headed back to their room, both digesting the Marines' conversation. In the room, they sat on their racks and said nothing. They stared at the space where John's gear used to lay.

4

Bama unwrapped an Otis Spunkmeyer muffin. He anxiously awaited his next mission to retaliate for John's explosion, but something distracted him. Distant verses from the *Qur'an* filled the eating space with foreign songs. The mosque across the street from the base projected the morning prayer.

Man, I wish them damned Iraqis had their own chow hall. He took a bite of his banana nut muffin, knocking off some of the nuts, and sipped a cup of sludge coffee. *Why does that mosque have to play those prayers? They sound like a curse.*

Across the chowhall several Iraqi soldiers, *jundies,* filled their pockets with ketchup and sugar packets. One Iraqi shoved muffins into his camouflage cargo pockets.

Look at them bums, they're stealing all of the Otis Spunkmeyer muffins. Bama noticed the Iraqi stealing muffins staring back at him. The Iraqis all looked brown. Their skin displayed a tint that differed from the ethnic people he saw in the states.

For the first time he saw this *jundi* as an individual— he looked different. The Arab's head contained a greasy mess of black hair. His skin glistened from the constant layer of sweat every Iraqi carried. The Muslim's face irritated the southerner. On the Iraqi's left cheek a black mole with a single hair contrasted against his brown skin. *He looks like Gonzo the Muppet with that long pointy nose and those beady eyes.*

The lieutenant stood watch the day before, chained to the command post. After starving for an entire day, he was hungry. Before he took his second bite, Isaac approached the table with an interpreter.

"Bama I want to introduce you to your counterpart for your next mission."

Isaac looked over his shoulder and pointed to an Iraqi.

"*Salah,*" yelled the interpreter gesturing to the *jundi.*

Bama shook his head.

"I ain't working with no Iraqi, that one *Salah*, he looks like a Gonzo."

"Bama, yes you are. He's your Iraqi squad leader."

The southerner sighed as the Iraqi walked to the table. The interpreter said something in Arabic and the Iraqi stuck his hand out. The *jundi* sat next to Bama.

He slid down the bench moving away from Gonzo, who barely looked eighteen. The Iraqi moved closer. Bama tried to ignore him. *All I want to do is get my boys home, not mess around with these damned Iraqis, especially this one.* He looked at the coffee and wished for some grits. He took a deep breath. The aroma of the coffee and the thought of grits aroused a certain nostalgia and Bama forgot about Gonzo as his mind began to wander.

* * *

A nine-year-old boy sat at the kitchen table in a plantation mansion outside of Montgomery, Alabama. On the wall hung a framed picture of Paul W. Bryant wearing a checkered hound's tooth hat. At the stove his black nanny prepared him some grits.

The boy reveled in the smell as his mouth watered for the southern delicacy.

"Lil' Will, let me dish you up some of these grits I fixed up."

"Yes, Ma'am."

After he finished the grits, his nanny got him ready for private school. Today was a big day for Lil' Will. His dad was going to give him a ride to school in his Mercedes Benz. As they drove to school, Lil' Will's father gave him a lesson on how he viewed life.

Ten years later Bama stood on the sideline during a college football game. He was recruited to play tight end, but rode the bench behind a better starter. His father started for Coach Bryant several decades earlier and never failed to let his son know it. After the game his father took him out for a drink.

"Why does that idiot coach play that sorry black over you?"

Because he's ten times better than I am. Today was a big day for Bama and he did not want to discuss football. He decided to join the military.

He finally figured out what he wanted to do with his life. He wanted to be a military officer. His entire life his father pressured him to be a doctor, but he thought biology was a waste of time. His father then pushed him to be a lawyer, but Bama thought lawyers were as much fun as doctors. When he chose business as a major, his father was excited that his son could go on to get his M.B.A.

I'll become a military officer. Officers have prestige. Doctor Whiting yes, that sounds important; Mr. Whiting, J.D., too much work for the title. Lieutenant Whiting. No... Captain Whiting.

He thought about the military titles.

Colonel Whiting, now that sounds very important. Colonel, that's as significant as a doctor, if not more so.

He told his father his decision and they finished their drinks. His father seemed all right with the choice.

"Not quite as good as an M.D.," said the father, "but Colonel Whiting does have a nice ring to it. If that is the case, you've got to start taking what you want, no one's gonna give it to you."

Bama nodded.

"And, son, I hope you don't think being a Marine Corps Officer is going to be as easy as Alabama football."

* * *

Bama pulled his cammie bottoms over his white socks as he waited to get cleared from the company command post. First platoon sat staged in two rows along a sandbag wall.

The heat beat down on Ramadi. The sun's reflection danced across the *Habiniyah* canal. The temperature hovered around 110 degrees.

Among the platoon sat thirteen Iraqi Army soldiers. Bama understood why Heath pushed hard to work with the Iraqi Army. *If we can get them up and running, my boys won't have to go out on patrols and it will be the jundies getting hit. It's hard to work with the Iraqis, they're un-American.*

He sat next to lance corporal Nathan Evans who the Marines called "Nate." Bama put himself with first squad to overlook the young lance corporal who filled in as first squad leader.

"It'll be a few minutes, the command post is checking with adjacent units," yelled the large lieutenant to his Marines.

He yelled next to his Arabic interpreter.

"Hey terp, yo Moody. Can you relay that to the *jundies,* and where the hell is Gonzo?"

"*Khamsa dakika enta doriah,* Five minutes until your patrol," said Moody.

The *jundies* nibbled on Otis Spunkmeyer muffins they stole from the chow hall and nodded back to Moody who they viewed as the Arabic equivalent of an Uncle Tom.

Bama sweated profusely in his gear under the sweltering heat. *Where is Gonzo?* He looked for the late comer.

He drank a large amount of water waiting to get cleared and walked over to a porta-John to relieve himself.

He opened the door. A *jundi* crouched on top of a seat. Gonzo stood atop the toilet rim with his legs spread and his bottom crouched down in the hole, conducting business.

Bama slammed the door.

"Damn it, Gonzo! No wonder all the porta-Johns are broken."

Bama fumed as the radio chirped out, "Golf one, you're cleared."

5

Out in the ville, first platoon bumped and bounded from house to house. Their mission was to conduct an IED sweep at John's vehicle accident site. Higher was convinced if they continued missions in southern Ramadi, they would deter attacks on the upcoming elections.

To walk straight down the road to clear for IEDs ensured death, so Bama's squads alternated taking a house in overwatch. The other squad bumped and bounded along the road trying to spot any suspicious items that might be IEDs.

The *jundies* were intermixed with the squads and despite being hard to manage, they seemed to be keeping up with the patrol.

Bama yelled, "Marine entering," and walked in the house. He crouched down on the roof and looked out over Ramadi. A refreshing cool breeze blew in his face. *We'll never get hit on a day like today.* The tension that normally gripped the lieutenant faded away and he relaxed, taking in a breath of fresh air.

The southerner took in the landscape. Ramadi sat in between the *Euphrates* River and the *Habiniyah* Canal. The big Ramadi sky reminded him of Alabama with its flat terrain and lush foliage.

From the roof tops, Ramadi looked like it may have once been a beautiful place. There were palm trees and the abundance of green plants created a desert oasis. Several small adobe and cinderblock shacks stood throughout the city, but there were also a wide assortment of miniature Arabic palaces.

The architecture of the mini-palaces differed from any house design Bama remembered from the states. The front of the houses displayed high pillars with flat roofs.

Bama looked to the southeast and saw his squad moving from a covered position.

Past his squad, Bama looked at the flowing water of the *Habiniyah* Canal, lazily carving its way through the Iraqi desert.

As Bama's thoughts drifted to a nice summer day in Tuscaloosa, a loud explosion abruptly interrupted his thoughts. It threw him back into reality.

* * *

A large plume of smoke rose behind the mosque. Bama's stomach dropped as he tried to focus. Straining, the dust and smoke blinded his vision. He grabbed the radio.

"Golf command post, this is Golf one actual, we have an IED explosion at Buckeye and A Street. Spin up the casualty evacuation crew, but hold them until I confirm or deny. Golf one is developing situation, over."

Bama scanned the area from the rooftop. Other than the single explosion, nothing else happened.

"They're not answering, Nate!" yelled Bama. "I think the radioman's hit in the IED blast. You stay here, I'm gonna run over with the corpsman and assess the site."

The lieutenant pulled the corpsman up with his left arm and jumped to his feet.

"Doc, let's go."

Bama ran down the first flight of stairs, and then jumped from the halfway point slamming onto the ground. He kicked open the door and ran 100 meters into the haze.

He rounded the corner of the mosque— BOOM! Another explosion detonated on the road. He barely began to see the silhouettes of his men, but the second explosion blackened the area with dust and smoke retarding his vision.

"Second squad, second squad?"

He strained to see in the fog of chaos. Suddenly a silhouette appeared from the dust.

He crept towards it and saw an AK-47 aimed in at him. Bama pointed his weapon back at the unknown silhouette, but resisted his first instinct to shoot. He lowered his weapon, utterly confused.

"*Oguf, oguf, mulazim, mulazim, sadiki,* stop, stop, lieutenant, lieutenant, friend," yelled Bama, surprising himself with own his pig Arabic.

He grabbed the barrel of Gonzo's weapon.

"*Muzien ani sadiki* very bad, I'm your friend. *Ween* Marines, *Ween* Marines, where Marines, where Marines?"

A timid Gonzo pointed a shaky finger. Bama pushed the Iraqi in frustration and ran to the direction he pointed.

When he got to the top of the berm, the smoke and dust cleared to reveal one Marine lying on the ground. Bama kneeled down, wiping the sweat and dust from the man's face and took three deep breaths. He looked down and saw massive amounts of blood. The radioman bled profusely from shards of shrapnel pierced in his skin. Bama looked him up and down and grabbed the handset.

"Golf command post, this is Golf one two. We're located at Buckeye and A-Street. I have one Marine injured. He has multiple shrapnel wounds from an IED and is an urgent surgical. Recommended ingress is West on Buckeye, don't go further south than A-Street. I'll have a ground guide waiting."

Bama un-keyed the handset and the snap of rounds started to fly over his head. He grabbed the Marine and carried him off of the road.

"Where's the squad leader?" asked Bama to the private who administered first aid to the casualty.

"I don't know, sir."

The private knelt in a security position as rounds continued impacting outside the courtyard. Suddenly Bama heard multiple bursts of friendly machine gun rounds being shot into the city.

I shouldn't have run to the casualty. I should be focused outboard. Where are these rounds coming from and where is the squad leader?

At that moment an exhausted corporal yelled, "Friendlies entering," as he and four other Marines came through the courtyard gate. Bama grabbed the squad leader, pulling him within inches of his face.

"How'd you find us?"

"Sir, the *jundies* pointed us in here."

The jundies? God damn it, I forgot about them bums. So much to do. All right, keep calm, keep steady, Will, get your Marines out of this, keep your cool, and keep your head.

He took another deep breath and gathered his composure as the rounds snapped against the courtyard wall.

"Okay, you stay here. Keep one fireteam on security, have the other fireteam round up the *jundies* and secure this courtyard and house. I have a casualty evacuation coming inbound. I'm going to link back up with Nate and see where these rounds are coming from."

Bama yelled to the corpsman to get ready to move. He ran back over and took a knee next to the injured Marine who faded in and out of consciousness. Bama squeezed his arm.

"Stay with me."

* * *

The lieutenant and the corpsman ran to Nate's position and found private Mallard, a machine gunner, on the roof curled up in the fetal position. The firing stopped.

"What the fuck-dickens happened here?"

"Well sir, when the few pop shots started to come inbound, this dipshit lost his cool and started dumping 5.56 bursts into every single house on the block," said Nate. "I was up here seeing the same shit Mallard was and I couldn't see any muzzle flashes or anything, so when he opened up for no reason I told him to cease fire."

"So, why's Mallard in the fetal position?"

"Well sir, he opened up again on nothing. He shot into random people's houses because he was scared and I wrestled the machinegun away from him, punched him out, and told him if he ever did any shit like that again, I'd kill him."

* * *

That evening back in the lieutenants' room, Bama peeled off his drenched cammies and put on a fresh dry set.

"So you got in some shit today, huh?" said Cash.

"Yeah man, it was fucked up. Those fucking *jundies,* they were all over the place, two IEDs, small arms fire; we didn't know our assholes from our elbows for a minute there."

Cash nodded solemnly.

"A Marine got hit badly. Blood everywhere. No accountability of the Marines. I never thought we would get hit today, never. Now that poor kid's fucked up. He's gone to Germany and probably won't be back. He was cut through and through in so many places. I don't know if he'll walk again."

"You sounded cool on the radio, Bama. To me from the command post, it sounded like you put the situation under control."

"I fucked up. I got focused in-bound. I ran to the casualty, instead of staying on the roof, and those *jundies* were all over."

"What was wrong with the *jundies*?" asked Cash, genuinely interested in how Bama managed the chaotic situation.

"Why do you like them Iraqis so fucking much? Today that asshole Gonzo stole muffins!"

"They were stealing muffins?"

"GONZO STOLE OTIS SPUNKMEYER MUFFINS OUT OF THE CHOW HALL!"

"Who cares about the muffins?" said Cash in a low voice. "And who's Gonzo?"

"GONZO STOLE THE MUFFINS; HE SHIT ON THE FUCKIN' PORTA JOHNS, FOR FUCK'S SAKE, HE ALMOST SHOT ME TODAY!"

"What are you talking about?"

Bama calmed down, realizing his emotional outburst, it was something he tried to avoid.

"You think they were actually trying to shoot, you know to kill you?"

"No, yes, I don't know. Gonzo, this *jundi* no shit, pointed his weapon at me. My Marine was hit, he was right there. I don't trust them Cash, especially him. I know you love them greasy fuckers but I—"

Cash grabbed Bama and pulled him outside the lieutenants' room into the night and sparked up his smoke.

"Bama, you know these Iraqis signed a death warrant to work with us?"

"Oh hogwash, Cash, I'm about getting them off their feet, but I don't trust them!" said Bama. "I don't trust the Iraqi people either. Today, as the shit was going down, we started to get shot at on top of everything else. If these people gave a fuck, they'd throw the enemy out."

6

John woke up confused. His vision was blurry. He squinted and saw a hospital room. He was in pain. He looked at his arm and saw an IV. His head was cloudy. He reached down and felt his sweltering hot leg. He lifted up his gown and saw his bruised mangled skin stitched together. Pus oozed from the wound. He smelled stale blood and became light headed. He shut his eyes and fell asleep.

"You okay sir?"

A male nurse plopped something down on a tray next to the hospital bed. John strained to turn his head. Something moved on the tray. Green Jell-O wobbled next to a bowl of steaming rice.

"Where am I?"

"Sir, you're at Ramstein Airbase in Germany."

"What happened?"

The nurse started to speak when a doctor entered the room interrupting him.

"Good, you're awake," said the doctor.

John's head remained cloudy. The doctor started to touch his lower body and spoke quickly. John tried to comprehend the doctor's words, but only knew his leg hurt. He felt a pressure building as if it was going to burst. The doctor continued to prod him and ramble on. John only heard the last sentence clearly.

"Son, you understand— we may have to amputate."

* * *

Two weeks later a private knocked on the door and handed three letters to the lieutenant. Bama smiled. He loved getting mail.

He enjoyed reading about Alabama football, the weather in the south and how his aunt went through a stressful time selling her house. *I can't wait to get back to the states and worry about these problems.* Waiting in traffic never sounded so good.

He looked through the three letters. The first was from his father. The second letter was from his aunt. He looked at the third letter and jumped out of his seat. *Awesome, I got a letter from John.* He felt a moment of regret. Weeks had passed since the incident and he had failed to write John. He tore open the letter.

Bama and Cash,

First off before I forget, my return address listed on the envelope is correct.

I wanted nothing more than to protect my Marines and I wasn't able to do that. I wish I could give my life and leg and hand to them, I really do. Bethesda was packed full with the wounded Marines, literally full. So many horrible wounds. No arms, legs, horrible.

Saw the back scar for the first time ever... it is freaking gnarly— goes from the hip to my butt, real jagged and zigzaggy, but at least I got to keep my leg.

There are two scars on the front of my leg up by the upper thigh/hip area. They are gross too, about 6 inches long. There is still some packing in there and a little oozing but it will go away in a few weeks.

My hip is still swollen like a bowling ball. I can't walk. I try every day. The other day I said, "Screw it, let's give it a try," and attempted to walk with the walker...bad idea.

Leg gave out and I went down! Not ready yet. I will get there eventually.

The other big thing is the drug withdrawal. Holy shit, it is bad. If I had known what it would be like, I would have said, "Fuck give me some Advil and ice packs," rather than deal with this crap. They had us on some powerful stuff, some kind of morphine drip...diluted it was called for a lotta days, and then percasets, and a few others.

Well, a little over a week ago, I said I feel better, I think it is a bad idea to keep taking all this stuff so I am gonna stop....24 hrs. later... felt like I got hit with a dump truck....like a crack head going cold turkey.

I just thought, I don't have a headache, don't take headache medicine. Not the case for opiate type narcotics.

Please tell Isaac and Captain Heath I say hello. Tell Isaac thanks for pulling me out of that truck. I tried to thank him at Ramadi med but I don't know if he heard me.

I think about the attack all the time and can't get past it yet. Isaac was there too...if he could send me an email I would greatly appreciate it.

Tell him he was great, a seasoned vet. And he saved my life. Please tell him for me.

Keep on hanging on Golf.

Semper Fi and God Bless,
Lt. John Magruder

7

A fluke storm pelted rain down on the roof. Cash sat in the occupied Iraqi house, safe from the rain. The platoon prepared to extract from a counter-IED ambush until they received the report. The Iraqi family effectively held hostage in their own home would be just as disappointed about the report as the Marines. The message from higher caused the lieutenant to question extending his ambush another twelve hours against the wishes of his men and most definitely the Iraqis.

"We recently received intel that there is a high probability the enemy will lay in IEDs on this route to disrupt the upcoming referendum."

"Sir, we've already been out here three days," replied the sergeant, "Let some other platoon come take over for us."

The decision belonged to the lieutenant; higher's orders did not mandate that they stay. Another platoon could easily replace them and they could go back to the Snake Pit. At the base, they could enjoy hot showers and sleep in the comfort of their own bunk beds.

Drained, hungry and running low on smokes, he wanted to go back and go to sleep. He also wanted to do the right thing. *We have to keep the route clear for the referendum. We've got a good position. If another platoon comes in, the enemy will see them setting in.*

He looked in his carton of smokes and saw two left. He laid his map across his lap and looked at the main road. He traced his finger along the next platoon's ingress route in. The extreme fatigue made it difficult for him to concentrate.

"Sir, we've got nothing to gain by staying out here," pleaded the sergeant. "I'll start having my squad break down and prepare for extract."

"Hold on," replied Cash in a firm tone, "give me five minutes to think about this."

He inhaled and blew out a cloud of smoke. Some of the smoke drifted into his nose and triggered memories of his father. His mind began to wander from the decision.

* * *

Courtney Cash started his Marine Corps career when he was five years old.

Pacific rain pelted the windshield of the beat up truck as it trailed through the muddy logging road on the Oregon coast. The truck filled with smoke, matching the heavy fog that floated outside. Cash's dad held a Marlboro Red with his left hand. The hardened logger gripped the wheel with his right hand, his arm like iron after years of manual labor. The timber jack's forearm showcased a faded green eagle, globe and anchor tattoo with the letters, U.S.M.C. stamped below it.

Courtney looked up to his hero. His father explained to his young son the proper breathing techniques for shooting a rifle. The other kids at school teased Courtney about his name and his father wanted to take his son shooting to make up for it. The pickup truck pulled into a gravel lot.

"Well, Courtney, it looks like we won't be shooting anything today."

The rain continued to pour down outside. His father smiled and tossed his son an orange from his lunch pail.

"Why am I called Courtney? It's a girl's name."

The boy smelled the fruit and bit into a juicy slice.

"I'll explain it someday when you're a little older."

He looked at his son with sad eyes, "This rain reminds me of when I was a sergeant in Vietnam in '69 in the An Hoa Basin. I'll have to tell you the whole story when you're a man."

The Cashs' double-wide trailer sat nestled in the middle of giant Douglas fir evergreens. The humble plot of land sat twenty miles up the Yaquina River from the nearest town of Toledo.

His father didn't have much, but he invested everything he owned into his son. He read to the boy every night; *Huckleberry Finn, The Wizard of Oz, Animal Farm* and Courtney's favorite *Moby Dick*. Soon his son read on his own and read everything he could get his hands on.

The summer after his senior year of high school, his father took his son on a camping trip next to a lake to celebrate his son's achievement. Courtney received a Marine Option NROTC scholarship to Oregon State University, and his father burst with pride.

Cash always wanted to join the Marine Corps to follow in his father's footsteps, but he was not so sure about logging. He saw the years of hard work grind away at his old man's soul.

This is my shot out. I'll go to school and get my education and the Marine Corps will pay for it. I'll do four years in the Corps and then I'll move to a city and get a good job and a nice house. No more logging, no more living in trailers, no more Toledo.

His father barely graduated high school and now his only son owned a ticket to college to become a Marine Corps officer.

"Well heck, I must have done something right," said the father.

He always told his son he could do anything despite his upbringing from a blue-collar background.

"I had great lieutenants," said the beaming father.

They sat on the bank of the lake, fishing. His father handed his son an ice cold beer.

"When times got tough, my lieutenant remained cool and calm. He always listened to us squad leaders, but wasn't afraid to lay the smack down. He always asked me something personal, you know, like he gave a shit about me. I'll tell you what Courtney, the biggest impression he left on me was that he always did the right thing, always."

"I knew you would be a Marine because, well, it's the right thing to do to serve your country. When you were growing up I knew you would be an officer because you're so bright, but I want you to understand the responsibility that comes with this leadership. Remember, leading other men, and especially leading other men into combat, is the greatest privilege, yes a privilege that any American could have. When you're out there talking to your sergeants, remember your old man in '69 slugging it out in Vietnam, do what's best for him."

In college, he resented the rich kids. The chip on his shoulder pushed him to work extra jobs to pay for his meager apartment and a clunker dark-grey pick-up truck. The NROTC scholarship only covered the tuition and books, not the cost of living. *You'll have to work harder, but in the end you'll be the better man.*

The same chip on his shoulder caused him to hold a severe grudge against the people given the easy road. *They're the lucky ones and they don't even understand how fortunate they are.*

When he stood in front of his platoon for the first time, the chip on Cash's shoulder fell away as he looked into the faces of the young men in his platoon. A coal miner's son from West Virginia, a ranch hand's son from Texas, a carpenter's son from Nebraska and a mechanic's son from Arizona.

When he stepped in front of them he saw himself and he saw his father. *I'm the fortunate one. I received the opportunity to go to school. These men are no different than me. Well they are different; they didn't join up for the educational benefits.* Nearly every Marine in his platoon joined after September 11, 2001. They knew full well they would soon enough be in harm's way. *I owe it to them to get them back to the States so they can do whatever they want in life.*

* * *

As he stared at the lantern, mesmerized by the warm glow and reminiscing about the past, Cash snapped back into reality.

"Lieutenant?" said Rock Durbraw.

The sergeant anxiously waited to get the word down to the Marines. They wanted to go back to the Snake Pit and be done with the mission.

"Yeah, yeah, I'm still thinking," said Cash as he opened his eyes wide trying to shake off the sleepiness.

He looked down at his watch, which indi-glowed 0221. It stopped raining and started to warm up in the middle of the night.

"Sir, you actually think we're going to catch the enemy laying an IED in this ambush?"

Third platoon had yet to kill a single enemy in an ambush. The sergeant's point was valid.

"Well, I don't know, but if we're already in a good position it seems like the right thing to stay here."

Rock disagreed with the lieutenant's reasoning. Cash knew if he told him he decided to stay, the squad leader would back his call. He hated to operate that way. If possible and time permitting, he liked to reason out the best solution with input from his men. This decision could wait.

* * *

Cash stood up and stretched his legs. He made his decision. He arched his back, holding up his bulletproof vest with his thumbs. He tried to lift the weight of the flak off his back if only for a moment.

The lieutenant looked at the map one more time and then back at his watch. The sergeant saw he analyzed every aspect of the decision.

"Sir, it makes no sense to stay."

He looked at the sergeant. *A Marine died to prepare for the referendum; we can stay out another twelve hours to keep the route clear.*

"We're going to stay," said Cash. "If we have the report and we also have a good position, it makes no sense to swap out because we're tired and want to go back. If we can stay in, we'll keep the roads open for the referendum and I'm willing to have us be inconvenienced for another twelve hours to keep some other Marine from getting blown up."

The sergeant looked at him and saw that he reasoned it out and that he at least considered his input.

"All right sir," said Rock. He let out a sigh, "I'll let the boys know."

8

Cash looked down at his hand. His wedding ring glimmered in the night. *I've got to call her when I get out of this ambush. It's been three weeks since we've talked.* He wondered what his wife was doing at that moment. He looked out the window at Route Michigan; the pavement of the road reflected the moonlight, still wet from the earlier rainstorm. He breathed in and refocused on being in Ramadi.

He thought about the monotony of another twelve hours in the ambush— dirty, tired and hungry. *It's the right thing to do.* He craved a smoke but only had one left. *I'll save it for later.*

For two hours Cash and the sergeant sat in silence. A slight awkwardness hung in the air. The sergeant recommended a course of action and the lieutenant decided against it. This rarely occurred, but when it did the sergeant realized the lieutenant was a professional. Situations like this amplified the distance and the closeness in their relationship. In this time and setting they were something other than friends. They sat in silence until the radio chirped.

"Sir, battalion is calling to see if we have a fifty-cal," said Rock.

"Why would we have a fifty-cal?"

"Sir, they say that an Army convoy got hit on Route Michigan and they somehow lost it. I don't know how you lose a fucking heavy machine gun, but leave it up to the Army."

"Have each squad conduct a sweep around their house towards Route Michigan."

"That's what I figured sir," replied Rock.

The sergeant passed the message and rounded up a four-man team to investigate the missing fifty-cal. Both Cash and Rock were glad to have something to think about besides staying in the ville another twelve hours.

"I'm going with you," said Cash.

* * *

The five men prepared to go into the Iraqi night. They huddled in the courtyard and then bounded across the street by twos to the next house. In no time they were at the main route.

"Do you see anything?" asked Cash.

He scanned the road with his night vision goggles.

"The only thing I see is the other team up the road."

All of a sudden the radio chirped a message from the Marines in the house.

"Golf three actual, we have two men carrying something onto the road behind you. We did not engage because you're on the ground."

"Rock?"

The sergeant heard the message and one of the Marines saw the unknowns. *What's going on?* From Cash's point of view the courtyard wall blocked the back alley road. He crept along the wall next to the two Marines watching the unknowns.

"Holy shit, sir," whispered Rock, "I think that might be the fifty-cal."

Cash peeked over the courtyard wall and saw two men dragging the silhouette of a square object with what appeared to be a barrel sticking out of it. He crouched down and his heart rate picked up. The men were thirty feet from the courtyard. He peeked again. *I can't tell; it might be some kind of IED or Improvised Rocket Launcher.* The pucker factor escalated. The stakes were no longer unknown.

"Should I shoot?" whispered the Marine aimed in through the door at the silhouettes.

"Wait," said Cash and Rock simultaneously.

The Iraqis knew to stay indoors at night. The Marines issued a curfew and any Iraqi who broke it knew they risked getting shot. The Marine only hesitated due to the leadership's presence.

"Something's not right," said Rock.

"What do you think we should do?" asked Cash.

"Let's keep two guys back in overwatch and three of us will white-light them with our flashlights. If they've got anything, we'll shoot them or detain them."

"Sounds good to me," said Cash.

The sergeant, lieutenant and a third Marine stacked on the wall.

"On three," said Rock, the lead man, "One, two— three."

The three Marines peeled around the corner and moved swiftly towards the men in the street. The men continued to carry the unidentified item. They were unaware of the Marines gliding towards them in the night.

At twenty-five feet, Rock shined his Surefire flashlight and yelled.

"Oguf, oguf, kiff aramick! Stop, stop or I'll shoot!*"*

The three Marines aimed in at the Iraqis blinding them with their flashlights. One of the Iraqi men carried the object. When the Marines yelled, the man dropped something and several items rolled in the street. Rock continued towards the men. He stopped one of the rolling objects with his boot. He kneeled down and picked up the item.

"Hey, sir," said Rock.

He tossed the mystery object to Cash.

9

Cash shined his light on the item and discovered the identity of the object. *An orange?* He chuckled to himself and smelled the citrus fruit. Rock stood with the two Iraqi men and picked up a broom and box of oranges, several of which were now rolling in the street. Cash walked up and saw the Iraqi men pointing to a fruit stand across the street.

"*Beyiti*," said the frightened Iraqi man pointing a shaky finger back across the alley.

"He's bringing these oranges and the broom to his fruit stand," said Rock.

The Marines apologized and warned the Iraqis to obey the curfew.

* * *

Back in the house, Cash checked on the other Marines standing post, asking each of them to show him their fields of fire. He quizzed the men on their actions if they actually saw an insurgent putting in an IED.

On the first floor, the Marines gathered up all of the Iraqis and put them in one room. All of the women and children were sleeping, but two men were still awake.

"Moody, how are they doing?" asked Cash.

He looked in the room and an older Iraqi man smiled. The other younger man glared back at the lieutenant.

"They're good, sir," said the interpreter. "They asked how much longer we would be here and I told them we were sorry for inconveniencing them, but we need to be in the city to protect them from the enemy."

"*Zein* Good Moody, *Shoukran* Thank you," said Cash.

"*Afwan Sadie.* You're welcome sir."

Cash turned to walk away and then his subconscious forced him to turn around and ask one more question, "Moody, what's with the two men who are still awake? I don't remember them from when we came in yesterday."

A Marine stopped looking at his fields of fire and turned to address the lieutenant.

"Sir, they knocked on the door about 1800 this evening and per standard operating procedures we yoked them up."

If the Marines were occupying a house covertly, and an Iraqi civilian unfortunately came to the house, they were pulled inside. The Marines forced the Iraqi to stay until their ambush was over in order to keep them from giving away their position.

Cash looked into the room at the older man. The 45-year-old Iraqi wore a salt and pepper beard. He analyzed the man's face, along with his height and weight. *That's it!* The Iraqi man's left hand, short three fingers, formed the shape of a claw.

"Sir!" exclaimed the Marine.

The Iraqi man with the claw stood up and walked towards the door of the room. He wore a white *dishdasha* with gold silk lining. On his head sat an Arab headdress. Cash turned back and saw the man smiling.

"Lieutenant, yes?" asked the man with the claw, in semi-descent English.

Cash nodded surprised.

"Would you like some Chai tea, lieutenant?"

"No thank you," said Cash. "Sir, please go back to the middle of the room."

"Lieutenant, this is Arab hospitality to offer one's guest Chai."

"Sir, I apologize. I have some work to do right now. Lieutenants are busy. Thank you for your hospitality. We will be out of your house shortly."

The man smiled and walked back to the center of the room. Cash walked over to the Marine and leaned in close speaking in a low voice.

"You gents noticed he has a fucked up flipper for a left hand right?"

"Yes, sir," said the Marine in a guilty tone. "The man's a long haul truck driver who owns big rig trucks that ship from the Syrian border into *Baghdad*. He said he does a lot of the mechanic work on the trucks and his hand caught in a serpentine belt years ago. He keeps offering us Chai. He's nice."

"Sounds good enough, but did you ever think he might have got it blown off making an IED."

The Marine mumbled no.

41

"Did you at least get his name?"

"Yes, sir, off of his ID card," said Moody.

He pulled out a piece of paper and handed it to the lieutenant.

"*Zein* Moody, keep an eye on him," said Cash.

He grabbed the piece of paper and headed up the stairs.

* * *

Upstairs Cash pulled out his green notebook and looked at the name; *KHALID ALI DOAD ALWANI*. He grabbed the radio and called the company command post.

"Golf, this is three actual, I need you to run a name to battalion intel and see if they have anything on this man. This is important. I recommend the S2 intel officer himself cross-reference the name. Stand by to copy— *KHALID ALI DOAD ALWANI*.

Cash spelled out the name phonetically.

"First name; Kilo, Hotel, Alpha, Lima, India, Delta.... Do you copy?"

On the other end of the radio, the tired radio watch put down his *Maxim* magazine, looked at his watch, and wrote in the logbook: 0330-G3A- Request info on *KHALID* ALDOWA. "Roger, that's a solid copy."

He relayed the request for intel to the battalion command post whose radio watch wrote down KHALIN ALDOWA.

The battalion radio watch sent a runner to the intelligence section with a note containing the name KHAL NADOWA that read *Golf Third Platoon Commander requests intel on this person, recommends intel officer action.*

The private intel clerk grabbed the note and typed in the name to the database computer. The screen flashed back NO MATCH, NO MATCH. The intel clerk looked at the note then looked at a typed piece of paper the captain intel officer posted in the intel office.

Okay, thought the private intel clerk, looking at his superior's standing message. He put the note in the captain's box, only after he spilled coffee on it.

Back in the Iraqi house in the ville, the radio chirped, "Battalion intel has no information on your requested individual."

"Battalion, did the intel officer look at the name?" asked Cash into the radio.

His intuition told him the Iraqi must have a record.

"Wait one," chirped the radio.

The message went through the chain to the intel clerk who typed in the name again and received another no match message. The word traveled back down the chain and chirped out the radio.

"Ran name second time, no match, no intel on requested individual."

"What about the family name?" responded Cash.

The telephone game continued for the third time, and the same response came across the radio.

"We have nothing on that name."

This is bullshit. He remained in an ambush for an additional twelve hours against the wishes of his men because it was the right thing to do. He pushed out teams to search for the fifty-cal and placed himself and the Marines in danger because battalion asked him to look for it. Now he asked for help to find out if this Iraqi was known enemy, and he received the run around from higher. He attempted three times to get the information and figured it was useless.

He went back downstairs and asked the Marine if the man carried anything that warranted detaining him. The man had nothing, and Cash's gut feeling did not justify detaining him.

* * *

With his rounds done and now wide awake and fully frustrated, Cash threw in his last cigarette and lit it off the lantern. Rock pulled out a smoke of his own and did the same.

"I put the radio watch to bed," said the seasoned sergeant.

The two men sat side-by-side. From the opening that looked down into the first floor, light poured up to the second floor from several lanterns glowing below. The light projected shadows on to the walls of the second floor as the platoon commander and squad leader sat in silence. They stared at the shadows on the wall, pondering their situation. Finally Cash broke the silence.

"So what do you think?"

"Think about what, sir?"

"The war, this ambush, whatever?"

"Well, sir, I think we are all fucked up in several ways."

He puffed away on his smoke and spoke to the young officer in a respectful but matter-of-fact tone.

"Take this ambush for one. I don't think that we're going to kill anyone tonight. I don't think the sneaky bastards lay in IEDs in the middle of the night. I'd say it's hardly ever, maybe twenty percent of the time and only if that's their only option."

"How do they lay them then?"

"Well sir, they either dig them in during the middle of the day when we're not around, and if we show up they say they're working on the road or some bullshit, or they drop them out of the bottom of a vehicle that has a hole cut out of the floor, making it damn near impossible for us to ever catch them doing it."

The sergeant's theory interested the lieutenant.

"The problem is we can't catch these guys doing shit if the people hide them from us," said Rock. "We might as well be boxing blind-folded, trying to hit an opponent we can't ever see. We live on these big castle bases with air conditioners, hot chow, television and gyms, isolating ourselves from the people. We only leave our comfy fortress to roll into the ville with overwhelming firepower which intimidates the shit out of the people. We do raids at night, crashing into these peoples' homes, maybe taking one bad guy to Abu Ghraib, which he'll sit in for three months, networking with terrorists, then be back on the street a God damn Mister Miyagi of guerilla warfare, with the people protecting him."

Cash looked at the sergeant. *He's probably right; we aren't doing much good on the big bases.*

"The problem is, we can dominate these guys if they ever chose to fight us heads up; we would slaughter them with our weapons and training," said Rock. "I've never lost a fire fight in three tours, not one. But I also think that we can win every fire fight and still lose the war. Big operations, weapons, and ambushes— they are not working. If we can't walk the streets without getting shot at, blown up or worse, how the fuck are we winning and what the fuck are we doing here?"

The sergeant looked at the lieutenant and breathed heavy from his diatribe. He may have said too much.

"I don't know what we're doing here," answered Cash, "but while we're here it's our duty to make a difference at least in the things we can affect. Even though we didn't kill anyone tonight, we probably deterred the enemy from laying in an IED."

The sergeant looked at him. He had never really thought about it like that.

"Today that fruit stand vendor will tell everyone how we held our fire, but he will also tell them we were out in the night policing the streets and maybe, just maybe, we deterred one IED layer for the next night by saving that man."

The lieutenant took a hit off of his cigarette and pulled a Red Bull energy drink out of his cargo pocket. He cracked the tab on the can and guzzled the energy drink. He handed the Red Bull to his squad leader. His watch glowed 0653. Both men stared at the shadows moving on the wall, letting each other's words soak in.

"How do we find a way to win this war?" asked Cash.

Moody let the Iraqis get up and move back and forth from the kitchen to bring food and water into their room. As they walked back and forth in front of the lanterns on the first floor, their shadows painted their movements on the upstairs wall.

"Look at these giant shadows. What if they were actually as we perceived them?" pondered the lieutenant philosophy major. "Imagine that we are prisoners who can only look forward and that we don't know the cause of the shadows. To us they are real and we believe that everything they do is what is actually happening. Because we can't look back and see the cause of the shadows, the people walking around down stairs are like puppet masters. We think that their giant casted images are real."

Cash looked at Rock lowering his eyebrows with a confused look.

"Stay with me," said Cash. "You gotta smoke?"

He slammed the rest of his Red bull and fired up another smoke. His mind raced as he thought of the dynamics of the war, the people, the enemy and his Marines.

"That scenario I gave you, now think of that as if we in actuality are the prisoners and the enemy are the puppetmasters. They control the will of the people through murder and intimidation making them anonymous to us, their anonymity gives them great power to make us and the people perceive things that aren't actually the truth. What we need to do is realize that they are only casting shadows. We need to figure out a way to stop them from doing it."

"Sir, I think you drank one too many Red bulls," replied Rock.

He looked at the shadows on the wall taking one thing away from the lieutenant's tirade. Rock wrote in his green book, *how do we stop their anonymity?*

10

John tossed and turned in his bed. He dreamt about being in intense pain. His whole body felt building pressure like a balloon over-inflating, getting ready to pop. Confused, he felt lost. All of a sudden a doctor looked over him.

"You'll be out of pain soon, son."

He dreamt of laying in a hospital bed in Germany. A piece of shrapnel obstructed an artery in his leg. His body healed the artery closed but the shrapnel blockage caused blood to swell back up into his leg. The doctors feared if they removed the shrapnel it would cause too much internal bleeding. If they didn't remove it, he would most likely lose his leg.

The doctor removed the shrapnel to avoid amputating the leg. John felt a gush come out of him. *Ahhh, relief.* He nodded in and out of consciousness. Somebody shook him. He looked up still disoriented. A Catholic priest stood over him.

"This is the Lamb of God who takes away the sins of the world. Happy are those who are called to his supper."

John barely understood his surroundings in the cloudy room.

"Son, are you worthy for the Lord to receive you?"

The priest motioned the sign of the cross against his forehead.

"May the Lord Jesus protect you and lead you to eternal life."

* * *

John sat up wide awake in his fiancé's apartment in a cold sweat ripped from his dream. He looked at Amy sleeping next to him. He got his walker and hobbled into the front room grabbing a bottle of pills off of the shelf.

He popped two pills and sat in the living room with the lights off. *Why didn't I do more? It should have been me who is dead, not Flynn. I'm the lieutenant for Christ's sake.* He popped two more pills and felt a wave of emotions rush him before he went emotionally numb. *I should have died, it should have been me.* The thought consumed him. He put his head in his hands and sat in the dark. Two hours later the lights switched on and Amy came and sat next to him.

"John, what's going on?"

"Ehh, I'm having a hard time with all of this, you know me here chilling and everyone else still over there."

"Do you want to talk about it?"

"No I— I don't think you would understand."

"Honey, I think you should talk to somebody. You don't have to talk to me, but I very much think you should talk about it. I'm worried about you."

"WHO SHOULD I TALK TO?" snapped John. "Who is going to understand this, you? You think you know what I'm feeling?"

"No, John," replied Amy rubbing his back, "Nobody knows what you're feeling, honey, except for you. That's why you need to talk about it or it will never get better."

He sighed and looked at the schoolteacher. She wore her pajama bottoms and one of his olive drab green Marine t-shirts. *I'm a wreck and she still loves me.*

"All right. For you, I'll go see somebody."

"I also think you should go to that baseball game with the wounded warrior program," said Amy. "It would be good for you to see some of the other Marines and get out of this apartment."

He sighed. He would think about going to the game.

11

Bama smoked a cigarette in the staging area of the Snake Pit as his platoon finished pre-combat checks. He looked over at the lieutenant from Washington D.C.

A few feet away, Greg, the new platoon commander that had replaced John, joked with a couple of *jundies*. The new lieutenant kissed Gonzo on the cheek, a sign of Arab hospitality. Bama threw down his cigarette in disgust.

What is wrong with this guy? He's even more in love with the jundies than Cash. He's definitely not John. A couple of Marines from Mobile saw their new platoon commander joking with the Iraqis.

Greg struggled to get mobile back in the saddle. The platoon remained cold to their new lieutenant who appeared squeaky clean.

"Ensure all of the windows are clean before we push," ordered Greg to one of the Marines, "I saw truck four's windshield was muddy."

Bama observed Greg's actions. *I guess he's a stickler for keeping the windows clean. That's good; the windows are how the mobile guys view the world.* The lieutenant's discipline on keeping the vehicles in good shape surprised the Marines in mobile.

"Bama, have you heard about the Hit and Haditha investigations?" asked Greg. "They're getting tried for murder."

"I heard some Marines killed a few Iraqis after an IED blast or something."

"I'm worried about the Marines," replied Greg, "You know we have reports that two stolen taxis are car bombs."

"Gentlemen, we're ready," said the section leader, interrupting the conversation.

Bama thought about the investigations. *On trial for murder? No Marine comes to Iraq wanting to murder somebody.* He shook his head and thought about the car bomb report as his Marines climbed in the seven-tons.

None of my men will be tried for murder, not if I have anything to say about it.

* * *

The convoy rolled through the ville on Route Michigan and stopped just short of checkpoint 295. As first platoon dismounted, third platoon burst out of three courtyards and ran to the trucks.

First platoon inserted into counter-IED ambushes as third platoon extracted from their ambushes. The two platoons high-fived each other as they swapped out in the ville.

Cash and Bama ran past each other during the switch.

"Fuck you, pussy," yelled Cash.

"You wish," yelled Bama as his platoon bumped and bounded into the city.

Third platoon loaded up on the seven-tons and returned to the Snake Pit. First platoon continued to push into the ville.

The platoon's three squads moved through the city to three houses overlooking In Between Path and Route Michigan. Their mission was to observe the roads in order to deny the enemy the ability to lay in IEDs. Higher continued to demand the routes stay open to prepare for the upcoming referendum.

Bama went up onto the roof. He peeked over the edge of the house keeping his profile low to avoid snipers.

"Hey, Mallard," ordered Bama to a machine gunner, "set in right here overlooking In Between. See that telephone pole, that's your trigger line. If a car passes it and you think it's a car bomb, you are cleared to shoot. Two of those taxi car bombs blew up last week. There's an intel report for a stolen taxi with two men wearing white *dishdashas*. Two Marines from Echo Company were killed last week, so stay alert."

* * *

The lieutenant checked on his men searching the house.

"Sir, I got three dudes digging on In Between," said the private.

"Nate, send a fireteam to check it out," said Bama to his squad leader.

Ten minutes later the fireteam returned from their mini-patrol.

49

"They said they are working on the road," explained the fireteam leader, "they said that the plumbing to all of the houses in this area is all jacked up so they need to dig down and fix the pipe."

"What do ya'll think?"

"Sir, I checked their water from the sink and it is dry. They have no running water. It sounds legit to me that they would be trying to open it back up," said Nate.

"Yeah, I think you're right," replied Bama. "We'll keep an eye on this here area and tell people to be careful moving on In Between."

* * *

Bama and Moody continued to help the Marines search the house. In one bedroom they found Gonzo.

"Sir, this Iraqi is acting weird," said Nate.

Gonzo motioned with his hands for the Marines to leave the room.

"What's going on here, Moody?"

"Sir, the Iraqi says the room is good and we shouldn't search through the people's personal items."

Bama looked at Gonzo.

"Moody you tell this here Iraqi that's exactly what we're going to do. Our job is to search through their personal items."

Bama looked around the room searching for any sign of the enemy. The Marines often found IED making material and anti-American propaganda inside the Iraqi's homes.

He lifted up a mattress revealing a bright red book. The hard back cover contained multiple gold criss-crossing oval shapes that resembled the infinity symbol. He opened up the book and saw Arabic handwriting. Bama put the book inside his camouflage day pack.

Gonzo started to speak rapidly in Arabic. He paced around the room excited.

"What's he saying now?" asked Bama.

"Sir he says you can't take that book; it doesn't belong to you."

Bama grabbed Gonzo and pulled him to the door.

"Now you listen here, Gonzo."

He pulled the Iraqi in close.

"I'm in charge, got that. Me, not you."

He pushed the Iraqi out of the room and slammed the door. Outside, the Iraqi yelled in Arabic and tried to get back in the room.

"Nate take care of that *jundi* for Christ's sake."

50

The squad leader nodded.

"I also need you to get some pictures of In Between Path," ordered Bama. "Heath wants the company to put together a report on why we should pave it. He thinks if we pave, it will stop them from putting in IEDs."

"All right, no problem," replied Nate.

The squad leader opened the door and pulled the sullen Gonzo away from the room.

* * *

"Moody, let's take a look at this book."

The interpreter grabbed the book from the lieutenant who held it upside down and backwards. The interpreter held it correctly with the spine of the book facing to the right. He opened up the book and began reading the Arabic script from the right to left on the first page.

"Sir, it says;

> *To: Salah Khalil Yusef June 1st, 2002*
> *From: Khalil Yusef*
>
> *In the name of Allah, Most Gracious, Most Merciful. Praise be to Allah the Cherisher and Sustainer of the Worlds. Most Gracious. Most Merciful. Master of the Day of Judgement. You do we worship, and your aid do we seek. Show us the straight way. The way of those on whom you have bestowed Your Grace, those whose portion is not wrathe, and who do not go astray.*
>
> *Son I hope I have not pressured you into following your father's path. I give this to you as a gift on your first day of secondary school. Being a writer and teacher has given me the utmost joy in life, followed only by being your father. I hope you too can find joy in writing stories, a daily account of your activities or whatever comes from your heart and fills the pages of this blank book.*

"It's a journal, sir."

"Ehh, I thought it was something worth a damn," replied Bama.

"No, sir, this is important."

"How do ya figure?"

"Sir, in Iraq writing is serious. If one writes, it is usually an expression of their family, culture or religious beliefs. The Arab writes in tales that are full of wisdom and truth," explained the interpreter.

"All right, find me some truth."

Moody turned the page of the journal and read directly while translating the passage.

> *August 3*
> *In the name of Allah, Most Gracious, Most Merciful.*
>
> *A young man grew up in a poor house next to a wealthy neighbor.*
>
> *The young man's father only had a donkey, while the rich man owned several beautiful white horses of Arabian Lore. Everyday the young man would conduct his chores with the old donkey envious of the neighbor's equestrian beauties.*
>
> *One day the father caught his son looking at the wealthy neighbor's horses and told his son, "BEWARE THIS SON. I'D RATHER HAVE THE DONKEY I KNOW THAN THE HORSE I DON'T."*

Bama stopped the interpreter after the first passage.

"What the fuck, Moody. You said that this would show me the truth."

"Sir, these words are wise, I'd rather have the donkey I know than the horse I don't is a proverb the young man wrote. His father must be an Imam or a teacher."

"Well, I don't like that there proverb stuff so put it back under the bed."

"Sir, I looked past the first page and there are also accounts of the young man's day to day activities like a diree," replied Moody in an Arabic accent.

"You mean a dia-a-ree," said Bama. "All right give me the damn thing."

He tucked the book back in his day pack. *Maybe Cash would like to read about this young jihadist praying to Allah before he goes to bed every night.*

Bama got up from the bed and started to walk towards the door. On the nightstand a picture frame lay face down. The lieutenant picked it up and stared at a father and son. Something caught his attention.

"Hey, Moody check out this picture."

The interpreter walked over and looked at the frame surrounding the photo of a young man and his father. The younger Iraqi in the photo had beady eyes, a long nose and a black mole on his left cheek.

"Doesn't this Iraqi look like Gonzo?" asked Bama.

Suddenly machine gun bursts rang out from the roof.

12

Mallard sat on the roof and looked down over the wall at the road. He hated Iraq. The eighteen-year-old wanted to go to war for excitement, but now that he was in the country the majority of his time lacked excitement. It was boring. *Sure there are intense moments every now and then, but for the most part, it's private, watch this, private, watch that. It's just boring.*

The private watched a cow mosey across the dirt road led by a young Iraqi boy. The pair walked to a drainage ditch where the Holstein bent down and took a drink. The cow's ribs stuck out of its belly.

That cow looks like it is starving. The thin cow stepped into the ditch and shook around splashing water on to its back.

That's gross. The cow stood in "Shit Creek." All of the houses' raw sewage drained into the creek. The ditch ran parallel to In Between Path. The boy sat on the side of the road next to Mallard's defined telephone pole and watched the cow.

Flies surrounded the cow and the Iraqi boy broke off a cat-tail reed from "Shit Creek" and waved it on the cow's back to disperse the flies. *He actually looks like he's having fun.* For a moment, the private was jealous.

Suddenly a taxi appeared from the east traveling down the road. Mallard yelled down to two *jundies* on the ground level.

"*Oguf Sayyaara Qumbula* Stop Car Bomb."

The two *jundies* ran into the street and held up their hands and yelled in Arabic. Mallard looked in the windshield and saw two men wearing white *dishdashas*. The vehicle continued to drive forward.

* * *

Bama heard gunfire. He ran out of the room and collided into Nate.

"Grab the radio," said Bama, "I'm headed up to the roof."

Bama climbed the stairs and heard several more machine gun bursts. Shortly after, he heard a woman screaming.

"What's going on, Mallard?"

The screaming became louder. Bama breathed heavily from climbing two flights of stairs, and consciously tried to slow down his breathing.

"Sir, that orange and white taxi came down In Between right toward the house. I called down and two *jundies* tried to stop it but it kept coming towards the house. After it crossed my trigger line, I shot two bursts into the tires," said Mallard. "It kept coming— so I shot two more bursts."

Bama peeked over the railing and saw the beat up orange and white taxi crashed into the courtyard gate of the house. The front of the windshield was shattered and partially shot out from Mallard's machine gun bursts. Bama called to his other squads and put them on alert. He told them to watch out for the follow on small arms attack he expected if the car blew. He continued to hear the woman's screams.

Bama peeked again. In the car two Iraqis were both badly injured. Red blood soaked their white *dishdashas*. Two *jundies* cautiously looked at the car, circling around it with their AK-47s pointed at the injured men. The *jundies* hunched over in anticipation of the explosion that might occur.

"You did the right thing," said Bama grabbing the private's shoulders looking him straight in the eyes, "I told you to do just that. You saved the squad, Mallard, good job."

"Sir?" said Mallard in a questioning tone.

He questioned the lieutenant. The private pointed over the wall of the roof. His shaky finger aimed behind the taxi to the telephone pole. Bama looked over the edge and saw where the screaming originated.

Twenty feet behind the taxi a woman stood over the Iraqi child who still gripped the cat-tail reed. The woman screamed hysterically. The boy was caught in the cross-fire. In the ditch the cow lay shot as blood dripped down its black and white coat.

Bama ducked back down behind the wall and gagged at the sight. *What the fuck have we done?* The woman continued to scream.

13

Back at the Snake Pit, Bama walked into the lieutenant's room with his head down. He threw his day pack. The red book came half way out as he plopped in a chair exhausted from the whole experience. He was confident his platoon had done the right thing, but worried they might be questioned for the events in town.

"How you doing?" asked Cash.

He heard about the mission.

"Bout as good as crawfish on the griddle," said Bama. "You're damned if you do, damned if you don't. We let that there taxi come through and we're all blown to bits and you're crossing my name off, putting NEXT LT over my gear."

He shook his head.

"We shoot that son of a bitch, kill two Iraqis, and some poor kid and we're fucked up. We're out there trying to do the right thing and we get put in these no-win situations. I feel trapped. This is so damned frustrating."

"Did you go out there wanting to murder those people?"

"No, you know that's not what we're about. But with the Haditha and Hit investigations and them Marines getting charged with murder, it feels like the man is throwing me out in the street to get fucked," said Bama. "We're in like a catch something or other, you know what I'm talking about right?

"A Catch-22," said Cash. He walked over to Greg's bookshelf and pulled out the Joseph Heller book. He handed it to the southern lieutenant.

"Oh, that there reminds me," said Bama grabbing the red book. "I thought you'd want to check this out, Cash. It's like an Iraqi kid's diaree or some shit."

"You mean diary," said Cash opening up the red book to see the handwritten Arabic script.

"Yea, I think it may be that *jundi* Gonzo's."

* * *

Moody scanned through book and stopped midway.
"Sir, this journal says the man was kidnapped by the enemy!"
The interpreter was pleased with himself for finding the entry.
"What?" asked both lieutenants.
"Sir, it says:

> *October 10*
> *In the name of Allah, Most Gracious, Most Merciful, I beg forgiveness for what I have done.*
> *Today I was approached by an albino man who asked me to meet him with him. Albino men are revered as being messengers so I went to the house where the man had asked.*
>
> *Inside the house were three bad men and no albino. The first bad man told me that he would give me money if I helped them. I said no.*
>
> *The second bad man told me that I must do what he says or he would kill me and my family.*
> *They brought out a known man who lays with other men and held a gun to his head. The men forced me into a back room where they told the known gay man to force himself upon me or they would kill him.*
>
> *They brought me out of the room and told me if I did not help them they would slander my family name and the man who lays with other men would testify that he had me.*
> *They made me dig on In Between and told me to tell people it was for the water pipes. They said not to ask questions or talk to anyone or they would do worse to me.*
>
> *They shame me Most Merciful, I beg your forgiveness.*

"I reckon that is crazy," said Bama. "What should we do?"

A knock interrupted their conversation.

"Gents, sorry to interrupt, but I need to talk to you immediately," said Isaac.

"Isaac, you'll never believe what we read in that book that Bama found," interrupted Cash.

"I need you in my room now!" ordered Isaac, "If he found that book in the ambush, bring it too."

* * *

"This only involves Bama, but I wanted you to hear it as well, Cash," explained Isaac.

He sat as his desk rifling through some papers. Both lieutenants respected the executive officer. He seemed to understand that the impossible demands placed on the Marines created less than ideal situations.

Both lieutenants sat in anticipation. As they waited they looked up at several white boards hung on the wall. One board showed the word "THINK" in red dry erase marker. Below were several phrases from previous Ramadi executive officers.

"YOU HAVE FIREPOWER. FIREPOWER ALONE WILL NOT WIN."

"THE BEST SHOT IS THE SHOT YOU NEVER HAVE TO TAKE."

"THE MARINE CORPS IS A GOVERNMENT BUREAUCRACY. YOU WILL BE JUDGED BY LAWYERS WHO HAVE NEVER SEEN A FIREFIGHT."

The lieutenants digested the words on the whiteboard. The executive officer turned around after having found whatever he looked for.

"You're going to be investigated for those Iraqis deaths. The lawyer is here in the briefing room and wants to see you, Nate and Mallard."

Bama's head dropped.

"It's only a preliminary inquiry so it's not a full blown JAGMAN investigation yet, but he is probably going to ask you some tough questions."

Bama shifted in his seat. He wished he and his Marines could avoid the lawyer. *We did not do anything wrong. There is nothing else we could have done.*

"Cash, you can leave now. I wanted you to know that this was going on."

Cash left the room.

"It's hard to think that they are doing an investigation to protect you, but that's why they do these," explained Isaac. "Go in there and tell them the truth and everything will work out. Whatever you do, don't lie."

Bama's face questioned the executive officer's advice. Isaac reinforced his point.

"You have nothing to hide. We, the Marine Corps, put you in that situation, you were doing what the situation demanded and that resulted in innocent peoples' deaths. War is an unpleasant thing."

They should be investigating them two car bombers who killed the Echo Marines. Yes, the man put me in this situation and now he is going to try and fuck me.

"All right, Isaac," said Bama. "You want me to go first?"

"Yes, he's waiting for you in the conference room."

14

"You're sure this is the room?" asked the lawyer.

"Yes, sir," replied the private, "This is where the executive officer told me to put you."

"This won't do. I need some place where I can have some privacy."

The private laughed.

"Sir, this is all we got out here in the Snake Pit, maybe at the big base you've got more room, but out here this is it."

"All right, private I'll make it work."

"Sir, I'll be waiting in the chow hall whenever you're ready to leave."

The lawyer looked at his watch.

"Stay in the truck, private. I don't plan to stay here long."

* * *

"Come in and have a seat, Will," said the major.

He used Bama's first name and spoke in a welcoming manner. Bama sat down placing the red book on the desk. The lawyer was a tall, skinny man. He appeared professional and educated.

"This is a formality. It doesn't mean anything, you know, just one of my rules," said the lawyer in a friendly tone. "I have to read you your rights."

"Well, sir, if it don't mean anything, why you going to do it?"

"It's a rule, we have to do it."

The lawyer read Bama his rights.

"I understand that you don't get eight hours of sleep every night and make your decisions in an air conditioned room like this one. Tell me what happened yesterday and we'll go from there."

Bama liked the lawyer's statement. He felt more comfortable.

"Well, sir, we were out on a counter IED ambush and…"

He told the story highlighting the key information; mainly that he ordered Mallard to shoot if a taxi crossed the trigger line. While he told his story, the lawyer nodded and took notes.

"Did Mallard have any reason to shoot the vehicle other than that it crossed the line that you defined?" asked the lawyer. "How would the driver of that taxi know that you were in the ambush?"

"That's what we're taught at Infantry Officer Course," said Bama. "How would I know what the driver was thinking? I never thought of it like that, but we were only doing what we've been trained to do."

The lawyer saw that Bama was becoming defensive.

"Lieutenant, I'm trying to figure out what happened. This is only a fact-finding investigation to protect you."

"Sir, we did what we were trained to do."

"And now an innocent Iraqi child is dead," muttered the lawyer under his breath.

"Sir?"

"Listen, I honestly don't believe you intended to murder those people, lieutenant. But I do hope you can provide some more insight as to how we can operate differently in the future to avoid more deaths. "

"Sir, with all due respect, this ain't no God damn tactical decision game ya'll get run through at The Basic School. This was a real life scenario. The intel report said that the taxi was a car bomb! Two Marines from Echo were killed last week by a taxi car bomb!"

The lawyer sat back in his chair surprised by the lieutenant's aggressiveness.

"I had a defined trigger line, like I was trained to do, and we sent them *jundies* out to conduct hand and arm signals. There's nothing else we could have done," said Bama.

"Lieutenant, don't forget you're talking to a major," said the field grade officer.

The lawyer folded his hands together and bounced his fingers off his knuckles. They sat in silence for a few minutes. The lawyer wrote something down on his notepad then looked up at Bama.

"I think I have enough information for my initial report. I will inform your company commander of the results. And lieutenant— I really am here to protect you."

Bama nodded his head. He grabbed the book sitting on the edge of the table and the major asked one more question.

"What is that red book, lieutenant?"

In the intel report, he read that the patrol confiscated a red book with Arabic handwriting.

"It's a journal we found in the house."

"Well, I'll need it for my report."

"But it's got nothing to do with what happened," said Bama. "We think the person who wrote this is a *jundi* here on this base who was working with the enemy."

"I need the book, lieutenant. I assure you after I'm done with my report, I'll give it to the battalion intel officer who will have it properly analyzed," said the major. "Any information that is applicable to your area, I'm sure you will get a brief on."

The major reached out took the red book.

* * *

Bama went to Heath and explained the situation.

"Are you sure it was the same Iraqi in the picture?"

He wasn't sure. Without positive proof, Heath's hands were tied. Bama walked back over to the lieutenants' room defeated. He craved a smoke.

Outside of the lieutenants' room, stood a fledgling date palm. The lieutenants smoked thousands of cigarettes next to the date palm, trying to figure out how to get their platoon through each day.

Bama looked forward to some alone time to go over the last 48 hours. As he approached, he saw Greg sitting on the cement block smoking by himself. The new lieutenant had grown a mustache.

"I didn't know you smoked, Greg."

"I didn't but I almost got hit by a mortar yesterday, so I figured fuck it."

With all of his own excitement, Bama overlooked the Snake Pit's mortar attack.

"Heard you had a rough go of it yourself yesterday," said Greg.

"You know it's part of being over here I guess. How's everything coming about in mobile?"

"They are apprehensive— still feeling me out I think."

You're a complete douche; of course, they don't trust you.

"I had my parents' friends send over flight suits for the entire platoon. They are flame resistant. I figured that if they are saying they need them, they need them. The boys say they have been asking for them for a while, but Skinner keeps telling them they are on order."

That the new lieutenant bought his platoon flight suits surprised him.

"Bama, don't tell the Marines I got the flight suits from the States— I want them to think the Marine Corps gave it to them. With the investigations and all, I think the Marines feel like we're getting hung out to dry."

Greg wore one of the tan flight suits and with his blonde hair and new mustache he resembled a naval aviator more than a Marine officer. Bama moped about as he lit his smoke.

"Bama, forget about that lawyer; he doesn't understand. I'm sure nothing will come of it. Keep your head up."

"Yeah, I suppose so."

"What's with the first sergeant, Bama? He keeps telling me I need to keep my mustache within grooming standards. Who gives a shit about those meaningless rules?"

"Well, I reckon it's important," said Bama, who wore a high and tight haircut and displayed immaculate grooming standards, "but not as important as the tactical shit. I see your Marines doing gun drills and that's good. Greg keep pushing them. That's what they need to get them their confidence back."

Bama looked at the new lieutenant who loosened up quite a bit. *Ehh, I guess he's not that bad after all.* He gave him one last piece of advice.

"Oh, and, Greg, watch out for them IEDs on In Between."

ACT II
LEARNING CURVE

Those who do not battle for their country do not know with what ease they accept their citizenship. — Dean Brelis

The senator nodded his head, acknowledging the information; he had heard it before. No other country in the region would intervene with China backing Malaysia.

"The Chinese have become masters of indirect influence," explained the first man. "There is widely known intelligence that they have a 5, 25, and 50-year plan to take control of the Pacific. Their build up of submarines in the South Sea of China is only the first step, in the next 25 years they wish to push their naval dominance to include all of the South Asian Pacific and in 50 years they hope to control all of the Pacific."

The next man held notes and studied them before he spoke.

"Sir, if we intervene in Brunei against Malaysia; it will send a clear message to the Chinese we will not sit by idly as they..."

The senator had heard enough. The arguments were valid, China was the ultimate threat. The country was at a critical point where they could stop the bleeding in the South China Sea. If the United States did nothing, China may also have to be stopped closer to our borders as they reached out to satisfy their ever-growing needs. Yet he was still troubled.

"Gentlemen, I agree China is a threat. However, I am unsure of the grave national interest that should lead us from a softer strategy to a unilateral war with lasting unintended consequences. Would this war and its repercussions actually increase our security and economic interests? I agree that China is a threat, but are they an urgent threat? If no, we should not hurry to get our young men killed."

15

"Gents, we have to jump through our ass to get this thing off the ground," explained Heath. "The clock is ticking."

The Golf Company staff sat in the briefing room and discussed the upcoming referendum. Cash looked at his watch and saw how little time they had.

The United States Ambassador and the State Department were responsible for the planning and execution of the event. Little information was passed to the military. Within the final 72 hours, the U.S. Army and Marine Corps quickly disseminated a semi-produced plan down to the battalion, company and platoon levels. The ground troops worked feverishly to produce some semblance of an execution plan. It would fall on the men who patrol the streets to secure the elections intended to ratify the fledging Iraqi government's first constitution.

"The enemy is going to use five stolen ambulances to hit the polling centers. They will attack these sites."

The company commander aimed a laser pointer at a Ramadi map projected on the wall.

"The mastermind behind the attacks going on in the city is an Iraqi named *Khalid Ali Doad* of the *Alwani* Tribe."

The name sounded familiar to Cash. The company commander clicked the power point presentation to the next slide. The name appeared on the screen. All of the Marines wrote down the information.

"*Khalid* controls several enemy cells whose activities include laying IEDs, sniping, rocket teams and multiple murder and intimidation gangs. His physical description is shown in this photo."

The screen displayed a picture of an older man.

"One key indicator is this high value target is missing three fingers on his left hand—"

Cash looked closely at the man on the screen. He struggled to find his connection to the Iraqi.

"What the fuck!"

Everyone in the room looked at Cash. He jumped up out of his seat and rapidly flipped through his green book.

"Cash, what's going on?" asked Heath.

"Sir, I had this fucker," answered Cash, still fumbling around with his green book.

"What do you mean?"

"Aha!"

He pointed to the name in his green book: *KHALID ALI DOAD ALWANI.*

"Look, I had him. I had this fucking guy with the flipper; I called it into the CP and they said that they had nothing on him."

How can this be possible?

"Are you sure?" asked Heath. "If you called it up, it would have been reported—"

"I called that name up to the command post and they came back and said 'nope nothing'. They said, 'we got nothing on him.' Check the logbook."

The company staff walked from the briefing room into the command post in the adjacent room.

"Where's the latest log book?" demanded Cash.

"Sir, it says the name was called up but there was no info on that Iraqi," replied the staff sergeant who looked up the event.

Heath looked at the Cash.

"Let me see the log book," said Cash, "hmm I don't think this is right."

"Well lieutenant they would have written it down correctly," said the first sergeant.

The staff sergeant looked cautiously at the company commander.

"Look at what I have in my book," said Cash.

Heath looked at Cash's green book.

"First Sergeant it's different between the two books," said Heath.

"It must have been reported wrong," replied Skinner.

"First sergeant I'm looking at the damned book right here," said Heath, "This is unacceptable."

Everyone stared at the desk.

"Gentlemen, gentlemen, if it was written wrong there is nothing we can do about it now," said Isaac.

The executive officer had become the buffer between Heath and Skinner. He intervened to avoid a public outburst that would be better handled behind closed doors and out of sight of the junior Marines.

"We'll mark that house. Okay, Cash? And we all need to tighten up on our command post procedures in the future. Let's get back to the task at hand."

16

Cash peered through the courtyard gate at the empty building. The *Al Fawta* School, which the State Department dictated to be a polling center, was locked. *Obviously no one heard there was supposed to be an election here today.*

The team paused as Cash thought about what to do. His initial thought was to ram the courtyard doors open with a humvee. After further consideration he decided to jump the courtyard.

The team waited while two bomb-sniffing dogs checked the building. The dogs ran in and around the building and then returned. They sat directly in front of their handlers with their heads held high. The canines' sign indicated the building was clear of explosives, but there was something else.

"Sir!" exclaimed one of the handlers. "There's something behind the building."

"What do you mean something?" asked Cash.

"The sign is for a non-aggressor, but who knows," replied the handler. "It might be a kid or another dog."

Two Marines stacked in a SWAT formation as they cleared along the outside of the school. They pointed their weapons at every window visually inspecting them as they glided along the outside of the windows. They paused on the last corner near the back of the building. A non-aggressor to the dogs may be a spotter for the enemy or worse.

The team rounded the last corner and saw the non-aggressor. A donkey yelped, startling the Marines. It neighed loudly with its front two hooves up in the air. Cash stopped struck by the donkey's actions. He looked at the animal's dark, black eyes. The beast stared back at him as if to warn him. *He's telling us some bad shit is going to happen.*

* * *

Cash escorted the *jundies* and 30 Iraqi civilian election officials back to the school. The military flew the civilians in from *Baghdad* to run the polling center.

He looked at his watch which read 0600. *We can't waste any time getting the building fortified.* The enemy would not wait till the defense was in place to attack.

Outside of the building the Marines parked a flatbed truck that carried hundreds of sandbags. Outside the school two seven-ton armored vehicles parked facing outboard. Two *jundies* stood in the back of the vehicles using them as pillboxes.

Word was passed that the international media intended to cover the referendum closely. The Marines were told to avoid having the wrong message sent, it should be portrayed that no Americans were running the elections or the polling centers. It was impressed upon them that the polling centers they were tasked to run, needed not to be run by them at all.

"Get the Iraqis down there and let them run it," said Heath. "It needs to be them doing it, but if they can't do it you need to do it."

Cash thought about Heath's statement. *Well, am I doing it or not?* The order seemed to be a mixed message. Nothing was clear in the way things were being run in Iraq. From the top down, there were no black and white orders. Gray seemed to be the color of every mission.

How is this enormous burden passed all the way down to the platoon level? The higher powers that be struggled to come up with a unified strategy, not only for the referendum but for the entire war. Despite the lack of a plan, the military forged ahead. Fractured from the top down, the overall plan seemed to change weekly, daily, and hourly. The changes were so drastic that each unit, in an attempt to make some progress that was worth risking their lives, came up with their own plan that they thought best fulfilled the wishes of their higher.

Implementing national foreign policy literally fell on the platoon level to decide what was important enough to make an effort. There was no unison. Each unit tried to do what they thought was the right thing. With no overarching realistic solutions, a unit could easily go astray. Each commander at his own level tried to make the best with what they had. Cash looked at the situation and was unsure if he could pull off setting up the site.

"Moody, tell them they need to reinforce all of the windows in the building and set up an entry control point leading from the road into the school," ordered Cash. "We need to get out of here so they can start setting up; they need to be the face on this thing."

Moody relayed the message to the Iraqi Army major. The two men ran back over to third squad's position leaving the Iraqis alone in the school. Cash plopped down next to the radio relieved that the Iraqis were at work in the school.

He pulled out a cigarette and went to light up. He stopped himself. *Too much to set up.* He held the unlit smoke in his hand. The platoon needed to mark the areas where Marine engineers planned to place barriers to disrupt car bombs. All of the windows needed to be reinforced. He calculated the time to complete all of the tasks. He put the unlit cigarette back in the box.

Over the radio Cash delegated what he expected each squad to have done by certain timelines. He issued one standing order, "Stay out of sight." He agreed with higher that it was important the polling centers have an Iraqi face.

After he issued his guidance, he looked out the window and saw that the Iraqis had accomplished nothing. *What is wrong with these people?* He grabbed Moody and his corpsman, Doc Mac, and ran across the street to the school.

* * *

All of the Iraqi civilians milled about inside the school. The election civilians from *Baghdad* were supposed to be trained in running a polling site. Cash looked at them. *Apparently they missed the training.*

In the center of the courtyard several ballot boxes sat unopened. Next to them other election materials sat untouched. In the middle of the courtyard several *jundies* huddled around one Iraqi.

"Moody, ask them what is going on down here."

"Sir, one of the *jundies* opened up an MRE and drank water out of one of the heaters," replied Moody.

The Meal Ready to Eat contained a liquid heater. A chemical reaction heated water when it poured into the device. The warm water was intended to heat up the prepackaged food contained in the MRE, so Marines could eat hot meals.

The *jundi* dumped water into the chemical heater thinking its purpose was to heat the water to drink. After the water warmed, the Iraqi drank the liquid. Cash looked at the *jundi* grabbing his stomach and moaning. *He might as well of drunk a can of Drain-O.*

"We can't be dealing with this shit."

The absurdity of the situation frustrated him. He looked at the Iraqi's languishing. *All right, you're going to have to make this thing go.* Cash called over to second squad's position where Isaac maintained communication with higher. He requested a casualty evacuation for the sick Iraqi.

"Moody, tell the *jundies* a CASEVAC's enroute, and for *Allah*'s sake tell them don't drink the damned heater water out of the MREs."

17

"*Jundi taal, jundi taal,* soldier come, soldier come."

He spoke in pig Arabic and waved for a squad of Iraqis to follow. Cash led the Iraqis outside to the flatbed truck. He motioned to the *jundies* to start unloading. The *jundies* did nothing.

"*Jundi!*" yelled Cash pointing to the Iraqis.

They stared at him confused. He climbed up on the truck and started throwing sandbags to the ground. The Iraqis followed suit and unloaded sandbags off of the truck.

The sandbag pile grew as the *jundies* threw them down. Through a series of pig Arabic phrases and rough sign language, he managed to convey to the *jundies* to carry the sandbags from the truck into the school. The sandbag operation was a minor victory.

Cash stood behind the truck directing the offload with the corpsman assisting him. He was pleased the Iraqis were doing their own work. He pointed to the truck—

BOOM!

An IED exploded five feet from their position. The blast threw Cash against the courtyard wall. Dust filled the air. He tried to gather his composure. PINGGGGG.

The ringing filled his ears.

Cash knelt from being knocked down and felt out the corpsman. He grabbed him and looked at his face as the dust dispersed slightly.

In slow motion Cash yelled, "DOC, ARE YOU OKAY?"

The doc looked back at Cash and yelled the same thing. *Am I okay?* His back was wet. He reached back and felt warm liquid running down his spine. He felt no pain. *Am I hit?* He pulled his hand back wet from the warm fluid.

Water. His Camelback burst when he impacted the wall and drenched the back of his cammie blouse. He wiped the dust off his face and tried to focus.

In that instant Cash's instincts told him something that sat in the back of his mind for some time.

John hit two IEDs— back to back.

Bama hit two IEDs— back to back.

Every time an IED exploded— a secondary followed.

"Get back in the school!"

He winced in anticipation of the secondary blast that he knew would occur. He and the corpsman ran towards the school. He stopped and looked back—

CHAOS!

Through the lifting dust cloud, several *jundies* lay in the fetal position screaming. He stopped, pausing to look at the Iraqis. Behind them the IED blast created a crater five feet deep. The blast hit a water pipe which sprayed water out of the crater. The fountain rained down on the stunned *jundies*.

Cash looked back at the school and pivoted running back towards the Iraqis.

"Get up, *ta'al jundi syrah, ta'al jundi syrah,* Come soldier hurry! Come soldier hurray!"

The Iraqis lay shell-shocked, stagnant.

"*Khatar- Qumbalah ta'alu we ya yeh,* Danger- bomb, come with me!"

The *jundies* were paralyzed by the blast. Muddy drops rained down on his face. *You've got to get out of here, that secondary is going to blow.* He kicked a *jundi* in frustration. *You've only got seconds. God damn, get up!* His muscles tensed in anticipation of the explosion he knew would go off. *Get up, get up.* His adrenaline raced. *They're not going to move!*

He grabbed a *jundi*, drenched from the water, and threw him in a fireman's carry. As he ran towards the school with the Iraqi soldier on his shoulder, the corpsman ran out of the school.

Cash dumped the Iraqi next to the entrance of the school. He ran back to the IED blast site, where the secondary had yet to blow. Doc Mac ran past him towards the school carrying a soaked *jundi*.

The lieutenant and the corpsman did the exchange another two times, carrying all of the *jundies* into the courtyard. Inside Moody, confirmed that none of the *jundies* were badly injured, only shell-shocked.

The enemy intended the IED to blow up on a vehicle. They buried it deep in the ground in order to force the pressure of the blast directly under a humvee, as it had done with John's vehicle. If the IED had been buried a foot shallower it would have killed the lieutenant, his corpsman and several *jundies*.

18

Isaac saw the incident from the second story window of an overwatch house. He immediately called the explosive ordnance demolition team and ordered them to re-sweep the area. The bomb squad found the secondary IED un-detonated, three feet from the crater. Rock and Isaac were Cash's guardian angels. After the first blast went off they both immediately sent out fireteam satellite patrols. The patrols deterred the enemy's triggerman from blowing the second IED.

Twenty minutes passed as the bomb squad conducted the second sweep. Waiting inside the school, Cash contemplated the situation. *Should I even be in the school? The Iraqis are supposed to be doing this. If I don't interject my force of will nothing will happen.*

"Moody, tell the Iraqis we have to go back out and continue to off load the sandbags," ordered Cash, "we must reinforce the school before any more time goes by."

Moody relayed the message to the Iraqi Army officer.

"Sir, he says someone is out there actively trying to kill us. He says they will be waiting for us to go back out there."

Cash sighed and looked at the Iraqi.

"Moody, tell them that Isaac and Rock are overwatching us. They won't let that happen. We need to get back out there. Every second we wait, their ability to attack us and hurt us gets stronger while we become more vulnerable."

The Iraqi listened to the translation.

"Sir, he says they are staying in the courtyard and they will not leave the school."

Cash looked at the election workers crouched in one corner of the courtyard. Every box remained closed and untouched. They were visibly shaken from the explosion.

He looked at the ragtag *jundies*. They ranged in age from 15 to 48 and appeared helpless. *They look like bums.*

Paul Bremmer, the first U.S. Iraqi Ambassador, disbanded the original Iraqi Army after the invasion. When the U.S. tried to rebuild the Iraqi Army the only people they convinced to join were the disenfranchised and uneducated Iraqis. These men were in such dire straits they signed their name to a death warrant by working with the coalition forces. They lacked leadership, and without training were as capable as 40 New York City bums dressed in fatigues.

Cash rubbed his temples. *This is hopeless. This thing was poorly organized by people way higher than me. How can I be to blame for what occurs or fails to occur here today?* All of a sudden he thought of his father in the An Hoa Basin in Vietnam in '69. *What would old Sergeant Cash do in this situation?*

"Cover me," said Cash to Doc Mac.

He went outside the courtyard and climbed up on the flatbed truck. He started throwing sandbags off. He worked in a fever. The lieutenant knew Isaac and Rock had him covered but his asshole still puckered. He knew the enemy watched him waiting for another opportunity to kill him.

Cash looked down off of the truck and saw Moody and Doc Mac carrying sandbags back and forth from inside the school. *I love those sons of bitches.* The burst water pipe continued to spray water into the air. Mud covered them all.

For twenty minutes the lieutenant, corpsman, and Moody unloaded sandbags. Suddenly something happened.

Cash looked down and saw a young *jundi* carrying sandbags into the school. *He cares! Holy shit this Iraqi cares about the referendum.* When he came back for his second trip, Cash jumped off of the truck and grabbed the young Iraqi. He pulled Gonzo in and kissed him on the cheek, hugging him tighter than he had ever hugged his own mother.

"Shukran jundi, shukran."

He held his hand against his heart, a gesture of thank you, holding back the tears. Gonzo smiled and continued to move the sandbags.

Several minutes later the entire Iraqi squad unloaded sandbags. They continued to reinforce the school.

* * *

After they jump-started the Iraqis, a muddy Cash, Doc Mac, and Moody ran back over to third squad's position. Rock grinned ear to ear as the lieutenant entered the house.

"Sir, you got your cherry popped huh?" joked Rock.

The sergeant had experienced multiple IEDs over his three tours to Iraq. He endured enough shrapnel to be awarded two purple hearts but still kept in the fight.

"Yeah, where were you on that one, Durbraw," replied Cash, "I thought you said you were my guardian angel."

"Why don't you think they blew the second one sir?"

He winked at the lieutenant.

19

The lieutenant plopped to the floor eager to catch his breath from the chaos. He looked at the cigarette anxiously awaiting the nicotine vacation from Ramadi.

Boom.

He sighed. *What now?*

"Sir, Gonzo's hit by a rocket and is badly injured," said Moody.

Cash dropped the unlit smoke on the ground calmly squashing it with his boot out of habit.

"Tell the *jundies* to bring him to the front of the school," ordered Cash. "We'll bring in a mobile section to extract him."

He looked down at the school. *This won't be easy.* In order to fortify the school, several strands of concertina wire surrounded the school creating an eight foot high fence. The only way to get out was on the back side of the building in an area mobile could not access. If the *jundies* wanted to get Gonzo out to mobile, they needed to figure out a way to get him over the fence.

The *jundies* appeared in the door of the courtyard with the casualty and stared at the obstacle. Suddenly explosions started raining down from the sky. Three mortar rounds impacted on the road fifty feet north of the school on the other side of the fence. The *jundies,* seeing the explosions directly in front of them, shrunk back into the school, disappearing from sight.

"Golf mobile this is Golf three actual," reported Cash. "We have mortars incoming just north of the school; you will not be able to go directly to the school due to the barricade. The *jundies* will get the casualty to you on the other side of the fence."

A few small arms fire shots went out from the courtyard of the school. Shortly after, machine gun bursts snapped from a building east of the school. A few houses away, second squad returned fire. They kept the enemy at bay, providing cover for the *jundies* to evacuate Gonzo.

"Sir, we've got to get Gonzo out of here!" yelled Rock. "I saw him when they brought him out to the doors and he looked messed up."

Another barrage of mortars landed thirty feet from the school. Cash looked at the dust clouds from the impacts. *They are dialing in on the Iraqis.*

"Mobile can't get in there," yelled Cash. "Tell the Iraqis to run the casualty out to the trucks; Moody, it's less than 30 feet."

"Sir, the Iraqis said they are not going out to the street."

"Tell them to move Gonzo out to the street! NOW!"

"Sir, they said no."

"I'll go get him," said Rock.

Cash grabbed the radio.

"Gents, we have mortars coming inbound; they are 82 millimeter mortars, so they are probably about two clicks out," said Cash. "I haven't heard the thumps of the rounds dropping, but keep your eyes peeled for their forward observer."

He looked down from the second story window of third squad's overwatch house and saw Rock run over to the school. The lieutenant called to his sharpshooters to take out any Iraqis with binoculars or cell phones within 300 meters of their position.

* * *

In the school, Rock saw Gonzo bleeding out fast from being hit with the rocket. The sergeant turkey peeked outside the courtyard and saw Golf mobile less than thirty feet away. *Thirty feet, this might as well be three football fields.* Greg sat in the front seat of the lead vehicle. He opened the door waiting to receive the casualty.

While looking out the entrance, another mortar barrage hit the deck five feet from the front of the courtyard spraying dirt and debris in Rock's face. The mobile Marines closed their doors and hunkered down as the blast hit.

Rock stared at the concertina wire. *I've got to get him out to the trucks.* He knew the next incoming mortar rounds would be close to the courtyard gate. He grabbed a piece of plywood from the school and tossed it on the fence. The weight of the plywood was not enough to hold it down, but Rock figured if he ran across the board, it would push the fence low enough for him to cross.

He threw the *jundi* on his shoulder and started to run to the trucks. Shots came at him from the east, down the long axis of the road. Rock struggled to carry the *jundi* and ran towards the plywood board ramped against the fence. He wobbled across and tripped in the middle of the fence. He lay tangled fifteen feet from Golf mobile's trucks. Rounds impacted around him. Gonzo moaned in pain.

He looked back at the school and then at mobile's trucks. *Fifteen feet, get out of this fence.* The sergeant grabbed his Kabar knife and cut his clothes off the fence and then did the same to Gonzo. Mobile returned fire to the east covering the two dismounts. He picked himself up and bent back over to pick up the wounded Iraqi.

Finally cleared from the concertina wire, Rock lifted the Iraqi half way onto his shoulder struggling to boost himself up when he fell again. More rounds snapped around him. *Come on, come on.* He struggled to pick the Iraqi up for the second time.

Suddenly the weight was lifted off of him. Greg ran from the vehicle to help carry the Iraqi. The two Marines sprinted the last fifteen feet to the trucks with shots coming at them from the east and mortars impacting at the front gate of the courtyard.

Greg and Rock set Gonzo in the back of the casualty vehicle and looked at each other for a split second. Rock's eyes said thank you, but the men exchanged no words.

Greg jumped in the trucks and drove away as Rock ran back into his overwatch house.

20

Greg looked over his shoulder at Gonzo who moaned in the back of his vehicle. The lieutenant looked down at his watch. Nine minutes had passed since they put Gonzo in the truck. In the backseat a corpsman sat next to the Iraqi and bandaged his leg where the shrapnel punctured through his skin. The mobile section headed towards Ramadi Medical Center located on Camp Ramadi.

The vehicle pulled up to the gate and stopped. An Army corporal ran towards the vehicle holding his hand out in the halt signal.

"What unit is this?" yelled the Army corporal.

"Golf mobile," replied Greg, "we have an urgent surgical casualty who's been hit in the femoral artery. He's bleeding out fast and we need to get him to Ramadi Med!"

"Roger, sir," the Army corporal waved to another soldier who lifted the barricade opening the entrance onto the base.

The mobile section moved forward through the serpentine barriers to the entrance. As they approached, another soldier ran outside.

"We did not receive a call about a wounded Marine," said an Army captain.

"Sir, it's not a Marine," replied Greg, "It's a *jundi.*"

"A what?"

"It's an Iraqi Army soldier, sir; he's in bad shape we need to get him through."

The Army captain shook his head.

"Lieutenant, we don't allow wounded Iraqis on base unless it's an emergency."

Greg stepped outside the humvee. He opened the back door and blood spilled out on the ground.

"What the fuck do you call this?"

Gonzo sighed holding his bloody leg wrapped in gauze. The lieutenant slammed the door and got back in the passenger seat.

"Is he going to die?" asked the Army captain.

"What the fuck difference does it make?"

"Well, if he isn't going to—"

Greg turned away from the Army captain and yelled to the driver.

"Go! Fuck this guy. Go!"

The driver looked confused.

"Go! DRIVE, GOD DAMMIT!"

The vehicle started to drive forward. The Army captain ran beside the vehicle.

"Lieutenant. Lieutenant!"

The vehicle drove onto the base and headed towards Ramadi Medical Center. The Marine and corpsman looked at the lieutenant stunned by his actions. In the backseat a lightheaded Gonzo held his hand to his heart. The rest of the vehicles in Golf mobile section followed behind. Over the open net on the radio all of the lieutenant's Marines heard the Army captain's report. The radio squawked—

"A rogue lieutenant blew through the gate unauthorized..."

21

Back at the referendum site Cash contemplated the situation. Normally if attacked in a static position, they moved. Movement was their key to keeping the enemy at bay. It was nearly impossible to locate the enemy and initiate an attack. If they stayed in one place long enough, the people who actively supported the enemy let them know where the Marines were.

They were always hit, and then the enemy vanished as if they had never been there in the first place. An IED explosion, with no triggerman. The enemy adapted to find the weaknesses in the Marines techniques. The Marine Corp "The Man" answered the tactical problems with technical answers.

The higher ups' answer was to add more gear, add more technology. The enemy with only his wits and the support of the people found the chink in each piece of additional armor the Marines added. *I don't need another piece of fucking gear, I need language training.*

The U.S. invested millions of dollars to create a system that jammed radio waves. They blocked the enemy from using cell phones and garage door openers to detonate IEDs. In return the enemy, with no money and a critical look at the problem, adapted and started creating pressure switch IEDs. The new bombs required no triggerman. The IEDs were victim actuated. You step, you trigger the bomb that would kill you, no enemy.

A machine gun ambush with no perceived shooters. The enemy forced the people to shoot from a house. They spread a sheet on the floor to pick up the shell casings. Two men waited out the back to run with the weapons. The Marines, one out of a thousand times, located the house and maneuvered on it. In their training schools they were over-taught the tactic to maneuver on the enemy. *What if you can't ever find them?*

After the shots, the enemy disappeared. If the Marines shot back they killed innocent civilians who were victims of circumstance that day. By the time they found the house there were no shells, no trace, and no shooters, only injured or dead Marines with no one to shoot back at.

A mortar attack, with no mortar-man. A technique the insurgents used was to put the top half of a mortar shell in ice and then set the popsicle mortar in the tube. When the ice melted off the top, the mortar fell in the tube releasing the trigger. The projectile launched, dialed in at a firm base. No shooter.

With all of the United States' might, they could not locate the enemy because the enemy hid within the people. For all intents and purposes, the enemy was the people.

And so the Marines patrolled and they moved. They bought time not really affecting the status quo. They hung on to a notion of hope that somewhere, someone did something different. Hopefully, their plans on a bigger scale might help them win or at least bring them out of the unclear state. What made sense tactically in the way they were trained did not make sense pragmatically on the ground. A tactical win often equaled a strategic loss.

Today's different— we have to stay and defend the polling centers. The enemy did not want the polling centers open. *Good, at least we get to square off against these guys instead of them constantly hitting us and vanishing.* The election forced the insurgents to act at a known place and time. Normally they chose the place and time which was equivocally the worst time for the Marines.

The referendum was a rare anomaly, where the tactical and strategic levels aligned, and the outcome of good tactics keeping the site open would be a strategic win, a rare occurrence but it would be a good boost for morale if the Marines kept the polling site open. *We finally get our shot.*

* * *

He stood up and walked over to a window. Through the glass, Cash saw two Marines from second squad on the adjacent roof. Their entire upper bodies were exposed to the whole world; random civilians, the other Marines and most importantly the enemy.

Are they insane? We know that there are enemy out there actively trying to kill us.

"Two-one this is Three Actual," ordered Cash into the radio, "you'd better get your Marines' heads down on the roof or I'm personally going to take a shot at them."

He fumed at the Marines' total lack of respect for the enemy. Rock looked at the lieutenant sensing his disappointment.

"I don't get it Rock. You'd think that the threat of being killed is enough to keep them on point."

"Sir, I can't truly explain it, but gunny broke it down for me once that made good sense. He said you can't prove a negative."

"What?"

"Basically you can't prove a negative. So the private standing on post knows that he might get shot. So the first day he stands post, he ensures that he stays behind the bullet proof glass fearful of getting shot. The second day he does the same thing still fearful. But on the third day, he has yet to get any reinforcement on his actions, that he is doing the right thing so he gets lazy and stands outside of the bulletproof glass."

Cash nodded his head.

"The third day nothing happens. He receives no negative reinforcement that his actions may kill him. So for the next thirty days the dumb fucker stands with his head exposed. On the thirty-first day, *kapow* he gets shot in the grape. The act kills him instantly without warning. He has no indications that what he is doing is wrong until he is already dead. Pretty high stakes."

The lieutenant had never thought of it like that.

"So how do you get him to keep his head down?"

"Well sir, the dumb fuckers won't keep their heads down out of fear of the enemy so I make them fear me. When I walk the posts, if I see a mother fucker with his head up I strike him with the fear of God. I tell him if I ever see him do that shit again, I will kill him. Normally I have to fuck a dude up like three times before he fears me enough to keep his head down. What happens is the little bastards will do the right thing, not because they are worried about getting shot, but they are worried I'm going to come fuck their world over."

The lieutenant nodded his head. In all his training no one had ever conveyed the concept so clearly.

22

Not much happened until nightfall. Explosions and gunfire echoed throughout the rest of the city while other units called in IED hits and other contact. The rest of the day, the enemy tried to find another polling center to exploit, leaving third platoon in relative peace.

When nightfall came, Isaac ran over from second squad's position to talk to Cash. The philosophy major, the physics major, and the sergeant sat next to each other monitoring the radio and discussing the day's events. After they took care of all the tactical discussions and plans, the talk inevitably turned to the absurd. These types of discussions usually only made sense to the men in the war zone, who high on nicotine and Redbull, were just trying to make sense of it all.

"Do you know what Chaos Theory is?" asked Cash, sparking up a smoke.

"Yeah, I saw it on *Jurassic Park*," said Rock, "a butterfly flaps his wings in the Bahamas and it causes a storm in New York City or some shit."

The sergeant thought for a second.

"What are you saying, sir? The Iraqis are going to turn into dinosaurs! Ha, if that happens I'd say we're gonna need some bigger fucking guns."

The sergeant laughed out loud. *These dudes are fucking ridiculous.* During the previous conversation, Isaac explained pieces of the second law of thermodynamics and how entropy related to the amount of resources the U.S. expended towards the war to achieve their overall strategic goal. *Fucking lieutenants. I'll play along, but only out of sheer boredom.*

"Everything tends towards disorder?" replied Rock, humoring his platoon commander.

"Yeah, yeah, everything goes towards disorder— well, not actually. The general belief is the opposite. Everything tends towards order."

Isaac nodded his head.

"Small events can have extreme ramifications."

Rock looked at the lieutenant and shook his head. Cash continued.

"Us holding this one polling center open might literally be the tipping point in the entire war. It's probably not that dramatic obviously, but what we're doing here at the small unit level can have impacts far above what is normally associated with the shit, at let's say the platoon level and below."

"I can somewhat see your correlation here," said Isaac. "Had Arch Duke Ferdinand not been assassinated it could have changed the course of world history. I get what you're saying about us having a bigger impact, but I don't necessarily see how that relates to chaos theory."

Rock was in awe they were having this conversation. He wondered if they actually knew what they were talking about and decided they did not.

"In its most precise rendering chaos can only arise when the possibility of any given state repeating itself is potentially zero, a situation in which the orbital..."

"For fuck's sake! I'm not speaking in literal terms," interrupted Cash, cutting off the physics major.

"I'm trying to make a damn point. Isaac, I swear, if you say anything about—"

The two lieutenants started to wrestle.

"I get it," said Rock breaking up the lieutenants' scuffle, "it's the strategic corporal. A Marine on patrol looks at a butterfly flapping its wings, he isn't paying attention and BOOM— he gets killed by an IED. The next day, on a patrol, his squad leader at the tactical level, revenge murders some innocent Iraqis, 'cause his buddy got smoked the day before. Then the shit goes sideways.

"A reporter happens to be standing there and catches the whole thing on videotape. The tape then airs on mother fucking CNN and the excitement goes all the way up the chain. Everyone goes berserk with the story, the locals go nuts because the Marines murdered some innocent dudes and start rioting. Oh, by the way, CNN happens to video all this as well.

"Pinko faggots in Berkeley start protesting the war using this event as a catalyst. The story builds momentum and college kids and soccer moms across the nation You Tube the shit and jump on board. Generals make blurred statements not demonizing the Marine, but not protecting him either. The President at the strategic level sees this fuck storm and fears he won't get re-elected cause of it all; this causes him to pull all of the troops out of Iraq. Basically butterfly flaps his wings in Ramadi, Iraq you get a shit storm in DC."

* * *

Several hours later, Rock walked the posts as Cash and Isaac slept. He was happy to have the lieutenants out of his mojo. He toured four times in two hours, stopping at the radio to think in between tours. *The shit those dudes say is unreal at times, but at least the big-brained fuckers are thinking. If we can make it out of here with no casualties and keep the polling centers open that would be badass.*

He mulled over his second deployment in *Husaybah, Iraq* along the Syrian border. They were ordered to patrol the streets with no mission statements. *We walked around and got blown up. It makes no fucking sense. At least now we got this one mission that seems to mean something.*

"I have two military age males pushing something into the street 200 meters to my east in between our house and Echo's pos" interrupted the radio.

"I'll be right there," replied the sergeant into the handset.

He climbed up to the roof feeling his way through the darkness and crawled up to the ledge. His fireteam leader and Gaines looked over the ledge into the night. Rock peered through the thermal scope and saw that heat signatures of two Iraqis dragging something into the middle of the street.

"Good job maintaining fire discipline."

The private held his fire.

"So, what do you think?"

"Well, there is a curfew and the people know that if they are moving shit out into the street in the middle of night, we define that as a hostile act," said the private quietly. "I think they are laying an IED to disrupt the logistics trains running to Echo's polling center."

The sergeant looked at the private.

"Well, what do you think?" whispered Rock in a serene tone.

"Let's take them out, sergeant."

"All right, you take charge."

"You want me to do it?"

"Yes, I want you to coordinate the ambush."

His tone encouraged Gaines. The private's confidence grew as he hurriedly called over two other Marines. Gaines placed them in on the roof, putting the machine gunner next to him. Their actions remained cloaked by the darkness of the night.

"Take your time," whispered Rock. "Be tactically patient, don't blow your chance to kill these shitheads."

The private ordered the four Marines to aim in. Their infrared lasers now glowed on the men who were still in the street.

"Be sure to clear your fields of fire," whispered Rock.

The sergeant gently lifted one of the Marine's barrels that pointed at a piece of rebar directly in front of him. The Marine looking through his night vision goggles did not see his barrel blocked by the rebar until the sergeant corrected him.

"Okay," said the anxious Gaines, "once everyone is set I'll give the countdown, then open with my M16; you'll all immediately follow."

All four Marines lay in the prone position on the roof. They arranged their bone structure getting in the proper position. They wanted to ensure their fires aimed straight with the lasers. The Marines' anticipation grew as they waited for the countdown. Through the night vision goggles, the street glowed green and the two men continued to mess with the IED. The green pixilated image sharply contrasted the white lasers which floated through the image all intersecting directly on the men.

Gaines whispered, "Four, Three, Two" and on one he opened up with his closed bolt rifle. The other Marines immediately followed suit and the machine gun gave out two bursts.

Rock looked through the thermal scope and saw the two heat signatures drop in the middle of the street.

23

The sound of the machine gun blasts interrupted Cash's dream. He talked to his wife, Jill, about having kids, saying he wanted a boy and suddenly he was pulled back into the fight. He stood, fully geared up and straightened his Kevlar helmet. He shook off the sleep then moved quickly to the roof.

"What's going on up here, Rock?"

He identified his squad leader's silhouette intrinsically by the way he stood.

"Sir, Gaines ambushed two IED layers. He did it all by himself, he spotted them and coordinated the whole thing. We saw some men drag away their bodies but we couldn't see anything in their hands for hostile act, positive identification so we didn't shoot."

"Good job, Gaines," said Cash reaching out into the dark to squeeze the private's shoulder.

"The bomb squad is on site right now disposing of the IED."

The lieutenant looked to the east and saw the sun creeping over the horizon painting the Iraqi rooftops with light. The first portion of the morning went by fairly uneventful. Three mortar barrages went by without any casualties. The radio squawked.

"Sir, battalion is calling to ask if any Iraqis have voted."

"Seven voted."

He called down to the school every half hour to see how things were going.

"Seven of the election workers we flew in from *Baghdad* voted, does that count? Oh, wait it is actually eight, the interpreter says he voted as well."

By mid-morning no civilians from Ramadi entered the polling station. The lieutenant looked at the concertina wire strung around the school. *How are these people supposed to vote? They are probably scared that we will shoot them if they come up to the polling site.* Down the road an Iraqi man appeared. He walked in the middle of the street a few hundred meters away towards the polling center.

"Sir, an Iraqi man's coming from the east," reported the fireteam leader.

He observed the man through his scope.

"He appears to have two small girls with him holding his hands. He also does not appear to have Down's syndrome," said the corporal.

Cash thought about the Marine's bizarre report. The enemy frequently used disabled people as suicide bombers. The Marines were tense about people with mental handicaps and always looked for them.

In Iraq there seems to be a lot of incestuous breeding. It seemed common place for Iraqis to marry their cousins. *I wonder if that is why there is a disproportionate amount of mentally disabled people.*

He looked through his scope at the man who was now fifty feet from the entrance of the polling center. He did not have any bulky clothing, an indication of a suicide vest and he did have two six-year-old Iraqi girls holding his hands. He focused his right eye through the scope examining the Iraqi girls whose black hair shined in the sun. *They have such big doe eyes.* Something about the girls connected with the idealistic lieutenant. He was pulled to their innocence, in the world of violence and chaos.

"Sir, that dude's a fucking *muj*, I know it," said Rock.

The man entered into the polling center.

"How do you know it?"

"Well, sir, why do you think he's got those little human shields with him? If he was truly trying to vote the enemy would be mortaring his ass right now. He's one of them I can feel it. He's casing out the joint so he can see our defensive set up."

"No, he's got the girls with him so, we don't shoot!"

The man exited out of the polling center. Several minutes later the *jundies* reported nine votes ratifying the Iraqi constitution. Cash sensed his sergeant was right. *There is no way he could walk in without everyone seeing him and then not be murdered.* Something lingered in the lieutenant's thought process convoluting his logic. To him the girls were too innocent to conceal the enemy.

* * *

Several hours later a muffled explosion boomed in the distance. The radio squawked, "CAAT Blue hit an IED south of checkpoint 295 on Moonlight."

The lieutenant climbed to the roof and saw a plume of smoke to the north. He looked up the street and could not see the mobile section around the bend. In the distance he heard the wail of a siren.

woohrauu...woohrauu...woohrauu...

An ambulance came from the north and the distant siren slowly grew louder as it drove closer. During the last 15 minutes, no guidon calls reported an ambulance coming down the road. Guidon calls were a general announcement that battalion called over the radio to announce any thing that pertained to all units. Before the referendum it was passed that when an approved ambulance traveled through zone, battalion would make a guidon call with the ambulance's information.

Fuck! Cash remembered the warning about the ambulances. He looked around the roof and saw Rock's Marines in position. He ran over to a radio.

"Golf CP, are there any guidons and is CAAT Blue's vehicle off of Moonlight?"

"Wait, one," squawked the handset.

Silence. The seconds ticked by. The moment slowed down. Cash anticipated bad things. *Come on, come on.* Rock positioned a corporal and Gaines to aim north towards the street. They waited for the vehicle with the siren to appear. The corporal held an AT-4, a modern day bazooka rocket.

"Rock, an IED blew up on a weapon's company humvee about 300 meters up the road from our pos. It's out of sight. Watch it, if we have to engage to the north, our fires might hit them if they haven't moved," ordered Cash.

The sergeant nodded slowly without looking at the lieutenant. Rock became motionless examining the road. The siren's wail continued to grow.

Woohrauu...Woohrauu...Woohrauu...

"Sir, are there any guidons?"

The sergeant now saw the mystery vehicle 250 meters away turn south onto their street. The white ambulance showed a red Muslim crescent on the hood and slowly progressed closer towards the Marine's overwatch position.

"Sir, are there any guidons about an ambulance coming south?"

The ambulance started to drive faster. The siren became louder as the vehicle moved towards the Marines, now 150 meters away.

WOOhrauu... WOOhrauu... WOOhrauu...

"THERE ARE NO GUIDONS FOR AN AMBULANCE," squawked the radio, "CAAT BLUE IS STILL ON MOONLIGHT"

"NO GUIDONS, NO GUIDONS."

Cash dropped the handset. His knuckles were white from squeezing the radio. He ran to the ledge of the roof. The ambulance closed in at 100 meters.

"If you have to shoot, DON'T SHOOT NORTH! Move to shoot across so your impacts go northeast. DO NOT shoot directly north, we have friendlies north, we have friendlies to the north!"

Rock, the corporal, and Gaines all aimed their weapons at the ambulance waiting.

The siren wailed even louder and the ambulance was now 75 meters away.

WOOHRAUU!!!WOOHRAUU!!!WOOHRAUU!!!

Rock looked at the ambulance, perfectly aimed in, and yelled, "Sir, Sir?"

The ambulance continued to drive and hit the first cone the Marines laid 60 meters from their position.

"Engage, Engage!"

Rock took four shots, shooting out the tires of the ambulance. It continued to drive through the barriers. Cash looked over at the corporal trying to cock the AT-4 rocket.

"Quit fumble-fucking around," yelled Rock.

The ambulance continued to move towards their position.

"Get that fucking rocket up!"

As Cash yelled, Gaines opened up with a thirty round machine gun burst into the grill of the ambulance. Rock took the AT-4 rocket from Doset and aimed the rocket on his shoulder ready to fire at any moment. His right thumb and index finger gently rested on the depress trigger.

"Cease fire! Cease fire!" yelled Cash.

Gaines's machine gun bursts disabled the vehicle. The siren continued to scream.

WOOHRAUU!!!WOOHRAUU!!!WOOHRAUU!!!

The Marines looked at the disabled ambulance anticipating an explosion to rock them. Before Cash stopped them, the *jundies* ran out in the street and assessed the situation. Thirty minutes later the Marines and the *jundies* were extracted.

* * *

The next morning Bama and Greg sat in the chow hall. The two lieutenants finished their eggs and hash browns and listened intently to the events of the referendum. Cash's food sat untouched as he struggled to tell them what happened.

"The siren is screaming, WOOHRAUU!!! WOOHRAUU!!! WOOHRAUU!!! It was the loudest thing I've ever heard. I can't get that damned siren out of my head. So we shoot the ambulance. One civilian woman who was sitting in the front passenger seat was shot in the leg. It was a minor wound only a graze."

Cash stared at the floor hesitant to continue.

"Another lady in the back of the ambulance was shot in the chest and stomach— killed instantly. We evacuated the other two and extracted."

"You killed a lady?" asked Rogue.

Cash sighed; he did not want to tell them.

"We killed a pregnant lady."

He exhaled and felt as though he dumped the weight off of his shoulders.

"That's fucking crazy," said Bama. "You worried about getting investigated?"

"No. Isaac said that because there were no guidons call out and because there was so much other shit going on in town that it won't get investigated. I wrote a nine-page statement last night and Isaac sent it to the judge. I think we did everything in our power to prevent it."

"So, you don't feel bad about it all?" questioned Rogue. "You shot a pregnant lady."

"Well, I honestly feel we did our best. It is an unfortunate situation."

He hid his emotions. The three lieutenants sat in silence. Cash shook the thoughts of the ambulance out of his head. *I was almost killed by that IED blast.*

He looked down at his cubed eggs and freezer-burned hash browns which were cold from sitting untouched for forty minutes. He realized he failed to eat a single thing in two days, his remorse changed to hunger. He was starving as he thought about his near-death experience. He looked at the cold eggs and his mouth salivated. For the first time in their deployment, despite the complications, he felt like they had made some progress. *We did it! We kept the polling center open.*

Before he took his first bite, a story that his father once told him flashed into his head. A man that almost died while climbing Mount Hood in an Oregon winter storm years ago, told his father that the morning after the event, he ate the best meal of his life. The climber told Cash's father that if he had captured the ingredient of that meal, he could have made millions by serving it in a restaurant. His entire life he never recaptured the ingredient.

"The ingredient," said Cash's father, "is the experience of near death."

Cash took the first bite of the cold eggs and then enjoyed the best meal of his life.

24

A white van with "Wounded Warrior" printed on the side pulled up in front of the apartment building. A reserve gunnery sergeant drove the van; he wore his uniform. John climbed in the van with his walker. He looked at the six other Marines, all of whom were junior enlisted. The oldest Marine barely looked twenty-one. The sight of them warmed his heart. *God damn, I love Marines!*

"Hey, how's it going, sir," said a Marine who recognized the lieutenant from Bethesda.

"Good, good; just call me John today."

He wore jeans and a polo shirt. All of the other wounded Marines were dressed in jeans and sweaters, no uniforms.

"How are you doing?" asked John to the wounded veteran sitting next to him.

"I'm doing good," said the lance corporal who lost his leg in an IED blast in Fallujah. "They told me I was the fastest Marine they've seen move from walking therapy to running therapy. Also I got three of these bad boys."

The nineteen-year-old pulled up his left pant leg and tapped on his prosthetic. A Marine Corps sticker covered the manufacturer's name.

"One for running, one for hiking, and one for everything else."

The van pulled up and the motley crew limped their way inside the stadium. The youngest-looking Marine of the bunch was named Paul. He was excited. He was going to get to throw the opening pitch of the game. Private Paul looked normal in jeans but walked slightly hunched over with a slight limp. In the van, on the way to the game, the Marines showed their scars and swapped stories. Paul's story involved being ripped open by a mortar round in Al Qaim. His stomach was a horrific site. John smiled at the private. *This ought to be good. These men deserve to get a little celebration after all they've been through.*

As they walked to their seats, Paul was escorted down to the side of the field. John looked out onto the green field as a military color guard presented the flag during the national anthem. He left his walker in the aisle and struggled to stand on his own.

As they started to the national anthem, John couldn't help notice the man in front of him did not remove his hat. The man looked thirty-something. He wore a Ralph Lauren windbreaker and khakis. He stood slouched seemingly disinterested as the national anthem played. His hat absorbed John's attention.

"Excuse me," said the Marine in a sharp tone.

"Yes," said the man turning his head back to look at the lieutenant.

"Can you take your hat off please?" asked John. "I find it disrespectful."

"Well I don't really give a damn what you think is disrespectful, this is a free country."

* * *

The security guards ran and pulled the gunnery sergeant off of the man. John spoke with the security guards. The man left on his own accord and as he walked away, John noticed blood all over his khaki's. *At least his khakis are ruined.*

The security guards left without saying anything to any of the other Marines. With all of the excitement they almost missed Paul's opening pitch. John did not want to miss the crowd's reaction to the Marine's moment in the spotlight. *This will be awesome.* The loud speaker projected,

"Tonight the opening pitch will be thrown by United States Marine Corps, Private First Class Keith Paul of Sandusky, Ohio. Keith was wounded in support of Operation Iraqi Freedom."

The wounded Marines in the eleventh row on the first base line hooped and hollered cheering for their buddy. John held his left hand to his lips, and gave a high pitched whistle.

Suddenly, John stopped and looked at the crowd. Several people clapped and cheered. Although no one stood, no one whistled.

He looked at the people sitting to his left who seemed annoyed by the Marines. He looked back at the other five Marines who were all still cheering. The jumbo screen displayed Paul. *Oh well, at least the Marines are excited.*

Private Paul limped off the field. The loudspeaker's announced the baseball team's starting lineup. The crowd cheered. Their noise filled the stadium. The announcer highlighted the starting pitcher recently won the Cy Young award. The crowd went nuts and several people gave a standing ovation. John shook his head. *This is sick.*

The lieutenant hobbled out to the aisle and grabbed his walker.

"Where are you going, sir?" asked the gunnery sergeant.

"I need some air."

"I need a smoke, I'll go with you."

The two Marines walked through the stadium to the outer balcony. John moved defeated, pushing his walker. The gunnery sergeant walked tall in his stiff and crisp Charlie's uniform, despite the scuffle. His green pants and shirt were freshly pressed and starched. His colored ribbons made a sharp contrast against the tan shirt.

The two Marines stood on the balcony smoking as a man walked by.

"Thank you," said the man, nodding his head toward the gunnery sergeant.

The lieutenant looked at the man as he walked away. *Thank you? How much do you thank me? Enough to walk by and say thank you. Geeze thanks; you're doing your part buddy. Not enough to take your hat off during the playing of the greatest country in the world's national anthem. Yeah right, thank you.*

These people don't have any idea. They don't care. To them this is just another day in paradise. They don't realize right now there are service members in harm's way sacrificing everything for them. They cheer for a ballplayer, an athlete who shows physical prowess, and call him courageous. That's something I guess, but it's surely not courage. Isaac running into fire, pulling out three wounded Marines, knowing he may get hit or burst into flames, that's courage.

Thank you. How much do you thank me? I'll put a yellow sticker on my car and I'm doing my part. It's almost insulting the majority of those sheep only have the sticker on their car so they feel good about themselves. Yeah, put the fucking sticker on your car but don't even stand up for a true hero. Cheer for some empty meaning like a ballplayer's accomplishment in a mere game.

These people are indifferent. In World War I and World War II, the Greatest Generation, the people cared. They supported the troops

100

wholeheartedly; the majority of the country was unified behind the foreign policy of the country. Gold Star mothers had strangers buy them groceries in the stores. The people cared.

In Vietnam the people cared. They cared enough to riot. They demanded the troops come home. They protested. They saw what was going on and objected against it, right or wrong they at least bothered to care.

Now you've got my generation's situation. A small disproportionate amount of people carry the burden and the majority is apathetic. We're out there risking our necks protecting their right to continue their lives in apathy. Thank you. I'll just go on protecting your right to not give a fuck.

Thank you. Not enough to cheer for a nineteen-year-old hero, a kid for any other relative situation in the states. A kid who carried a burden no young man should ever carry and has sacrificed more than any one person should ever have to. You know what, unless you want to sit down and buy me a beer and pay attention to what is going on in the world, next time don't thank me. He was disgusted with life, bitter by the atrophy of America.

He pushed the walker and hobbled back down and sat next to Paul whose face was full of excitement.

"Sir, did you see all of those people cheering for me, when I threw the first pitch? It was awesome; it was the coolest thing that has ever happened to me," said Paul.

He handed the lieutenant a baseball with a signature on it.

"The Cy Young winner even gave me a signed ball. He told me he wished he was as a brave as I was, said I was his hero. Can you believe that! I'm that dude's hero! Isn't that awesome, how much people appreciate what we're doing?"

"Yeah, that's awesome," said John trying to smile.

He was ashamed by his own arrogance, humbled by the innocence of the private.

25

"Today is a date which will live in infamy," said Greg.

He sat in the lieutenant's room wearing desert digital cammies instead of his normal tan flight suit. He read a book called *At Dawn we Slept* about the attacks on Pearl Harbor. His library included an assortment of economic course books, novels and military history. On Greg's bookshelf, sat ten times the amount of books that Bama and Cash owned combined.

"What ya talking about, Rogue?" asked Bama.

In the months since Greg blew through the gate taking Gonzo to Ramadi Medical Center, his Marines started calling him Rogue. The other lieutenants followed suit.

"Today is December Seventh," replied Rogue, "Sixty-four years ago today, the Japanese attacked Pearl Harbor."

"Hey, Rogue, that's fucking great, can I borrow your iPod?" said Cash. "I'm going to the gym. I've listened to mine so much I know every song by heart. I've got duty at noon so I'm trying to knock out a quick workout this morning."

"No problem."

He threw his music player to Cash who walked out of the room.

"So today's the anniversary of Pearl Harbor huh?" asked Bama.

"Yes. At the staff meeting last night Skinner said the Commandant was coming to the big base today. He said today was the anniversary of Pearl Harbor?"

"Oh, yeah," replied Bama, "what's he gonna tell us? Great job getting blown up. Anybody from your platoon gonna go hear the Commandant's moto speech?"

He tucked a dip in the bottom of his lip.

"No, they were all upset that we swapped our flight suits for cammies. It is ridiculous that we are going to change out of a uniform that has flame protection in order to be in utilities for the Commandant's visit."

"Yeah, I was gonna ask how come you're in cammies, I ain't never seen you in cammies, Rogue. That's stupid. I doubt he's even gonna come over here to the Snake Pit."

"Well, I guess the sergeant major ordered it in case the four star general wants to come over. His lap dog Skinner told all of the platoon sergeants the Marines must wear the same uniform. I told gunny to tell the first sergeant to go fuck himself, but he guilt tripped me into it. He asked if the Marines are going to do it. You know, I told him there was no way I was shaving my mustache though. That's going too far."

Bama nodded his head.

"What time are you giving your order?"

"I'll probably give it around 1400," answered Bama, "I plan on staging at Echo's OPVA then patrolling dismounted from there. Can mobile give us a lift?"

"No problem."

Bama and Rogue sat in silence. Bama read a *Maxim* magazine and thought about hometown hotties. Rogue read about Pearl Harbor and thought about how Japan achieved a clear tactical victory. Overall though, Japan's act was a strategic blunder. The event pushed the U.S. public opinion to back the war and ultimately make a formal declaration of war. The U.S. then exponentially increased the amount of resources and attention they had been focusing on the Pacific theater.

The Georgetown economics major pondered how the tactical and strategic goals were so convoluted in his current fight. *We can't go into mosques even if we think there are enemy using the mosques as staging areas for IED triggermen or weapons caches. If we did, it would enrage the Iraqi people and ultimately hurt us at the strategic level.*

"We're the good guys," preached Heath to his lieutenants.

"If the enemy is doing this it will ultimately hurt them. By taking advantage of the sacred places that the Muslims revere, the people will see that they are not holy warriors, *mujahedeen*, but common thugs."

Rogue was not so sure. *If the people support them they will continue to let them use the mosques. We might as well be fighting with a blindfold on and one arm tied behind our back. We are giving them a distinct tactical advantage.*

Cash came back into the room, laughing. He threw the iPod to Rogue.

"It smells like sex in here. What were you doing while I was gone?"

"Funny," replied Rogue.

"Hey, Bama, you'll never guess what happened to me," said Cash. "So I'm down in that shitty gym getting my lift on, jamming to Rogue's iPod. He's got some good music on there."

"Oh yeah?"

"So I hit the next button and this entrancing beat comes on like— bump, bump, bump. I think hmm this must be a good song. The beat's good then it starts and the words kick in. *It's Raining Men Hallelujah, It's Raining Men Hallelujah*, ha ha Rogue you are such a fucking queer."

"You a faggot?" asked Bama.

"Well, gents, some of us non-Neanderthals who are secure in our masculinity and sexuality can listen to whatever they want. It's a good song, Cash, you yourself said it's got a good beat."

"I don't thinks he's gay, he's a mattress-sexual," said Bama.

"The term you're looking for is metro-sexual," replied Rogue.

"Right."

26

In the company command post, Cash stood duty. Several maps of Ramadi hung on the wall. The watch officer's role was to know everything that was going on in the zone with adjacent units, higher, and his own units. The watch never maintained as good as situational awareness as the Marines on the ground. They only ever knew a sliver as to what actually happened on the ground. Despite not knowing everything, they would often know more information as to what was going outside of their own unit's immediate situation. This allowed the watch to best support the unit in the fight with additional pieces to the puzzle.

Whenever a mission was out, the command post took on the tone of a surgical operating room. The feeling in the room was more somber and serious than any church service Cash had ever attended.

The company had experienced enough bad events that the lieutenants who stood duty knew that at any moment horror could come crackling out of the radio. The man on duty needed to be on his best game. It was critical to be ready to coordinate assets to the man in the fight and shift units to them if they got in a hairy situation. If the watch was not paying attention to everything and tracking all units, down to the microscopic level, it might cost a Marine his life.

Rogue sat next to Cash. The quick reaction force unit went on two-minute strip alert when a unit was out in zone. The mobile platoon commander or section leader sat in the command post while the other unit was out. The Marines on quick reaction force stayed in their boots and uniform. They waited to mount up and roll out the gate at a moment's notice.

Rogue and Cash stared in silence at the large map of Ramadi.

"Golf mobile heading East on Route Michigan, past four story," squawked the radio.

Cash picked up a green thumb tack with GM2 written on the head of the tack. He pressed the GM2 tack into the map on Route Michigan.

* * *

Golf mobile two pulled into Echo's observation post, OPVA, and first platoon jumped out of the trucks and moved into the building.

The gunny who led the section failed to call the command post to let them know that they reached OPVA, he assumed Bama would call when he went inside. The mobile section exited the outpost and started west on Route Michigan back into the darkness.

Bama started to walk towards the building. His radio operator grabbed him.

"Sir, do you want me to call into the command post that we've reached OPVA?"

"No, gunny will call and let them know. Once we get inside here and link up with OPVA's watch officer, I'll call in."

Bama walked inside the Echo Company command post and linked up with the lieutenant.

"Hey Bama there is a possible IED on Michigan, they let your mobile know," said the lieutenant.

* * *

"Possible IED on Route Michigan at four story," squawked the radio.

Golf mobile two pulled out of OPVA and headed west on Route Michigan. They were five blocks from the possible IED. The gunny sat in the lead vehicle and quickly analyzed the situation as the trucks moved through the night. Then he did what leaders do. Based off of the information present to him at the time, he made a decision.

"Golf Mobile two, we have a possible IED on Route Michigan at four story," said the gunny, "We're going to turn south onto Hospital. We'll take In Between west around the possible IED on Michigan and then loop back up onto Michigan once we've gone around it."

The mobile section turned south onto Hospital.

"We'll bypass that IED on the main road," said the gunny.

The lead seven-ton turned west onto In Between and traveled approximately 20 meters down the road. The gunny looked at the window and saw a small child close to the side of the road.

"Hey driver watch out for that—"
BOOM!

* * *

In the command post, Rogue and Cash stared at the map where the GM2 green tack was still stuck on Route Michigan at four story. They heard a distant explosion.

"Golf command post, this is Golf mobile two, we've been hit with an IED on In Between just west of Hospital intersection, we have one downed seven-ton, and one Marine casualty and one civilian casualty," squawked the radio. "We're rigging for tow on the first seven-ton but are requesting an evacuation for the casualties."

Rogue and Cash looked at each other.

"What the fuck are they doing on In Between?"

"I don't know. First platoon might have more casualties if that was an initial assessment of the situation," said Cash.

He relayed the situation report to the battalion command post and told the runner to go get Heath. He wanted more information so he could help. His impulse was to call back and ask one hundred questions to help build his own understanding of the situation.

Asking immediately never helped the Marines in the fight, and he knew it. The unit on the ground never knew all of the events instantly. To call and ask only added unneeded additional friction on the leader. Cash looked at the map and waited for the next report. The time between reports, although only seconds and minutes, felt like an eternity.

"I'll get the rest of the info while I'm enroute," said Rogue.

He threw on his flak jacket, picked up his rifle and ran out of the command post.

27

The Marines pushed the gun trucks out to provide security around the downed seven-ton.

"Gunners, watch out for shit heads trying to back lay IEDs on the evacuation route."

The IED exploded under the front two wheels of the seven-ton demobilizing the vehicle's front axle. When the blast occurred, the explosion lifted the seven-ton into the air. As it slammed back to the ground the private assistant driver was thrown against the roof injuring his back and neck from the jolt.

The child standing next to the road when the IED blast exploded was badly injured. A corpsman attended to the body.

"What should we do?"

A senior corporal stood outside the vehicles directing the recovery and casualty activities.

"Put the child with the private for now."

The junior Marines all faced outboard on security as the small unit leaders moved to take care of the situation.

Two corporals rigged the downed seven-ton for tow. A corpsman and a third corporal examined the private about ten meters from the seven-ton. The corpsman told the private to take off his flak jacket and blouse and gave him an initial assessment.

A fourth corporal identifying a gap in security moved from the protection of his gun truck and took a knee a few meters from the downed seven-ton. The corporal posted security protecting the Marines who were attending to the casualty, filling an imperative break in security.

"We've got to get this vehicle rigged up and get it out of here," ordered the senior corporal.

He worked with nerves of steel, meticulously hooking up the downed vehicle correctly under the immense pressure.

A total of seven Marines and one naval corpsman were outside the vehicles in vicinity of the downed seven-ton. All eight men consciously knew they were in danger that night. They knowingly put their own safety aside to get the entire unit out of the less than ideal situation.

* * *

Golf mobile one headed east on Route Michigan into the night. The drivers looked through their night vision goggles and saw Echo company's green infrared lasers dancing on the road. Rogue wondered what the exact situation on the ground was. He did not hear another radio transmission from Golf mobile two. As his vehicle turned down Hospital and rounded onto In Between he saw eight men outside the downed seven-ton. He stopped his truck fifty meters from the downed vehicles and opened the door.

Rogue looked down the street and saw the child lying on the ground. Suddenly a flash of fire ignited the dark night engulfing the downed seven-ton. The eruption boomed. The Marines disappeared into the fireball. Flames devoured the vehicle. The force of the explosion blew past him. The open guntruck door shielded the lieutenant. He felt the warmth through the glass.

After the initial explosion, the fireball faded away. The downed seven-ton continued to burn. Flames shot from it. The Marines who stood in the vicinity of the explosion all lay on the ground. Rogue looked. They were in bad shape.

"Golf command post, this is four actual, we have a mass casualty on In Between. We're assessing the situation, request additional battalion assets to conduct mass casualty evacuation plan."

He dropped the handset. Rogue and his corpsman ran to assess the situation. Several Marines from the first mobile section dismounted their vehicles. They searched for all of the casualties. Several were thrown up to twenty meters by the blast.

Rogue came up on an injured Marine covered in blood and debris. The Marine's leg hung off from the rest of his body. His eyes were closed and his body lay still.

The lieutenant saw the private driver who looked confused and walked in a daze less than five meters from him. The private's badly burned upper body appeared scorched, bloody and blackened. The private's trousers burned off of him and he only wore his combat boots.

He started to move to help the private when he looked back down at the body of the Marine next to him. The face of the Marine covered in ash, debris and blood looked black in the night. Suddenly, the Marine opened his eyes and gasped. *It's the gunny.*

Rogue yelled for help as a Marine came up and took the lieutenant's tourniquet and starting tying it to the corporal's leg. Two Marines pulled the injured corporal to the back of a high back casualty vehicle. Rogue continued to help grab bodies. He tried to get a solid count on how many Marines were injured and what the severities of their injuries were.

Three Marines loaded the casualties into the high back. The senior corporal regained his consciousness. He looked at the other two injured corporals and spoke to them as they passed in and out of consciousness.

"Come on, men. Hang on, they're going to get us to Ramadi Med and we'll get out of this," encouraged the section leader. "You're gonna be all right, we'll make it."

He lay in the back of the highback. Suddenly he heard gunfire.

28

Rodriguez's humvee sat seventy meters west of the IED site. Rodriguez, a seasoned lance corporal on his second tour to Iraq and the private driver were the only Marines in the guntruck. Everyone else dismounted to provide security or help with the casualty evacuation. He kept his focus outboard looking though his night vision goggles scanning the area.

"Rodriguez, what's going on?" asked the private. "Who's hit? Do you know how many casualties there are?"

"Shut up, and keep your focus outboard. We need to ensure shitheads don't move in on us."

"The corporal said he was going to fill a gap he saw south of the seven-ton," said the private. "Was he over there when the blast blew?"

"I don't know, but right now our job is to keep looking outboard, everything is gonna be okay as long as we keep doing our job," replied Rodriguez. "If we get all spazzy and run over there, who is going to cover the unit? No one."

"But I want to help."

"You are helping by observing the perimeter," answered Rodriguez. "Now shut up and keep your eyes open. I saw something turkey-peeking from that house over by where the casualty came in."

Several minutes passed by.

"Rodriguez, I see someone by the road."

Through his night vision goggles, Rodriguez saw the shape of a man with something in his hands. The man crept towards the road where the vehicles would exit. The lance corporal's hands firmly gripped the handle of his .50 caliber machine gun. He trained the weapon at the figure moving through the night. His thumbs rested on the butterfly trigger. He paused, stopping himself from pressing the trigger.

The senior corporal had impressed upon his Marines that a .50 caliber machine gun's maximum range is 7400 meters. In the city, the rounds would tear through three or four of the Iraqis' poorly constructed houses.

Rodriguez reached down and picked up his M16A4 rifle and aimed in at the man who was on the edge of the road, waiting to lay in the IED. He looked through his night vision goggles and rested his elbows on the edge of the turret giving him a solid shooting platform. He lined the laser up on the enemy. He took a deep breath and squeezed the trigger at the end of his exhale. The man fell to a knee with the object still in his hands and crawled off the road. Rodriguez fired four more shots as the man fell to the ground, unable to put the deadly object in the road.

* * *

In the command post, Heath and Cash stared at the green GM2 tack now stuck on In Between. The last information they received was a mass casualty report.

Bama called in from OPVA so they knew the first platoon Marines were not the casualties. The lieutenant and captain waited in silence, restless for the next call to come across the net.

"Golf command post, this is the driver for first truck, they've— they've all lost their legs— they're in bad shape we need to get them— we need to get them out of here— it's bad— IT'S REALLY BAD," squawked the radio. The grainy radio noise amplified the nervousness and terror in the Marine's voice.

Cash and Heath stared at the green GM2 tack. There was nothing they could do from the command post. They had launched the quick reaction force and called in Weapon's company to reinforce. The radio chirped again, giving some clarity to the situation, widening their sliver of the horror that occurred on In Between.

"Golf command post, this is four actual. We have seven urgent surgical casualties and one Iraqi casualty. We are developing the situation on names. I'm launching Golf mobile one with three urgent surgicals to Ramadi Med', we've had a small arms engagement that disrupted an IED layer on In Between and Hospital. I'm linking up with Weapon's company time now to get the rest of the casualties out of here."

* * *

On scene, Rogue dropped the handset after giving the report to the command post. He ran to the section leader and told them to push to Ramadi Med.

"Sir, are you coming with us?"

"No push without me," answered Rogue, "I'm staying here to clean up this mess."

Golf mobile one pushed to Ramadi Med with the senior corporal and two other badly injured corporals. Rogue and Doc V rounded the corner of the gun truck heading back towards the seven-ton. The only Marine still in constant consciousness was the burned private. The private in his combat boots and boxers wandered in a daze talking to himself. The Marine stared at the lieutenant. His eyes pleaded to him.

"Sir, you have to get me out of here."

He collapsed to the ground. Dirt stuck to his scorched skin. A stray dog appeared and licked the burned private's sores. Rogue saw the mongrel and gagged in his mouth at the sight. He kicked the dog.

Rogue grabbed an uninjured Marine and ordered him to take the private to the casualty collection point.

At the casualty collection point, three injured Marines lay on the side of the road with the dead Iraqi child. The child had been killed by the second IED blast. The Marines bled profusely from multiple shrapnel wounds. The seven-ton driver, the initial corpsman, and the private lay in agony on In Between waiting to be evacuated.

"Sir, an Iraqi man is trying to get to the casualty collection point."

Several meters away, a Marine held back a helpless Iraqi man who screamed. Rogue shined his light at the man's face. *That's his son.*

Rogue knelt down next to the dead Iraqi child and felt his pulse. *Nothing. There is nothing we can do for him.*

"Let him through," yelled the lieutenant.

The Iraqi man picked up the limp child. He said nothing to the Marines and shook his head as he carried his son away. The man disappeared into the night.

* * *

With all of the injured Marines evacuated, Rogue assessed the situation. The Marines were loaded up and a Weapon's company mobile section was on scene. There was no reason for Golf mobile to remain there as well.

Something nagged in the back of Rogue's mind. *Did we get all of the body parts?* Several of the Marines' legs hung off, but he did not recall if any were completely blown off. Multiple feral dogs moved in on the destruction. They sniffed around and Rogue saw an animal with a piece of desert digital camouflage cloth in his mouth.

"Did we get all of the body parts?" asked Rogue to a group of Marines who were waiting on his call to exit the site.

No one said a word. They desperately wanted off In Between.

"We're not letting some fucking Iraqi dog run off with one of my Marine's legs," yelled Rogue. "I'll ask again, do we have accountability of all of the body parts."

"Sir, I saw a dog run to the south with a Marine's leg," answered a lance corporal. "The dog gripped the boot in his mouth."

"We're getting that fucking leg," ordered Rogue. "Alright the four of us are going to patrol down to find that mutt."

He told the remaining Marines from Golf mobile to strong point the area while he patrolled into the night. After forty-five minutes, they did not find the leg or the dog. During the hunt, they shot five other dogs in hope of finding the leg. Rogue would have searched all night, but Heath ordered him to leave the scene and get Golf mobile out of the ville and off of In Between.

* * *

Rogue climbed into a seven-ton that had not moved throughout the entire ordeal. The vehicle sat thirty meters behind the first truck and the driver had not dismounted. He had viewed the night's terror in its entirety.

"Okay, let's roll," ordered Rogue as the rest of the vehicles pulled away.

The Marine held his hands on the steering wheel but stared into the night with a blank look. The vehicle did not move.

"Hey, Marine, let's go," demanded Rogue.

The Marine kept the thousand-yard stare. The lieutenant smelled urine. He looked down at the floor of the truck on the driver's side and saw a puddle.

Rogue slapped the driver in the face.

"You'll have the rest of your life to think of this day, but now is not the fucking time. Get your shit together, Marine."

The seven-ton driver pulled forward. As they departed In Between, Rogue looked out the passenger's window and saw a mosque. He shook his head.

29

The following day Rogue stood in the briefing room and gave an order to both his mobile sections. He asked Heath to go out in the ville. They were going out on another mission to conduct snap vehicle checkpoints. Outside the briefing room the private and Rodriguez smoked a cigarette.

"I think its bullshit we're doing a mission today," said the private. "We should be paying our respects."

"No way, we have to keep going, if we take a pause we'll be overwhelmed by the event; we need to keep moving, that's how we honor them. Do your job and live up to what those Marines would want you to do. What did the senior corporal do when the first lieutenant got hit? He pushed on, that's what we're going to do," said Rodriguez.

Golf mobile conducted two snap vehicle checkpoint missions the day after the event.

* * *

Three days later the lieutenants sat in their room. It was their first time together since December Seventh.

"The private burned thirty percent of his body and experienced multiple shrapnel wounds, my section leader lost his left leg, the doc lost a leg, two other corporals also lost a leg, and another corporal lost both his legs and, and—"

Rogue's lips quivered and he quit talking and looked at the floor. He struggled to bring himself to say that the corporal who filled the gap in security died of complications while flying from Ramadi Med to *Baghdad*. Bama knew that one Marine had died. He hugged Rogue.

"I'm sorry," said Bama, "I'm sorry."

The lieutenants sat in silence for some time.

"While we were out in that ambush, we saw something messed up," sighed Bama breaking the silence.

He winced debating whether or not to tell Rogue what he saw.

"A Marine reported an Iraqi on a motorcycle with something dragging behind it."

He stopped and took a deep breath trying to find the words to describe what he saw when he went to the window.

"He was dragging a Marine's leg, Rogue."

"Did you shoot the MOTHER FUCKER?"

"We tried," said Bama. "Nate and another Marine were in a good spot and fired but he was moving and they missed him. We tried. I'm sorry man. I'm sorry."

The lieutenants sat speechless. After some time, Cash broke the silence.

"What about how you were wearing cammies, what the fuck, that private is burned 'cause of that stupid fucking sergeant major," said Cash. "That's bullshit, that son of a bitch should be relieved, and the commandant should get a fucking memo with four gold stars on it detailing how the secondary effects of his visit caused some poor kid to get burned."

"It would have happened anyway," sighed Rogue. "He took his blouse off to get checked by the doc. It was ignorant of me to agree to that."

Rogue looked at his flight suit, appalled by his decision to let the Marines wear cammies that day. *It's my fault that kid is burned.*

We need to be here but whatever we're doing isn't working. We're not winning; we're hanging on in a game that we're going to lose. On December Seventh, Rogue made a difficult revelation. *We must change the way we are fighting or we will lose this war and those Marines' sacrifices will have been all for naught.* The lieutenant hoped he was not the only one who knew this truth.

30

"Why are you smoking Virginia Slims?"

Cash reached up to his left blouse pocket and pulled out a pack. He looked inside the empty box. Bama and Rogue sat next to the fledgling date palm. Cash noticed they were smoking thin cigarettes. After three days in the ville, he wanted to catch up.

"Ain't you heard," said Bama, "an IED blast took out the logistics train that supplies Camp Ramadi with smokes. We haven't been able to get any American smokes for a week."

"Moody bought these Iraqi cigarettes for us out in town," said Rogue. "I think he is fucking with us."

"Well, shit, gents, I'm all out of smokes, can I bum one of those faggity ones from you?"

Bama handed him one. The three infantrymen stood next to the palm smoking thin cigarettes.

"We should quit smoking," said Cash. "Sooner or later we've got to go back to the states and it's not kosher for us to be smoking back there."

"I drive too fast to worry about my cholesterol," said Rogue.

He pushed his sunglasses down over his face.

"What the fuck ya talking about?"

"In *Taqaddum*, you know where we stayed for a couple of days before we flew into Ramadi?" said Rogue. "There is a big poster in the chow hall of a double bacon cheeseburger with grease and melted cheese dripping off of it, and underneath it, it says I drive too fast to worry about my cholesterol."

"Sooner or later we'll be out of this shit hole and Jill is not going to buy the whole, I drive too fast line," said Cash. "I'm done smoking next month. That will give us a few months of no smoking and then we'll be back home."

"You gents know what Heath wants to talk about?" asked Rogue. "I don't know if this whole mobile patrolling is working."

"Golf six is right smart," replied Bama. "If anybody gets it, it's him."

"I think he's giving us our reviews," explained Cash looking at his watch.

"Yeah, we'd better get on over there"

* * *

Heath sat at his desk. On the walls of his room hung several white boards marked up with company plans. On the wall also hung a picture of every Marine the company had lost.

I'm worried the lieutenants are losing faith in the way we're conducting the mission. Heath was a perpetual optimist and consummate professional who vowed long ago not to let his skepticism show to his men. He had lost faith months ago.

After a non-eventful tour as a lieutenant in the nineties, Heath taught lieutenants at the Infantry Officer Course. He promised his wife and four sons to leave the Marines after his tour teaching lieutenants. When the war broke out he felt a sense of duty to come back to the fleet and be a company commander.

He often wondered if he had made the right decision.

I don't understand why the brigade is focused on conducting operations in a World War II, conventional type of way. We're not going to win by sweeping through the city fifteen times. The Marine Corps is phenomenal at conducting missions that are focused on killing the enemy. The problem is we can kill a million insurgents on the streets and they will continue to re-emerge.

We need to focus on the root of the problem. He tried to convince the battalion commander to let his unit move out into the city. His commander received Heath's request with a positive mindset. Ultimately the idea was shot down by the brigade commander. The unit did not have enough troops to conduct those kinds of operations.

Golf Company's battlespace comprised all of southern Ramadi. The population for the single area included 100,000 people who dwelled in two kilometers of dense urban houses. The difficulty the company faced was that near the Snake Pit there was relatively no contact, but when they ventured south away from the base they were consistently hit.

For endless hours, every night and every day the company commander contemplated the way they were fighting in Ramadi. He was forced to have a unit constantly in an overwatch of Route Michigan. One mobile platoon remained in constant readiness for evacuations and logistics. Another stretched platoon protected his firm base and manned another checkpoint that led into the city. With all of the required tasks he barely had a platoon left for maneuver. Although he wanted to, he hardly affected the status quo in the ville because he did not have enough manpower.

We are great at conducting large conventional operations where we sweep, flank and attack. Whatever the operation is we swoop into the city, make an excellent action executed damn near to perfection, but then we don't exploit that action and we leave. When we leave we fuck it up. The enemy who lives in the city wins because we leave.

The company lost a Marine every time they ventured south and Heath had come to the realization if you were going to abandon each objective after you'd taken it, only to take it again and abandon it again, again, and again; well it wasn't worth the life of even a single Marine.

The thing that frustrated him the most was that these were not new lessons. On his desk he highlighted a passage from David Hackworth's *About Face*:

> *Marines were innately unfit for guerilla warfare ... The Warriors were trained for shock action- to violently close with the enemy and destroy him, and then go back to a rear area to marshal, refit, train, and wait for the next mission. They were eager motivated and aggressive all admirable characteristics in a conventional war, but on a guerilla battlefield they became too eager, too motivated too aggressive...*
>
> *The main thing I learned was there was simply no point in taking an objective you had no intention of holding, no point in using men... to taking of such objectives one by one if it wasn't going to lead you anyplace and if (as was also the case) you were going to abandon each objective after you'd taken it, only to take it again and abandon it again, again and again and again as the French did before us and as we were doing now- well, it wasn't worth the life of even a single soldier.*
>
> *I'd learned.*

On the side of the passage Heath wrote, "WE ARE FUCKING THIS SAME THING UP IN RAMADI!"

Today he was excited. He had some big news to tell his lieutenants. The news he was going to tell his officers gave him something he almost lost after December Seventh. The news gave him hope. But before he could share his hope, he had to address the Marines' fitness reports.

31

Heath looked at his lieutenants' fitness reports. He thought the Marine Corps report card for officers and senior enlisted Marines was broken. *I hate this system. I might as well just write a number from one to ten on a pink Post-it note and hand it to the lieutenants.*

When the superior showed a Marine their FITREP, it was not intended to be a counseling session. To Heath's knowledge that is what it inevitably turned into. He believed that a Marine should be evaluated with a 360 evaluation. Under the 360 assessment not only did the superior judge the Marine, but also his peers and subordinates. He thought this gave a more complete view of the officer instead of rewarding the teacher's pets.

He already counseled Bama and Rogue. The southerner was excellent tactically, the best in the company. His only problem was he needed to be more open-minded when it came to working with the Iraqis, both the civilians and the *jundies*. Bama's Marines loved him, not because he was easy on them. He worked them hard and held them to a standard. If he needed a performer for any mission, Bama was his lieutenant. The southerner easily affected any fight he was thrown into.

Rogue was also good tactically. He was head and shoulders above his peers academically, but he needed to learn how to work within the system better. The new maverick had a way of doing things on his own. The company commander liked this about him. *He's probably the best type of lieutenant to fight a counterinsurgency. It's not like the insurgents play by any rules.*

The only problem was, the Georgetown graduate had not yet mastered which situations warranted going against the Marine Corps. *Sometimes it is best not to go against the man.*

Then he had Cash. He was decent tactically and fair enough academically. His biggest flaw was that he was an idealist. Out of all of the lieutenants, he worked the most with the Iraqi Army. He did the best job keeping his Marines thinking about the bigger picture.

The only problem was Cash believed it. He bought in to all of the hype. Heath thought about his experiences. *Sometimes your higher is not always right. The Marine Corps is definitely not always right, look at the way we've been fighting in Iraq since the beginning of the war.*

Heath heard a knock on his door and Cash entered the room. He handed him the FITREP enclosed in a manila folder. Cash opened the folder and looked at the document.

"You can read that later," ordered Heath. "If I ranked you first or last, in actuality it makes no difference. Every lieutenant gets promoted to captain. If you're breathing you can get promoted to major. Here's my spiel that I give to lieutenants if you want to be a battalion commander someday. Be a stud, be perfect, work hard and never make any mistakes. If the timing is right, you'll make it. If you aren't, oh well, you'll just be in charge of a reserve battalion or chow hall somewhere."

Heath looked at the naïve lieutenant debating whether or not to tell him the truth.

"Do you love the Marine Corps?"

Cash thought about all of the Marines in his platoon and his squad leaders. He remembered his father pinning on his gold bars when he got commissioned. He thought about the other lieutenants.

"Yes, sir, I love the Marine Corps."

"That's what I want to talk to you about Cash," replied Heath. "How many times have you called your wife since we've been over here?"

Cash took a deep breath, he thought about Jill all the time, and wanted to call her every day. In Iraq five months had passed and he had only called five times. He did not answer the question.

"You see, I know we're busy and the shit we're doing is important. Hell, if you don't give everything you have to the fight, your Marines might pay the price. I know you know this and I see you give everything you have to the Marines."

Cash looked down at the ground.

"The problem with loving the Marine Corps is this. It will chew you up and spit you out, no matter how much you love it. No matter how hard you work."

The lieutenant looked up at Heath.

"Cash, the Marine Corps is only in love with one thing and that's the Constitution. It does not matter if you are a good man, the Marine Corps

123

will use you anyway it can to accomplish its mission and that's to defend the United States. The reason I'm telling you this is because I don't want you to give your whole life to something you love because I'm telling you now the relationship is doomed for failure. The Marine Corps will never love you back Cash."

The commander studied his protégé's face.

"We need men like you, Cash. I want to ensure you know what you're going into and I'm telling you as your company commander sometimes it's okay to take some time for yourself. If you don't, you'll get burned out and won't be as good as you could have been if you took some time to recharge. Also if you stay in the green machine, at the end of the ride, you have to get off. Sooner or later everybody gets off, and the question I often ask myself is when I get off the ride, will my family be waiting for me? Keep up the good work and remember this conversation the next time you go days without sleeping. Better yet, remember this the next time you go three days without calling your wife."

The lieutenant nodded his head.

"Cash, tonight you need to call your wife, that's not a suggestion, that's an order."

* * *

That night Cash stood in the lieutenants' smoking spot with the Thuraya satellite phone and dialed his wife's number.

"Hello," answered Jill Cash, 7699.50 miles away in California.

Her voice sounded grainy.

"Hey I—"

The phone cut out.

Cash felt awkward talking to his wife while he was in Iraq. He felt guilty for never calling her. When he did talk to her, it had been so long in between conversations that they were always hesitant. He could never tell her how everything was going. He could not tell her Ramadi was the Wild West and they were getting shot or blown up almost every day. He called again.

* * *

Jill looked at her cell phone. She loved it when Courtney called, but it was always awkward. She wondered if she should tell him. Her phone rang again.

"Hey, babes…I'm sorry about this stupid…"

"Honey, don't worry about it. I love you so much and can't wait to see you. I'm worried about you. There is all this crazy stuff on the news about Ramadi being the capital of the insurgency and they showed men in black masks patrolling with guns and explosions…"

"Jill, sweetie— don't worry about that— the news never— gets it right."

"I think you're sugar coating it, Courtney, you only tell me what I want to hear."

"No, it's not that bad here— honey, if the phone cuts out again— won't call back I have a ton of stuff to do—" The phone cut out again.

Jill knew he would call back, he never let the phone cut out without calling back to tell her everything was going to be okay, that he loved her, and that he would be home in a few months. Jill looked at the phone. *I'm going to tell him, what if something happens to him I want him to know.* Her phone rang.

"Courtney," said Jill. He interrupted her.

"Hey, babes, everything is going to be okay— I love you— I'll see you in a few—" The phone cut out. Jill knew he would not call back.

32

"Gents come in and have a seat. We have some big changes coming our way. I want to talk to you about the enemy we're fighting and then we'll go over my plans for the retaliation operation."

The lieutenants sat down and prepared their note-taking gear.

"We've got about a week left in the Snake Pit before brigade is having us move."

The lieutenants looked at each other and mumbled in despair. The Snake Pit was their home; it was the place they felt some semblance of normalcy in the chaos. Heath knew the sell might be hard. He needed to impress upon his young officers that it was overwhelmingly the best decision.

"I know I don't want to move either, but it is for the best. The brigade is halfway through a relief in place. The new brigade commander is an active duty soldier, not like his reservist counterpart who barely handled what was going on here. He has been in Iraq almost the entire war, this is his third tour and the Army does 12-15 month deployments. You do the math. This Army colonel gets it and he actually fought to get another Marine battalion in Ramadi. The new battalion is coming next week and they will take all of our battle space and our battalion will have everything north of Route Michigan."

"I've also heard from good sources the Multi National Forces Commander, the officer in charge of all of Iraq is changing next month. The incoming soldier is named General Petraeus and he understands counterinsurgency. He is a genius. When he commanded the 101st Airborne Division, they took Mosul from one of the worst cities in Iraq and made it Disneyland, no shit. General Petraeus and General Mattis literally re-wrote the military's publication on counterinsurgency.

"The general is going to push to do business differently in all of Iraq. Our new brigade commander is one of his men and the battalion commander says there are some big changes underway. The biggest change is that we will move out into the city. Petraeus' strategy is to push all of the troops off of firm bases and into the cities to live with the population.

"We will also start getting large amounts of money to conduct reconstruction projects at the company level. Previously these were only division or higher funds but Petraeus wants to push the money down. Most importantly, he wants to recruit local citizens to become Iraqi Police. All of these ideas I believe are for the better. You can have all the air, troops and guns in the world and still lose this fight. This is the right way ahead."

The lieutenants looked at Heath with wide eyes.

"I can see this is a lot of information to process. Why don't you gents take a smoke break and digest some of it."

* * *

All of the lieutenants sparked up the thin cigarettes. Isaac bummed a smoke from Bama.

"What's with the smokes?" asked Isaac.

"Don't ask," answered Cash. "So what do you think about moving to the ville?"

"It's crazy," said Bama, "those Muslims will kill us."

"I don't know," replied Rogue, "whatever we're doing is obviously not working."

The officers put out their slender smokes and walked back inside.

* * *

Heath looked his officers in the eyes making sure they were ready to receive the information.

"Who are we fighting in Ramadi?"

The lieutenants looked at each other.

"*al Qaeda.*"

"Yes, we're fighting *al Qaeda,* but who else?"

"The United States peoples' perception of the war and the media, sir."

"I like what you're thinking but we'll save that conversation for later. Gents, I want to talk to you about a friend verses foe theory. Here in Ramadi we are indeed fighting against *al Qaeda*. These are the same shitheads who put that sub-surface IED in the road on December Seventh. They are the same extremists who flew the planes into the World Trade Towers. *al Qaeda* in Iraq are the sick bastards who fuck men and impress them into fighting us. They are the number one enemy."

The lieutenants nodded their heads.

"Most of the leadership from *al Qaeda* is not from Iraq though. They infiltrated into the country. Right now they are kicking our ass in an insurgency fight. There is another group of people who attack us. These Iraqis are called the 1920s Brigade, has anyone heard of them?"

The lieutenants looked at him with a blank stare.

"All right, gents, I've asked the *jundi, Salah Khalil* to help explain this from the Iraqi's perspective."

The name sounded familiar to Bama.

"You mean Gonzo?"

"Yes, Gonzo," replied Heath, "you see Gonzo is from Ramadi and is *Sunni* unlike the majority of the Iraqi Army who is *Shī'ah*. He is actually going to transfer and become one of the new Iraqi Police."

The lieutenants nodded their heads as Moody and Gonzo entered the room. Gonzo walked with a slight limp from his wound.

"Gonzo, can you help explain to us what the 1920s brigade is?" asked Heath.

Moody interpreted and Gonzo looked at the Marines sheepishly. The young Iraqi replied with a one sentence answer speaking softly.

"They are patriots."

"Akin to Iraqi minutemen," said Heath.

The lieutenants stared at Gonzo and nodded. The Iraqi's posture became erect as he spoke more confidently. Moody's tone became more self-assured as well as he interpreted for the young *jundi.*

"They are Iraqi patriots who fight to keep Iraq from being occupied by anyone. Their militias predate *Saddam Hussein*'s dictatorship and have lineage back to the early 1900s. They resurrected the name 1920s Brigade from a revolt that happened when the British occupied Iraq."

Heath interjected.

"When the Brits occupied Iraq they were doing the same ops we're doing today, except they were no shit occupiers. They wanted Iraq to be a British colony. So the Brits parceled up the land and tried to push all of the nomadic Arab tribes into cities or onto permanent farmlands. They wanted to turn them into farmers, which the nomads were actually interested in, because they had never before owned a place where they constantly possessed food and other basic needs."

Gonzo nodded his head and replied with Moody interpreting.

"The problem was the British occupiers started to tax my people after they helped turn them into farmers. My grandfather didn't have a problem with getting taxed, but the occupiers also took their weapons, housed troops in their—"

Rogue interrupted.

"Sir it's the same list of grievances the colonial states had against the Brits."

"EXACTLY!" exclaimed Heath, "the Iraqis got pissed because the Brits were treating them like shit. So one day an *Ayatollah* became fed up and blew a British major's brains out. This act started the first Iraqi nationalist movement in history.

"Well, when the U.S. invaded Iraq, these revolters' grandsons and great-grandsons said, 'we aren't letting any gringos stay in our homeland,' so they aligned with *al Qaeda* to fight the U.S. occupation in Iraq. Over the last two to three years, we've hung on in Iraq and have shown the Iraqi people that we don't actually want to occupy Iraq. We legitimately want to help out their country. And we're not taxing them on anything.

"That's why I constantly preach to you all about being the good guy and not shooting people for no reason. Well, in these same years, *al Qaeda* has instated the Islamic State of Iraq and shown their true colors for what they actually are. They are the real occupiers. They have a murder and intimidation campaign going to keep the people in fear of kicking them out. They are enforcing strict Muslim law. Gonzo what's the name of it?"

"*Shar'iah* law," replied Gonzo through Moody, "it's a slanted view of the Islamic religious law. The Islamic State of Iraq forces the women to wear veils. Before the U.S. invaded Iraq, it was one of the most educated modern countries in the Middle East, here in Ramadi and even in *Baghdad* the women wore no veils. When *al Qaeda* entered they started making the women wear veils. They also started killing shop owners for placing tomatoes next to cucumbers, because one is the round symbol that represents the female ..."

"And," said Heath interrupting the Iraqi, "they TAX the people and treat them like shit.

"So what we've been seeing in the intelligence reports is that the 1920s Brigade is starting to fight *al Qaeda* in Iraq. Don't get me wrong, they are still taking shots at us as well, but they are trying to distance themselves from *al Qaeda*. The 1920s Brigade is not ready to marry up with coalition forces today, but if we move into the city and show them we actually give a shit about their safety, who knows?"

"There is one more important thing going in the city right now that I want to bring to your attention," said Heath. "Gonzo can you explain who *Sheik Ali* is?"

"He's the head *Sheik* of the *Alwani* tribe?" replied Gonzo through Moody.

"My tribe, the *Alwani* tribe makes up the majority of the 1920s Brigade in Ramadi. *Sheik Ali*'s father, the elder *Sheik,* was killed because he told *al Qaeda* that they had become too violent and the *Alwani*s would no longer pay tax to the Islamic State of Iraq.

"*al Qaeda* hung the elder *Sheik* in a field with his head cut off like a scarecrow. In our world, this means that the dead person's soul won't make it to heaven."

Heath interrupted.

"This is the largest 'fuck you' that *al Qaeda* could have done to *Sheik Ali*. The *Sheik* said he wanted to meet with the battalion and brigade commanders to discuss having the 1920s Brigade possibly work with the U.S. forces."

Cash and Rogue nodded at Gonzo thanking him for his insight. Bama shook his head. The Iraqi smiled back at the Marines.

"Gonzo, thank you for your help. All right, gents, I can see that Bama's head is about to explode, so take another smoke break."

* * *

"This shit is crazy," said Bama, "come hell or high-water, I ain't working with none of them fucking camel jockeys, especially that one. Did Heath forget, these are the same Iraqis that blew up John?"

"I don't know, what's the alternative?" replied Cash. "We're not winning now, if *al Qaeda* fucks it up with these 1920s chaps, we'd be stupid not to exploit it."

They puffed away in silence. Each lieutenant's mind raced as he tried to grasp all of the new information. The lieutenants crushed out their skinny smokes and headed back into Heath's room.

"Let's talk about this retaliation op for December Seventh."

33

Jill met Courtney her sophomore year waiting tables. She loved Courtney because he loved life. Despite being dark and rough, he was charismatic and exuded a contagious optimism. She loved him because he was an idealist.

The two dated throughout college and the week after graduation they flew down to California and got married in San Diego. Courtney wore his dress blues, and they rode to the reception in a horse and carriage. She felt like Cinderella.

She did not hate the Marine Corps. The few Marine Corps balls she attended in college were entertaining. The events were so proper and the soon-to-be officers looked so handsome in their uniforms. Then Courtney started active duty and she realized the fairy tale was only at the balls.

One week after their wedding, she stayed in California while Courtney attended The Basic School and Infantry Officer Course in Quantico, Virginia.

She cried when her father took her house hunting in Twentynine Palms, California, where Courtney received orders to be stationed.

"It's a blessing, it's only a few hours from San Diego," said her father.

Courtney and Jill lived in a two bedroom rental house for four months till he deployed to Iraq. One of the months she sat alone while he went to the month long pre-deployment exercise where the company was in the field the entire time. She regularly counted how much time they actually spent together during their marriage. Three months, one week with some additional weekends here and there. They would be married two years in May, a month after he returned from Iraq.

* * *

"How's Courtney doing," asked her father.

"Oh, he's good."

"Did you tell him about the big news yet?"

"No, the phone cut out before I had the chance."

Her father walked over and kissed Jill's six-month pregnant belly. Jill feared telling Courtney she was pregnant due to a previous miscarriage shortly after they were married.

When he found out about the pregnancy the first time, he was so excited. After their miscarriage, she knew he felt awfully bad because he was at The Basic School and not there to console her. The day Courtney deployed, Jill took a pregnancy test, and found out. She did not want to tell him until she passed the three month mark and now she was six months pregnant. She tried several times to tell him. He hardly ever called and it was always so brief, she never felt like it was the right time. She wrote him several letters telling him the big news but every time she went to send them, she started crying and threw them away. She must tell him when he called; she couldn't quantify the news in a letter.

I wonder if he'll be different when he comes back. She sat in a rocking chair and looked at pictures from their wedding. She looked down at her stomach and suddenly became scared. *What if— What if he does not come back.* She started to cry, then wiped her tears and said a prayer. *He'll come back. He has to.*

34

Cash and Moody jumped out of the back of the seven-ton and ran towards the school. The lieutenant carried his plastic Pelican laptop case. *I can't believe I'm bringing my computer into the ville.* He ran through the night juggling his rifle and the case. Third platoon ran to the entrance of the school, briefly stacked, and then flowed into the building and systematically cleared it. The action kicked off the retaliation operation.

Cash and Moody went to work trying to hook up the laptop through converters to the Iraqi power outlet. On the second deck of the school, Heath and Isaac set up a forward command post.

* * *

Rogue's mobile platoon cordoned off the area and waited for the bomb squad to sweep through the streets. Bama dismounted his platoon at the first house and set up an overwatch. He quickly detained the six military aged males who resided in the house.

Bama took all the men to the front room and looked at his blown up map of the four block area. The map was an enlarged aerial image that he downloaded off of Google Earth. The quality of Google Earth imagery was as good as or better than anything the military produced. The benefit in using the program was that Marines downloaded it directly from the internet. Bama looked at the map. Each house was numbered one through forty-three. *Forty-three houses; it's going to be a long night.*

One of his fireteam leaders filled out a tag and numbered the detainees. He put the corresponding house number on the tag. Each detainee received a numbered tag. He wrote on the tag MAM 1, House 1. MAM 2, House 1...

While the fireteam leader filled out the tags, Bama did the mental math; forty-three times roughly four men per house. *Holy shit, if Heath was right, we're going to detain 173 men tonight.* Rogue called Bama over the radio.

"EOD's cleared the roads in the cordon."

Bama's Marines escorted the detainees out to Rogue's trucks. They loaded them into an open highback and left them un-blindfolded. The mobile section drove from house one to the IED blast site. At the blast site they stopped the highback and the Marines brought the detainees to the edge of the truck and shined their flashlights on the crater. Bits of metal and tire surrounded the blast site. The ground was still red from the blood of the Golf Marines.

Rogue looked at the men and said, *"Leish* why, *Leish?"*

Once they forced the detainees to look at the bloody crater, they drove them to the school and dropped them off.

After December Seventh, Nate, had been combat meritoriously promoted to sergeant. He was transferred from Bama's first platoon to Golf Mobile to help supplement the leadership they lost that night.

* * *

In the school the Marines took the detainees and lined them up against a wall.

"Enta schismick, howea Your name and ID," said the intelligence sergeant.

The Marines wrote the Iraqi's name, tribe, house number, and tag number on a small white board. While the Iraqi stood with his information, the sergeant took a mug-shot on a digital camera.

On the roof Heath looked at his stop watch when Rogue left the first house. It read 12:10. *Twelve minutes, we have to go faster than that or we'll be here eight hours.* He reported to battalion that they were conducting a company cordon and sweep. He looked back at his watch. *Those missions only last three or four hours, not eight.*

To make matters worse, the operations officer talked on the battalion net directly to Echo's company commander who also conducted a mission that night. *Damn it he won't leave the battalion command post with two units in zone.*

"Four actual, one actual, we've got to speed up the transit time," barked Heath into the radio.

Rogue ordered his mobile section to split into two, three truck elements. Split into two sections, the mobile elements delivered detainees to the school every five minutes.

After an hour and a half of runs, 48 detainees sat in the school. Cash and Moody uploaded pictures onto the laptop in the interrogation room.

* * *

To get some of the detainees whose houses weren't directly on the road, Rogue and Nate dismounted and moved on foot. They ran across a side street they had run across twice before and slowed to a walk as they hit the edge of the street. It was dark out, but there was enough illumination from the moon that Nate was not wearing his night vision goggles.

Nate took a step and froze. He stood motionless as he realized he might explode at any minute. He stepped on top of what he thought was a gray sack. *I fucked up.* In the night the object appeared to be a rock.

Rogue continued to walk and noticed his battle buddy no longer with him. He looked back and saw Nate standing like a statue with his left foot on an unknown dark object.

"Nate, let's go we've got to keep pushing to get these detainees back."

The lump in the sergeant's throat grew as he tried to figure out what to say and do.

"Nate, what the fuck is going on over there?"

"Sir, I think I stepped on an IED"

"What?"

"I'm standing on two mortar shells."

35

The sergeant kept the lower half of his body still and raised his flashlight attached under his rifle barrel. He cautiously squeezed the handle grip shining the light at his feet. Sure enough, he stood on what the Marines called a burrito wrap. The insurgents quickly planted these IEDs by throwing them out in the street.

Fortunate for Nate, the IED was rigged to a pressure switch hose that ran off the two mortar shells. In the illumination of his flashlight, he saw that he had only stepped on the shells.

Inside the hose were two hacksaw blades. If stepped on, the two metal pieces would touch completing the circuit that initiated the fuse to blow the IED. He studied the IED device and decided if he pulled his foot off, the bomb would not blow. He slowly pulled his left foot off of the burrito wrap cringing at the thought of the blast that could occur at any moment.

"Sir, I'm good. I barely missed it."

Rogue took a knee in the courtyard twenty feet away. He was sure the burrito wrap was not there ten minutes ago when they ran across the same road. *Somebody threw that in the street within the last five minutes*. At that moment an eerie feeling swept over him that someone was watching the whole thing.

* * *

Two houses down from where Nate stepped on the burrito wrap, Bama entered into a room. In the dark he shined his flashlight. On the floor several people slept on foam mats covered with blankets. Normally when Marines entered into a room the people immediately got up. In this room none of the people moved. There were four foam mats with four unknown people under the blankets.

The Marine picked up the blankets. Under the mats he found four twenty-year-old Iraqi males dressed in Abibas track suits, a knock off of Adidas. The men pretended to be sleeping and did not move.

"Sir, all of these Iraqis are fully dressed and wearing tennis shoes."

If an Iraqi military-age male wore tennis shoes, they were immediately suspect of being an insurgent. Most Iraqi men either wore Arab sandals or boots. Tennis shoes meant they were running places. Tennis shoes meant they were insurgents.

"Well, let's tag them and bring them to the school."

He looked down at his map.

"We're in house twenty-three," said Bama, "the military age males will be tagged MAMs 89, 90, 91 and 92."

* * *

"Blade command post, this is Golf six," reported Heath, "we are about 50 percent actions complete with our cordon and sweep."

"Golf, what is going on at that school?" squawked the radio. "Echo Company rolled by on Route Michigan and reported 50 men entering into the school."

Heath looked into the radio.

"Blade, we stumbled across a wedding ceremony and we think they are trying to have a reception at the school."

"Roger, keep Blade updated if anything occurs. What is your return to base estimated time of arrival?" squawked the radio.

"ETA, probably another two to three hours in the ville."

Heath looked at a clipboard. *We have a total of 92 men and we're only halfway done.*

"What do you think, Isaac?"

"Sir, I think we need to start having Cash and Moody interrogate the people or we'll get behind the eight ball with battalion and we won't get any information at all."

Heath thought about the possible courses of action. If he waited for all of the people from the forty-three houses to get tagged they might be pulled out of the ville early. If they were pulled they would have no information and they would have infuriated 200 Iraqis.

If they pulled the trigger and started the interrogations before they had all of the people detained, the people being interrogated would not see all of the line ups and they might miss some information. *Something is*

137

better than nothing. He walked down to the first deck and told Cash to interrogate the Iraqis.

* * *

Cash and Moody sat in the interrogation room with two additional Marines on security. He compiled the 92 pictures onto a power point presentation. Cash's plan was to have the Iraqi sit down at the desk and look at the laptop. Moody explained to the man he was a suspect in an IED strike. Moody told the Iraqi that if he cooperated and told the Marines any information on the other 92 men he would be let go. If he did not cooperate, or if other people narked on him, he would be detained and sent to Abu Ghraib.

The first man from house number one, who was designated tag number one, entered the room. Moody explained to him what was going on and they started to flip through the pictures. Twenty detainees later, the two legal pads were full of notes. All twenty MAMs dished out an abundance of information on each other.

MAM # 12 in house four was repeatedly called a simpleton. MAM #17 in house five was a former colonel in Saddam's Iraqi Army. MAM #60 in house ten had four wives and owed money all over Ramadi.

For the most part the information was only that, information. There was no intelligence to derive from it. Ninety percent of it was interesting, but ultimately useless. However, there were a few things that repeatedly came up. MAM's 89, 90, 91 and 92 found in house 23 were reported as being not from the area, known criminals, known rapists, or known to work with or for *al Qaeda*. Cash and Moody continued to cycle through detainees.

* * *

Although they started the process without getting all of the detainees in the forty-three targeted houses they continued to detain the individuals. Heath thought if he kept battalion from pulling him out, he would conduct a second wave of interrogations. Worst case scenario he would at least get all of the individuals in the area's name, house number, and picture. To have a photograph census of all the inhabitants of an area was priceless when conducting targeted missions.

In a classroom where they were keeping the detainees, the Marines continued to take the Iraqis' pictures with the mug shot information.

"Okay next MAM," said the sergeant. MAM 166 was escorted to a holding classroom. MAMs 93 through 174 would get their pictures looked at in the second wave of interrogations.

At the forward command post, Heath and Isaac sat next to the radio.

"Golf six, this is Blade three," squawked the handset, "I have multiple reports that there are now over 100 people in the school. I need to know what the situation is."

Heath stared at the radio. When they called for him, he was going to give up his plan to interrogate the people.

"Blade three, this is Golf six, we are rounding up all of the MAM's in and around the In Between IED Strike site to question them about that night; we have 174 people that we intend to question."

Heath and Isaac looked at each other knowing the next response. They waited for a couple minutes while the operations officer processed the information.

"Golf six, say again," squawked the radio.

"We detained 174 people, brought them to the school, and intend to question them all about the December Seventh."

Another minute passed.

"Golf six, this is Blade three, you need to abort that mission; you do not have permission to detain 174 Iraqi civilians," demanded the radio.

"Well, the gig is up," said Heath to Isaac. "You try to stall him while I see how much we can get wrapped up here."

* * *

In the interrogation room, Cash and Moody questioned MAM # 123, when Heath walked in.

"Cash, you have ten minutes to wrap this up," ordered Heath. "Did we get any good information?"

Cash pulled Heath into another room. He held the note card with the names of the detainees that Moody wrote from house 23 on in Arabic and English.

"Sir, the men in house 23, MAMs 89, 90, 91 and 92 are all getting reported as being shady," said Cash. "Are we going to detain them?"

"No. We can't detain people off of other people's comments; we need to have some hard evidence on them."

"Sir, if we aren't going to detain these men, why did we do all of this?"

He put the note card with the MAMs from house 23 back in his pocket.

"I'll explain later. You know what, gather up all of the people and bring them into the center of the courtyard."

* * *

Heath stood on a picnic table in the courtyard and addressed the 174 Iraqi men. The sun broke the horizon lighting up the city.

"Men of Ramadi, my name is Captain Heath and I command the Marines who patrol this part of town. I apologize for the inconvenience taking you out of your homes. As you know an IED exploded on a Marine convoy here last week. The explosion injured and killed some of my men."

Moody translated and the Iraqis stared at Heath.

"We are here to help the Iraqi people, but we cannot help if we are blown up driving on the streets. We know who blew the IED and we will bring justice to you. For the rest of you, I apologize for pulling you from your homes."

The Iraqi men looked at each other. They knew somebody in the crowd was responsible for December Seventh.

"There are going to be some big changes in Ramadi coming in the future. The Marines are going to leave their firm bases and push into the city. We are recruiting the local men of Ramadi to join a new police force and rise up against *al Qaeda* forces that murder and intimidate your families. Men of Ramadi we are here to help and we will show you this as we never have before, I ask you to join us. You are free to go back to your homes; if you have nothing to do with *al Qaeda,* you have nothing to worry about."

The Iraqi men looked puzzled. They mulled around in the courtyard for the next five minutes unsure if they could actually leave.

Slowly the men trickled out and walked disheveled back to their homes.

* * *

Back in the briefing room at the Snake Pit, the leaders of Golf conducted the debrief. Heath wanted to get all of the information out on the table before the operations officer reprimanded him.

"Sir, I don't understand." said Cash, "why didn't we detain anyone?"

140

"Sir, we know those men in house 23 threw that burrito wrap and they are probably the same people that made December Seventh happen!" yelled Rogue.

The captain knew they couldn't detain anybody before they went on the mission. His motives were not to detain Iraqis. He wanted to send a message to that neighborhood. The challenge was the Marines could not go in shooting guns. Conversely if they did nothing the populace would continue thinking *al Qaeda* was winning the war.

Golf six thought his roundup was a good compromise and he obtained the desired effect he wanted. He looked at the lieutenants.

"Gents, now they know we know."

36

In the low-lit Italian restaurant, Jill, her sister Andrea, and her sister's friend Danielle sat enjoying the ambience. On the walls of the restaurant hung cheap fake wine vines.

"Would you like an appetizer?" asked the server.

"Yes, we'll have some antipasto," said Danielle. "So, Jill, your husband Courtney is deployed somewhere?"

"Yes, he's in Ramadi in the *Al Anbar* province."

"I'm sorry," said Danielle looking at Jill with pity. "I've never heard of Ramadi. Is it in Iraq or Afghanistan?"

"It's in Iraq."

I wish people didn't look at me like he was dead when I tell them that. He volunteered to serve, he wasn't drafted. To her, this is interesting; she has no comprehensions that outside of Southern California things are going on in the world that could affect her. Her idea of being inconvenienced is that she has to pay a little more to fill up her Volvo. It annoys her that the segment on E True Hollywood Story is going to be moved for the President's national address tomorrow.

"So, how is he doing? Does he like the Army?"

"He's a Marine."

* * *

On the car ride home after dinner, Andrea apologized to Jill about Danielle.

"I know she is egotistical but she really is a good person," said Andrea, "She is you know—"

"Living in la la land," replied Jill.

"She's never been exposed to any hardship. So it is hard for her to relate that you are making a sacrifice for her, you know being apart from your husband," explained Andrea.

"Well, I'm all right with it; I have those conversations every day," said Jill. "I find strength in that I actually believe that what they are doing is important and worth something."

"Yeah, that makes sense," said Andrea. "When you really care about something it puts everything else into perspective."

"I'm going to tell you something I've never told anyone, not even Courtney. Did you know before he left Courtney's dad called me?"

Her sister shook her head no.

"He called to see how I was doing and then he started crying on the phone," said Jill. "He said he could not imagine the guilt he would feel if something happened to his son. He apologized and told me why he named his son Courtney."

Her husband never spoke about his name with anyone and he usually went by Cash. She was the only person that called him by his first name.

"He said that in Vietnam his best friend named Courtney died. When his son was born, they were going to name him something else, but when he saw him for the first time, he named him Courtney."

Jill looked out the window and continued to talk. She explained to her sister what his father told her months ago. Courtney's father told her that he did not envy what a wife experienced during a deployment. As a father and veteran, he knew what Courtney would see. This troubled him greatly, but he told Jill that he knew everything would be okay. He said what the wives and mothers experience is far worse because they can only imagine the unknown. He told his daughter-in-law that this burden that a warrior's wife must carry is far heavier than anything he or any soldier carried.

"Then he reassured me and told me about how all of the Marines were closer than family and that they only actually fight for each other. They fight hardest to bring each other home. He thanked me and said I was a true patriot for supporting my husband."

Jill's sister looked at her confused. The talk of her husband being in harm's way usually sent her sister into tears, but tonight she spoke calmly. In the car on that night as she spoke of her father-in-law's talk, she possessed a confident proud tone.

"It's hard with Courtney being gone, but I feel the most satisfaction by being a part of this than I've ever felt about anything before in my entire life. This is by far the biggest sacrifice I've made, but the funny thing is, I do feel an honor, a sense of satisfaction greater than anything I've ever felt. I think to serve, to sacrifice for others, to offer what you have is the most rewarding experience. I feel sorry for Danielle because I don't think she'll ever know that feeling."

37

Jill and her mom sat on foam mats in the Lamaze class being held in a yoga studio. In the corner of the room, a television sat on an elevated stand. Jill asked the instructor if she could turn the television to the news, when the President's address came on.

She sat cross-legged with her six-month belly resting on her legs. Her mom made small talk with a few other pregnant ladies. The conversation turned to Courtney being deployed and Jill explained to two uninformed moms-to-be that Ramadi was in Iraq.

The instructor started the class.

"Hee, hee, hoo, hee, hee, hoo."

"You're doing good, honey," encouraged her mom.

"Hee, hee, hoo."

She looked past her instructor to the television where the newscasters announced the President would give his address.

Jill stopped the breathing and walked over to the stand and looked up at the television where George W. Bush started to speak.

"What's she doing?" asked another pregnant lady.

She looked at the young pregnant lady staring at the President on television.

"Her husband is in Ramadi," answered one of the ladies sitting next to Jill.

"Where's that?" asked the first pregnant lady.

"Iraq."

On the television, George W. Bush wore a dark black suit. His lavender tie with purple imprints evenly spaced contrasted nicely with his crisp white shirt. On the collar of his suit he wore an American flag pin.

"The new way forward in Iraq," spoke the President, "is for America to change their strategy to help Iraqis carry out their campaign to put down sectarian violence and bring security to the people of *Baghdad*. This will require increasing American force levels... We will deploy 20,000 additional troops, the vast majority of them to *Baghdad* and one additional Marine Battalion to *Al Anbar* province... In addition to the troop surge we will diversify our political and economic efforts."

Shortly after the address, reporters spoke with some former generals. Some agreed with the new strategy and others openly opposed it.

Jill walked back over and sat down. Her mom held her hand. She listened to the Lamaze instructor and continued the breathing exercises. While she over-emphasized her breathing, she thought about the speech.

I wonder how that will affect Courtney.

ACT III
UNDERSTANDING

Only the dead and the infantry know the horrors of war. — Ernest Hemmingway

The Senator waited for his staff in the back of a restaurant and looked forward to hearing their input. It reminded him of his past comfort in meeting with his squad leaders. This decision was weighing on him heavily and he had not slept for weeks. He asked himself that if he did not have the experience needed to make this impossible decision, who did? He was reminded of a quote from Sam Houston that particularly resonated with him: "I have the right to speak on the soil of Texas because I have watered it with my blood." He had earned the right to speak, yet was unsure of what to say.

While waiting he watched the younger patrons cheer for a baseball game on the television. Years ago he would have been annoyed that U.S. citizens would cheer for a sports game on the eve of the country deciding whether to wage war. He smiled as the home team scored and the bar cheered. Along the way he had learned why people serve the public. We bear the burden so they can enjoy the games he thought. His aides arrived, ate, and then went back to his office to discuss.

"My fellow senators are all too willing to send the troops to war, but what next?"

His tone was not angry, but inquisitive. This was not a rhetorical question, for he did not know the answer.

"What next after it becomes an unpopular war? History tells us there has never been a popular war so is this to be the first? What happens when the people back home no longer support it, but we have already opened Pandora's Box? As a country, once we commit to an action, we have a moral obligation to the countries we influence to see that our actions will improve the status quo, not diminish it."

"But, sir, the Bruneian people..."

"I'm well aware of the people. If we go into Brunei and rescue them from Malaysia what happens when we leave early? Do we stay for two years or two decades? The problem is intervening seems to be the overwhelmingly correct decision, but a direct action will not be resolved within one year. If our country is not prepared to be in South East Asia for the next thirty years, then our knee-jerk reaction to intervene will not be worth it."

He stepped out of the doorway and sat on the sofa folding his hands together. He looked at his aides as he thought for a moment. A thousand-yard stare came over his face as he spoke.

"Believe me, there is nothing worse than telling a mother her son is dead for a war that we ultimately did not want to fight and accomplished nothing. I will not tell any service member's mother we decided to do

something and not commit to it fully later. There is nothing more pitiful then a country that cannot come together behind their foreign interests. Unity of command is required in these situations. If we can't guarantee a unified front from Washington through the duration, then it is a simple answer."

He broke the distant gaze and looked at his staff eye to eye.

"Imagine being an eighteen-year-old in a foreign land risking your neck for a purpose your country mandated necessary enough to send you overseas. Imagine picking up a newspaper after you've lost men fighting for their mission and seeing that back home your country doesn't really want you there. I can tell you from experience, you might as well just throw that soldier off a cliff."

He looked away again.

"You see, as a lieutenant I felt an ethical obligation to my men. As a senator when I think of this decision, I now feel that same obligation. I truly believe this obligation to the men is not something you can just procure from nothing. It's not as simple as whether you would send your own son, because when you become a senator you are a public figure, elected to take care of everyone's sons. So would you make a decision to send someone else's son to protect everyone's interests? That is the question. If the answer today is yes, it must be yes for thirty years."

"But, sir, the cold war was won through thirty years of negotiations and talks, not invasions..."

"You're right. People are demanding immediate action but to act without considering all of the variables that will impact the result is naïve. Do people realize the Brits occupied Malaysia up until 1984? What if this is what China wants? To bait us into a long drawn out occupation while they continue to pump money into other defense platforms..."

He continued to list considerations and then stopped and thought for a moment.

"Some situations require force. I'm aware this current situation mandates the use of force, but I'm not only looking at the immediate situation. That's what fools and the newspapers look at. I'm looking ten-twenty years down the road when I stay up at night questioning was it worth it..."

38

Bama handed the Iraqi child an American five-dollar bill. In exchange, the eight-year-old handed him a block of ice and a twelve pack of Coke. Although Bama was cold to the idea of working with the Iraqi Police, there was something about the local kids. Every time he saw this particular child, his eyes were filled with hope and excitement.

All of the kids were so innocent and optimistic. The adult Iraqis looked beaten by life. Their actions suggested they knew their destiny— to live a life of misery. For some reason Bama liked the small child from whom he bought the ice. He looked at him and smiled. *This kid's still hopeful.*

When the Marines moved into the city, the children started to change first. Months earlier, when the Marines patrolled out of the Snake Pit, the people avoided them. Now living in the city, multiple times per day, patrols left out of the forward base. With their increased presence in zone, the children warmed up to the Marines.

Moody told Bama that the children selling ice next to the Marine base was a good sign. Under *Shar'iah* law ice was considered an un-needed western luxury and not permitted. Since the Marines moved into the city, ice was being sold next to the bases.

Bama's Marines adopted the Iraqi child with the hope in his eyes and nicknamed him Little Camper. The child was a mascot for the Marines. The boy loitered next to the front of the base. The Marines sent the errand-lad for miscellaneous items that were unavailable through the logistics trains. In exchange they would pay whatever he asked. Both parties benefited from the relationship.

"*Shukran 'Lil* Camper," said Bama tussling the kid's hair.

"*Afwan sadie* You're welcome, sir," replied the child.

The southerner carried the ice from the entrance of the firmbase up to the chow hall. He chipped off a few chunks and put them in several Iraqi Cokes, then juggled the drinks down to the meeting room.

In the briefing room Bama handed each staff member a soda, as they waited for Heath's announcement.

* * *

"Gentlemen we're getting extended," said Heath.

The company moved to their new outpost *Sabatash* two weeks earlier and was still getting adjusted to their post which sat in the middle of the city.

The name of their new outpost raised some eyebrows at battalion. The operations officer pushed to have it named Seventeenth Street. He argued against using the Arabic name. Heath fought back and pressed hard to have it named; *Sabatash* the Arabic word for seventeen. Ultimately, the battalion commander sided with Heath, putting out an order that, "From now on we're using Iraqi names."

"I don't understand," said Rogue, "I thought the President would surge new troops into Iraq— not extend us."

"For simplicity's sake, let's say there are three battalions in the Marines Corps," explained Heath, "and for the last three years they've been doing a rotation to Iraq where one battalion goes in for seven months, while the other two battalions train for roughly fourteen months in the states then deploy back to Iraq."

He drew a diagram on the white board:

Month 1-7	Month 7-14	Month 14-28	Month 28-35	Month 35-42
BN 1 IRAQ	BN 1 States	BN 1 States	**BN 1 IRAQ**	BN States
BN 2 States	**BN 2 IRAQ**	BN 2 States	BN 2 States	**BN 2 IRAQ**
BN 3 States	BN 3 States	**BN 3 IRAQ**	BN 3 States	BN 3 States

"So, gents, at any given time you've got one battalion in Iraq. If you want to increase the troops you have to overlap the troops because you only have three battalions. The way they are going to get the 'extra troops' is to extend us and make the incoming battalion's time in the states shorter. We have to overlap in Iraq, therefore increasing the amount of troops we have on the ground."

Heath erased the first diagram and drew another one representing how the Marine Corps intended to come up with the additional troops on a ten month rotation.

Month 1-5	Month 5-10	Month 10-15	Month 15-20	Month 20-25
BN 1 IRAQ	**BN 1 IRAQ**	BN 1 States	**BN 1 IRAQ**	**BN 1 IRAQ**
BN 2 States	**BN 2 IRAQ**	**BN 2 IRAQ**	BN 2 States	**BN 2 IRAQ**
BN 3 States	BN 3 States	**BN 3 IRAQ**	**BN 3 IRAQ**	BN 3 States

The lieutenants stared at the white board trying to make sense of "The Surge."

"I want to go home as much as you do, but I think this is a good thing. We've been bitching the first six months that we needed more troops to affect what is happening in the ville and those troops come at a cost. If the cost is us being extended for another three months, I'm okay with that to accomplish the mission."

The lieutenants nodded their heads.

"In reality it is a lot more complicated than that; I want to give you a logical base so you understand the reasoning behind us getting extended. Also your families probably won't understand this dynamic. When your Marines call home and have to explain why they got extended, now they have a legitimate answer and not some half cocked rumor the lance corporal underground cooked up. "

Back in the lieutenants' room they discussed "The Surge."

"I guess I see how it makes sense to extend us," said Cash, "but I feel like we're getting fucked. We've been here in the fight for six months and we have one month to go; it is mentally defeating to know we have to stay for another four months."

"It's the right thing," said Rogue, "we're only now figuring out how to fight and if they pulled us out, the new unit might not be as willing to lean into a different way of doing business."

"Now we have to explain this to the men, and I ain't as good as Heath when it comes to explaining," said Bama.

"I have to go meet with Heath and the new Iraqi Police chief," said Cash. "We're doing an operation with them; he said you were supposed to come too, Bama."

"Good luck," said Rogue.

"Don't worry, we'll keep an eye on them," said Bama.

* * *

"Why we trying to work with the locals?" asked Bama. "We been working with the damned Iraqi Army for months and they ain't done much 'sides get blown up with us."

"The Iraqi Army has come to their limit of advance in Ramadi," said Cash.

As the lieutenants walked down the hall, Cash mulled over the conundrum that was the Iraqi Army. The people of Ramadi who were mainly *Sunni*s remembered Saddam's regime as the good old days when they were thriving. They viewed the Iraqi Army, mainly made up of *Shī'ah* Iraqis from the south, as dogs. It was essential to Cash that his Marines understood this dynamic. In training the *Shī'ah* Iraqi Army, he tried to instill in them pride in their service and a sense of chivalry and professionalism. When they went out into town they needed to be respectful to the *Sunni*s.

The people of Ramadi did not respond to the *Shī'ah* Iraqi Army patrolling their streets. As much as the Marines tried to make the Iraqi Army work in Ramadi, *al Qaeda* was able to pit the *Sunni* locals against the outsiders. Cash looked at Bama and tried to verbalize his thoughts.

"The answer in Ramadi was not to bring in *Shī'ah* Iraqis," explained Cash. "The Marines cannot bridge the security gap in Ramadi without the cooperation of the locals."

* * *

Bama thought about Cash's statement. He was still unsure about working with the same men who caused Golf Company so much bloodshed.

The two lieutenants continued to walk down the hallway towards the meeting room anxious to see the Iraqi Police chief. Outside of the room, stood the police chief's personal security detachment. All of the Iraqis were between the ages of 16 and 26. Each of them carried a weapon and wore old school green cammies.

Multiple Iraqis slung several belts of linked PKC ammunition over their shoulders like Rambo. Across from the ten Iraqi men stood two Marine lance corporals on watch. The Marines and the Iraqis stared at each other with solemn faces. Each looked somewhat hesitant to be in the presence of the other.

"*Salam shurta*, hello policeman *shurta sadiki, shurta zein* police friends, police good," said Cash.

He slapped a few of the Iraqis on the shoulder smiling at them. The Iraqis smiled back at the Marine lieutenant who spoke broken Arabic to them. The lieutenant looked at the two Marines.

"Lighten up, gents," said Cash, "we're about to be living with these Iraqis so we need to make nice."

"If you say so, sir," replied one of the Marines in an uncertain tone. Bama smiled at the Marines and patted them on the back. "Gents, it'll be all right."

39

Cash opened the door and the police chief *Malik* and his cousin *Abdullah* stood up. *Malik* was not your typical Iraqi. He stood six feet tall and portrayed a kingly statesmanship rarely seen in the local men. He emitted the same command presence that Marine colonels only carry after twenty years in service.

"*As-Salāmu `Alaykum sadie* hello, sir"

"*Mulazim Cashee Shlonik* lieutenant Cash, how are you?" said *Malik*.

The lieutenant and the forty-year-old Iraqi shook with their right hand and pulled each other in for a hug. While hugging they kissed each other's left shoulder. Bama sat down next to Heath barely acknowledging the Iraqis.

Sheik Ali delivered *Malik* to the brigade commander as the man to take back the city. The *sheik* and the brigade commander came to an agreement that the tribal leader would get his tribe to join the Iraqi Police if the Marines would support them with firepower. The brigade commander agreed to put two tanks in front of the *sheik's* house in return for his help. The day after the tanks were placed *Sheik Ali* went onto Route Michigan and gave a speech recruiting hundreds of *Alwani*'s to stand up against *al Qaeda*.

Now that the politics were done at the higher levels, it came upon the companies to put the plan of working with the Iraqi Police into action. The *Alwani* tribe lived in the area North of Route Michigan. The coalition forces never figured out why no contact had occurred in these areas. *Malik* kept the violence out. He did not have direct ties with the 1920's brigade— at least no ties Marine intelligence could trace.

When meeting with Iraqis, before the Marines talked business, they learned to conduct a certain level of small talk. If they tried to rush through the Arab formality the relationship suffered.

"You're my new friend *Mulazim* Cashee," said *Malik* through the interpreter.

They met a few times prior to their current meeting and the Iraqi seemed to like the young Marine lieutenant who spoke broken Arabic.

"*Cashee* means new again in Arabic," said the chief, "so to me you will always be my new friend."

"Sir, what does *Malik* mean?" asked Cash.

Bama looked at Cash and shook his head.

"It means king!" answered *Malik*, proud of his name.

The Iraqi lit up an imported Dunhill British cigarette and offered one to the Marines. Dunhills were a status symbol of Iraqi upper class.

"Sir, I want to decorate this room," said Heath.

The bare meeting room was an old classroom. With a sandbag wall, three gray drab walls, and the fluorescent light, the room felt like a prison cell.

"I want to make it an Arab sitting room so I can entertain my guests and new Iraqi friends," said Heath.

"Oh, you want to make it into a *modif*," said *Malik*.

"I'll bring you some Iraqi decorations and couches."

"I'll bring you purple wallpaper," interjected his cousin, *Abdullah* breaking his own silence.

Abdullah was equally as imposing as *Malik* but quiet. Heath, Bama and Cash looked at each other puzzled. Purple wallpaper?

"Purple is the color of royalty for the Iraqis," said Moody. "I think they picked it up from the Brits."

"Sir, can you tell us a little about yourself? We're curious to get to know you." asked Heath.

"I was born in the mid '60s I think. I attended the military college in *Baghdad* and was a captain for an infantry company during the Iraq-Iran war. I spent two years fighting on the frontlines. *Saddam Hussein* used to get on the radio and speak to all of the troops on the open net. He was an excellent military leader. He told the troops *Avia* which means excellent job. Does Bush talk to you?"

"Well, our generals do most of the leading of the military," replied Heath. "Bush has been to Iraq a couple of times though."

"Hmm, I am hesitant to stop the fighting," explained *Malik*.

His matter-of-fact tone suggested that at the snap of his fingers he could end the violence. He took a deep drag off of his imported cigarette and exhaled slowly letting the smoke billow out of his mouth.

"The Iraq-Iran War stopped on August 8th, 1988 after eight years, eight months and eight days of fighting. I was thinking we should try to do the same with *al Qaeda,* but after the *irhabin* killed *Sheik Ali*'s father, my wife threatened to pick up a weapon if I did not."

"You could stop the violence?" asked Heath sincerely.

Since Golf moved to *Sabatash,* the violence increased. The company lost three Marines patrolling the area in the center of the city.

"It has already begun," answered *Malik.*

The Marine officers looked at each other in disbelief. During the last month, they had experienced the most violence. Despite the increase something occurred in the city they could not understand.

* * *

"I will explain it to you," said *Malik.*

He looked at *Abdullah* hesitating before he spoke.

"When America invaded Iraq, *Saddam Hussein* released all of the prisoners from Iraq's jails. He also made a deal with the devil and invited *al Qaeda* into the country. We stood up silently waiting to defend against the occupiers. Although *Saddam* issued the guidance, the leaders of the local areas could have denied *al Qaeda* from coming into their tribes. *Sheik Ali*'s father invited *al Qaeda* into Ramadi with open arms."

Heath listened intently to the Iraqi Police chief.

"The *al Qaeda* members married into the tribes and recruited the locals to help fight against the Marines. But then something happened. They became too violent. They started terrorizing the people and forcing *Shar'iah* law. Then *al Qaeda* became arrogant and their power consumed them. They preached ideals that they themselves did not follow. The events that lost *al Qaeda*'s support were thousands of injustices done to the people everyday since they came into the country. The injustices started out small and grew until the people could not stand it anymore."

"So *Sheik Ali*'s father, after asking *al Qaeda* into Ramadi, then asked them to leave?" asked Heath.

"It is not that simple," replied *Abdullah* through the interpreter.

Malik continued to explain the events and the lieutenants listened in awe to the translation of Ramadi's recent history.

"*al Qaeda* broke some unwritten rules. When *al Qaeda* started to impress men to work for them, and the violence started to impact the people daily, *Sheik Ali*'s father asked them to not hurt the people. They curbed their violence after the sheik's request, but then *al Qaeda* did something that ruined them," said *Malik*.

He paused and took a hit off of his cigarette contemplating how to explain the change.

"They put an IED in front of a man named Nile's house. Nile is a breadmaker, a menial low status job for an Arab. Nile is the third son of the third wife of his father and is a peasant. He holds no real *wasta,* social capital, in the tribe. When a Marine convoy drove by, *al Qaeda* blew the IED in front of the breadmaker's house. The IED killed several Marines, which was no real loss, but it also killed Nile's oldest son, a nine-year-old who played in the street. To us death is a part of life and Nile viewed his son's death as *In šā Allāh* The will of *Allah*. The breadmaker thought his son's death was part of *Allah*'s divine plan to rid the holy Arab land of the infidels."

The Marines shook their heads.

"But shortly after, *al Qaeda* put another IED in front of his house. When Nile's second son, a seven-year-old child played outside, he feared he would also be killed leaving him with no children. He could not justify that *Allah* wished for him to lose another son. So Nile went to *al Qaeda* and asked them to move the IED away from his house, explaining that they killed his eldest son. The breadmaker told the hardened men that he carried no qualms about his first-born, but he did not see it as the will of *Allah* to lose two sons."

Malik looked at *Abdullah*.

"The *al Qaeda* members laughed at Nile and told him he was trivial and the *mujahadeen* Holy Warriors were blessed by the will of *Allah* to do what was necessary to fight the infidels. 'Bread maker you are but a small grain of sand in the desert, you mean nothing,' said the *irhabin*."

Malik picked up a piece of dirt off the floor and held in his fingertips gesturing the breadmaker's worth to *al Qaeda*.

"Nile told the insurgents he accepted killing Marines, but he forbade them to put another IED in front of his house. The breadmaker decided it was worth his own life to save his second son."

Heath leaned in.

"What did *al Qaeda* do?"

40

"Did they kill Nile?"

Malik's voice sounded rich as he spoke. The foreign words rolled off his tongue in a poetic sound, putting the Marines in a trance. Moody emphasized the highs and lows in his vocal chords as he translated.

"No. They told Nile to leave. They threw him in the street and shut the door. After banging on the door for hours, Nile finally went home defeated. The next day Nile opened his door. He looked for his second son, who played outside."

Cash looked at the chief and winced. *They kidnapped his son.*

"On Nile's doorstep was the head of his seven-year-old second son. The *irhabin* cut the child's head off and threw it on Nile's doorstep still dripping blood."

"What did he do?"

"The breadmaker went to *Sheik Ali's* father and begged the elder *sheik* for justice. The peasants to us are seen as pure people innocent of heart. The elder *sheik* felt shame that he invited these devils into his bed. The *sheik's* father, after hearing the story, went to *al Qaeda* and told them to stop the violence or he intended to rise against them and push them out of the country. They killed the old man and disgraced his body. That act caused *Sheik Ali* to start the Awakening."

"And now we sit with you today because *al Qaeda* killed the son of an insignificant breadmaker," said *Abdullah*. "We mark the day his first son was killed, December Seventh, as the day the Awakening started."

He sat with a mild smirk on his face, mesmerized by the will of *Allah*.

The Marines saw a tiny window into the horrors the average Iraqi citizen endured under the grip of the *irhabin*. *Malik* offered them another Dunhill and the six men lit up.

"So, how do we stop the violence?" asked Heath.

"You do nothing," answered *Malik*, "Stay out of my way. If I ask for your help, give it. Other than that, I can have the *irhabin* out in a few weeks."

"But how?" asked Heath.

"You're hunters, are you not?"

"Yes," answered the Marines.

"So I will explain this to you in terms of hunting."

He used the same tone a teacher uses with a student.

"When I was a child, my father took me hunting for jackals next to the *Euphrates* River. You know the jackal is like a small dog, but they run in packs of three or four. The jackals conceal themselves in the thick reeds next to the great river. When other lesser animals go to water, the jackals prey on them. The problem is they are undetectable in the reeds; they are a ghost to the hunter."

Cash listened to *Malik*'s story. He was anxious to hear him explain how to take away the insurgent's anonymity. He reasoned it would be effortless for the Iraqis to know who their countrymen were and were not.

"My father lay in the open, waiting still with his weapon. His hunting partner would sneak to the edge of the *Euphrates* and jump into the great river tucking his legs. While he was in the air, before he hit the water, he screamed loudly. The splash and the noise frightened the jackals. Before the ripples from the splash hit the shore, the ghosts appeared. After they lost their cloak of concealment, my father shot the frightened jackals with ease."

"That is a great story, and I understand we need to flush out the *irhabin,* but I want to know how?" asked Heath.

"We can't flush out the *irhabin* because they are a cancer on our people. They have infected our tribes and have now, in a large part, become our tribes. In order to truly get rid of the *irhabin,* we need to accept that some of the young men were only victims of circumstance. If we kill everyone who has worked with *al Qaeda,* in one way or another, there will be no one left."

Heath nodded acknowledging this idea. He was prepared to overlook people who had been insurgents, if they now pledged to fight with the Marines and against *al Qaeda*. Bama looked at Heath in disbelief. *He is actually going to forgive these same Muslims who killed our Marines.*

"What we need to do is issue a *fatwa* forgiving the sins of those who stood with the *irhabin*," explained *Malik*. "Then we issue a message that we are going to have a day of reckoning. On the day of reckoning, whoever stands with us will be for the country of Iraq, and whoever opposes us we will know are insurgents. This will be the yell and the splash that exposes the ghosts to us. After the splash, I figure we can be gone of the *irhabin* in less than seven days and seven nights of hunting."

"When do you want to do this?" asked Heath.

"I need some more time to mobilize the true Iraqi patriots," answered *Malik*. "Right now only some of the *Alwani* tribe has pledged to fight with me."

He looked at *Abdullah*.

"All of my second cousins have volunteered to be my lieutenants in the fight against the *irhabin*. This is not enough though. I gave them an order to each gather ten men to fight against the *irhabin*. The *Sheik* has issued guidance for the people of the tribe to stand up and fight but they are scared. My family will be the tip of the spear. Our strength will inspire not only the men of the *Alwani*, but all the tribes of Ramadi, and all the peoples of *Al Anbar*. We are the Awakening."

"So what do we do next?" asked Heath.

"We have already killed several *al Qaeda*. My cousins and I will continue to strike the *irhabin* in the night. We will hunt them as they hunt you, in the night with masks; we will go into the reeds and become the ghosts. Once we have killed a few of their leaders and have secured more men, the time will be right."

"We can help," said Heath. "We have air, communications, overwhelming firepower, and we can evacuate you if necessary."

"Yes, the United States is very powerful but the power is useless if you can't find the enemy," explained *Malik*. "If we work together we can use the power for great things. Tell your men to not shoot into town for the next few weeks; don't let your defense down by any means, but please no offensive operations or you may shoot us. There will come a time when we will need you. I will call for you then."

41

During the conversation, Heath contemplated how *Malik* verbalized all of his thoughts on killing. *This is not the first time he has hunted men.* He stared at the kingly Iraqi. *Malik* possessed an innate fatherly presence but also carried the eyes of a killer.

The entire meeting the Iraqis brokered the power. *Malik* had something the Marines wanted. He owned the key to stopping the violence in the city. The battalion commander told Heath to make this thing go, but to be watchful of *Malik*.

Well, am I doing it or not. Heath thought about the mixed message order. The company commander now felt nothing was clear in the way things were being run in Iraq.

As his lieutenants felt before, he now wondered from the top down why there were no black and white orders. Gray seemed to be the color of every mission. To Heath this was much harder than the actual combat he had seen. *There is much more to this than the physical side.* He wondered what to do and after convincing himself there was no right answer, he did what he was trained to do. He took a bias for action. The action was negotiating. He was convinced he could change his environment to put the Marines in the better position with words; weapons had only brought him so far.

"*Malik*, sir, you are a brave man for taking this burden upon yourself," said Heath. "We will reconcile with you and forgive those who have fought against us, but you must give me a guarantee. You must promise to defend the city against *al Qaeda* not only in the short term but for the duration you work with Marines. The people see you and *Sheik Ali* as the true leaders and we will help legitimize your power."

Malik and *Abdullah* nodded their heads agreeing with the Marine.

"To give you legitimacy, we will pull you towards the law. But if you turn on us, we will be ruthless in hunting you down and detaining you

162

and all of your cousins. When you say something is clear, I will take your word on it. If it is not, and my men or I are killed by a guise by you or your cousins, we will hold you accountable."

Malik believed what the Marine said. He gave up something he could never take back. He came out of the reeds and revealed his identity.

Cash pulled a note card out of his pocket with four Iraqi names on it and handed it to the Iraqi leader.

"We will forgive everyone except these men. Everyone is pardoned except them."

Heath nodded towards his lieutenant.

"You will find them and bring them to justice as a sign of good faith that we can trust you."

Malik stared at the note card and handed it to *Abdullah* who wrote down the names in his notebook. *Malik* took another deep drag off of his cigarette and let it billow out of his mouth as he exhaled.

He paused looking back at the note card as if he were deciding what cards to play in a poker game. He looked back up at the Marines nodding as if to say– *I'll take care of it.*

"As you wish," replied *Malik*, "this will be a sign of our commitment to working with you."

The meeting became less dramatic and the Marines and the Iraqis transitioned the conversation to tell stories of their families and upbringings. They drank Iraqi Cokes and the Marines and Iraqis in the hallway heard laughter coming from inside the meeting room.

For many hours the Iraqis and the Marines bonded only as warriors could. At the end of the meeting, they hugged and kissed goodbye. Both groups now felt intimately closer. Each party exposed some of their own vulnerabilities in order to work together.

Cash and Bama walked down the hallway and headed towards their room.

"What was on the notecard?"

"It was the names of the men from house 23."

42

Bama's Marines pushed out and set up security. They were only one hundred meters from *Sabatash,* but they were outside of the wire and he was unsure of the Iraqi Police with him. He took a deep breath. *Why does it always smell like shit?*

Bama recalled driving through the dairy farms of rural Lamar County back home in the heart of Dixie. The smell of the fertilizer normally triggered a sense of nostalgia and pleasant memories of his grandfather's farm would come rushing back. The smell he took in that morning was not the slightly pleasurable odor he associated with dairy farms and sweet grass. That morning, in the streets of Ramadi, he smelled human feces.

Bama choked as he looked down. He knelt in a running gutter where raw sewage flowed around him. The street was covered in trash. Fruit flies swarmed above the fruit skins on the piles of garbage. He looked up at the crude two story cement buildings that created an urban canyon. Outside of the second story windows, Iraqis dumped water and trash directly into the street. *These people are animals.*

"Sir, I don't see him," said a Marine.

"He's always on this corner," said Bama.

The patrol circled the ghetto area in between *Sabatash* and the *souk* marketplace. The locals called the area *Azzizziyah.*

"*Ween Qadir,* where's Lil Camper," asked Bama to one of the *shurta,* Iraqi Police.

"*Maku, la Qadir,*" answered the *shurta* shaking his head no.

Bama looked over to another *shurta* who took a knee on the corner of a building. The *shurta* looked over to the Marine with a sour look on his face. *What's that smell?* A more disgusting vagrant odor overpowered the smell of shit. Bama smelled stale blood and rotting flesh. He smelled death.

"*Ta'al Mulazim* come lieutenant," said the Iraqi captain now shaking from whatever he saw around the corner.

Bama stood up and wiped the human excrement off of his knee with a watermelon peel from the street. He walked over and stood behind the Iraqi captain, and prepared to turkey-peek around the corner.

He looked around the corner. Flies swarmed around the matted hair of Little Camper's head on a block of ice. The severed head dripped blood on to a pyramid of ice blocks. The blocks melted and the water and blood mixed as the ice thawed. The fluids ran towards the path of least resistance to join the sewer flowing in the street.

Bama and the Iraqi captain were the only two people that saw the head. Bama gagged and turned to look away. Suddenly, something told him to go.

43

"Bronco's, Bronco's, disperse, disperse!!!"

Bama yelled the brevity code for take down a house and establish a hasty defense. He grabbed the *shurta* and pulled him back around the corner and headed toward the building his Marines were preparing to enter.

Before his first Marine entered a house, BOOM, BOOM two explosions hit the street.

GRENADES!

Several explosions boomed as ghosts hovered from the rooftops.

Bama ran towards the house and tripped. The figures moved on the rooftop. He struggled to stand with all of his gear. His adrenaline rushed and he jumped to his feet only to fall again in the slippery sewage. A masked man stood directly over him. He aimed his weapon as the man ducked behind the edge of the roof.

Suddenly, as he tried to stand he felt a push and was knocked over. He fell to the ground and heard a loud explosion. Lying on his back, Bama fired several bursts towards the rooftop. The first explosion burst Bama's ear drums. PINNGGGG rung in his ears. He could not see anyone on the roof and he breathed heavily from the excitement. He looked at the door twenty feet away. A Marine yelled, "Come on."

Bama looked back and saw who had pushed him out of the way of the falling grenade. A few feet away, the Iraqi captain lay bleeding from the neck. Bama quickly dragged him towards the house. The Iraqi choked up blood and tried to say something.

"*Ašhadu an lā ilāha Illā-llāh, wa ašhadu anna Muhammadan rasūlu-llāh,*" gasped the Iraqi as Bama pulled him into the house.

The Arabic words burned into Bama's mind. *Ašhadu an lā ilāha Illā-llāh, wa ašhadu anna Muhammadan rasūlu-llāh.*

The other explosion sent fragmentation into one of his Marines and another Iraqi Policeman.

166

"They're on the roofs, they're on the roofs," screamed the Marine who bled profusely from his lower leg.

He aimed his weapon toward the rooftop. Two Marines cross-decked, aiming over each other's heads at the opposite rooftops but saw nothing. Two more explosions echoed from the blasts of grenades.

After pursuing the ghosts to no avail Bama, assessed the situation.

"Sir, we have to get this Iraqi out of here," said the corpsman, "and the— the Iraqi captain— sir, he's dead."

The Iraqi had bled to death. He lay with his mouth open. Blood drenched his blue button down shirt.

Bama's mouth was dry. He licked the roof of his mouth trying to think what to do. *If we call in mobile, there might be IEDs on the extract.* The Marine hit in the lower leg was good enough to walk out. *We're only one hundred meters from Sabatash, fuck it.*

"Give that Iraqi to me," ordered Bama. "Call the CP tell them to have Golf mobile ready to link up with me at the gate."

If we do not get this Iraqi out of here he is going to die! The lieutenant threw the injured Iraqi on his shoulder and ran a hundred meters back to the base. Two other Marines and a *shurta* carried the dead Iraqi captain's body behind. At the gate Bama threw the wounded Iraqi in the back of the casualty vehicle while the injured Marine climbed inside. They sent the dead captain back knowing that he was beyond help.

* * *

The next day Bama waded through *Malik*'s ten-man security detachment. Embellished rumors spread through the new *shurta* force of the giant Marine lieutenant. Hundreds had heard the story of the lieutenant who carried the injured *shurta* to the casualty evacuation under fire.

"*Mulazim, nom, Mulazim,*" said the *shurta* looking at Bama, as they nodded at each other.

"*Shukran Nasir,*" said another *shurta* reaching out to touch the large lieutenant. The *shurta* called the new Marine legend the 'Protector.'

"Don't touch me God damn it," said Bama.

He slapped down the Iraqi's hand. He did not appreciate his new status with the *shurta,* but was somewhat amused by the whole ordeal. Although he had been hesitant about working with the Iraqi Police, his attitude started to shift. The story that *Malik* told him about the breadmaker did not affect him too heavily.

The death of Little Camper though, enraged Bama. He also could not shake the thought of the Iraqi captain. *He didn't have to push me out of the way.*

On the entrance of the meeting room, "HOOKA ROOM" was written in bold black permanent marker. Bama opened up the door. Purple fabric wallpaper with dark violet roses outlined the shape of several hearts and decorated the walls of the room. Five gold lush Arab couches made a sharp contrast against the purple walls. The sofas sat low to the ground in eastern style. The lounge seating was even further accented with several plush bright pink pillows.

The Marines' new allies furnished the room with authentic Arab garb. Inside the room sat Heath, *Malik,* and *Abdullah.*

"Hello lieutenant, we were just speaking of the Protector," said *Malik* through the interpreter.

Bama reached out and shook *Malik* and *Abdullah*'s hands. He reluctantly hugged the Iraqi men who pulled the lieutenant in tight and kissed his left shoulder.

Out of safety the Marines monitored the new Iraqi Police chief to see if he planned to sell them out to *al Qaeda.* Above the door to the battalion commander's room hung a sign he called a tribute to Ronald Reagan. The sign read, *"Doveryai, No Proveryai"* and he impressed the message upon his company commanders. The Russian Proverb meant, "Trust, but verify," and the leader used the phrase liberally when speaking to his men about working with the Iraqi Police. Weeks earlier the same men had shot at the Marines. Through the phone tap, the Marines learned that *al Qaeda* called *Malik* frequently.

* * *

Since their last meeting, *Malik* energized the Iraqis. The charismatic leader mobilized the entire western side of the city, the area where the *Alwani* tribe lived.

The Iraqi commander pushed a dual mission. He set up a defense in depth around the *Alwani* area. Simultaneously, he left the safety of his defense to hunt the insurgents who lived intermingled with the other tribes.

The Marine officers knew that *al Qaeda* threatened *Malik.* The *irhabin* insurgents had called him three times with increasing bribes to dissuade the dynamic Iraqi leader from working with the Marines.

The first call, *al Qaeda* offered *Malik* $40,000 to quit working with the Americans. They offered him a position as a lieutenant prince in the *irhabin*. *Malik* said no.

The second call, they offered him $120,000. They guaranteed they intended to make him the commander of *al Qaeda* in all of Ramadi. He said no.

On the third call they offered him $2 million dollars to do nothing.

"Just stop and we will give you the money," pleaded the *irhabin*.

The phone cut out and the battalion commander wanted to verify that *Malik* would not switch sides. The Iraqi leader said nothing to the Marines about the calls.

"The *irhabin* are putting up flyers in the *souk* market condemning the *Alwani*," said *Malik*. "This is a good sign they are scared."

"I'm sorry to hear of your cousin's death," said Heath.

"Captain *Falah* was special," replied *Malik*, "we're having his funeral ceremony today at the *Al Boheim* Mosque."

He looked at the walls with a long gaze.

"I want to ask you a question," said the chief. "If I gave you my phone can you track a number that has been calling me?"

"I'd have to look into it, but we'll figure something out," answered Heath, "Why?"

"The *irhabin* called and asked me to switch sides," replied *Malik*. "I told them I chose my side and that I planned to track them down and kill them. I don't like to make empty threats—"

"I'll see what I can do," said Heath. "Sir, is it time to flush out the rest of *al Qaeda*?"

"After Captain *Falah*'s funeral, the time will be right," explained *Malik*. "I will let you know, and when we fight I want *Mulazim Nasir,* the protector, with me. In honor of Captain *Falah,* I want him at the funeral today."

Malik pointed to his watch.

"We have to go, there isn't much time."

* * *

In the hallway Bama and Heath spoke with their backs turned to the Iraqis.

"Sir, I ain't going to no funeral," said Bama, "they'll kill me."

"You're going," ordered Heath. "Take a fireteam with Isaac and post them outside. Bring Moody and the two of you will go into the mosque—"

"Sir?"

"Bama, you're going."

44

Several hundred members of the *Alwani* tribe stood in silence as they mourned the death of Captain *Falah Alwani*. A fireteam with the executive officer posted security inside the courtyard.

Bama looked up at the ornamental minaret of the mosque, overwhelmed by the situation. All he thought about were the Iraqi captain's last words.

"Moody, what does *Ašhadu an lā ilāha Illā-llāh, wa ašhadu anna Muhammadan rasūlu-llāh,* mean?" asked Bama.

"I bear witness that there is no God but *Allah*," answered Moody.

The lieutenant looked at the hundreds of Iraqis mourning the hero's death.

Malik spotted Bama and walked towards him.

"*Mulazim Nasir* come with me," ordered *Malik*.

The chief reached out and held Bama's arm.

"Bama, take your gear off before you go into the mosque," said Isaac over the radio.

"Come hell or high water, I ain't taking off my gear," replied Bama into the radio.

Isaac looked over his shoulder at Bama and chirped back into the radio, "If *Malik* wants you to go in, take off your gear and go in."

Bama looked back at the hundreds of Iraqis dressed in their white *dishdashas*. They all wore the *smog agul* headdress that covered their heads. A large group stood outside the entrance to the mosque.

"Sir, we aren't going into the mosque," explained Moody. "At the funeral they say the prayer outside. We should drop our gear by the courtyard wall though."

Bama took a deep breath. *Fuck it.* He pulled his gear off and set it down next to courtyard wall. *Malik*, Bama and Moody walked towards the crowd gathering at the front of the mosque.

On a platform lay a simple wooden coffin. *Malik* stood next to Bama and held his hand. Sweat poured off of the southerner's hand onto the chief's. The Iraqi held a tight grip on the sweaty palm and looked at the Marine.

Malik said something in a fatherly tone.

"What did he say?" whispered Bama.

"It's okay, son," translated Moody.

Bama nodded back at *Malik*.

"Sir, they will start the prayers soon," explained Moody. "The body of Captain *Falah* is facing *Mecca*. In a normal funeral they would have washed him and put him in new clothes, but because he is a martyr he is still in the same clothes he died in."

The Imam faced away from the crowd towards *Mecca* and said something quietly. The crowd stood silent and Bama bowed his head. *Malik* reached over and lifted Bama's head up towards *Mecca*.

After several minutes of silence Bama became bored. He tried to look out of the corner of his eye to what went on around him. Everyone stood frozen. After some more time, suddenly, with no warning, the Imam broke the silence and spoke loudly. The Iraqis started to hug and move around.

Malik released Bama's hand and moved to the coffin. He kneeled over, kissed it and turned to the crowd. The Iraqis quit moving and gazed at the leader with attentive respect.

"The eyes shed tears and the heart is grieved but we will not say anything except which pleases our lord!" exclaimed *Malik*. "Brothers, we will push out the *Irhabin*, the *Alwani*s will be the saviors of Ramadi!"

The Iraqis cheered.

The mosque played an Arabic verse over the loudspeaker and the Iraqis stood facing towards Mecca. Bama did the same. As he stood still, a breeze brought the aroma of dates across his nose. Outside of the mosque courtyard stood a large date palm orchard. Under the trees, fallen dates decomposed. *It smells like the inside of a Fig Newton.* He tried to recall the last time he ate a Fig Newton when an explosion erupted.

MORTARS!

The Iraqi crowd scattered as machine gun fire poured into the courtyard cracking over the crowd. Bama turned to run towards his gear. Two Marines crouched over the top of a Marine who bled profusely.

ISAAC?

The southerner scooped up his gear with his left hand and threw it on. He ran to Isaac. His body lay still.

"Golf CP, this is One Actual, Isaac's been hit; I need a CASEVAC to link up with my team and extract us at the entrance of the mosque ..."

* * *

After evacuating Isaac, Golf reinforced the *Alwani*s who were fighting the last surge by *al Qaeda*. *Malik* did not need to initiate the day of reckoning. The *al Qaeda* insurgents, in their last attempt to show they were in control, attacked the mosque during Captain *Falah*'s funeral. The city erupted in violence.

The *Alwani*s engaged in a three-hour battle with *al Qaeda* who massed in force to attack them. After the initial attack with several *Alwani*s being wounded and killed, they spread out in security around the mosque and repelled the insurgents.

Malik called Heath on a cell phone. He requested the Marines to fly helicopters over the mosque as a show of force to the insurgents. He told them not to shoot into the city. Heath directed two Marine Cobra fighters to fly over the city and when the *Alwani*s saw the air cavalry, it was an unforgettable symbol that the Marines would be there to help.

Cash's platoon reinforced the area around the mosque and helped to repel the attack. During the battle, the Marines evacuated several wounded *Alwani*s, which only further reinforced that the Marines and the *Alwani*s were now allies in battle against *al Qaeda*.

During the battle, Heath continually asked *Malik* what the Marines could do to help. The Iraqi leader requested that the Marines take out the enemy mortar position which continued to rain explosions down on the mosque.

Using counter-battery radar, the Marines located the enemy's firing position several kilometers away next to the *Euphrates* River. With an unmanned aerial vehicle, the Marines saw a two-man mortar team in a semi-truck lot launching the mortars. The drone showed the acre lot that was fenced in by a high cinderblock wall. Inside the fence one hundred parked worn-down semi trucks created ten rows.

Heath maneuvered Rogue's mobile section and Bama's platoon to the semi-truck lot. In the command post, Heath watched a plasma flat screen that showed the image the drone plane emitted. On the screen a lone semi-truck pulled into the lot.

Rogue's platoon drove en-route to the semi-truck lot. Heath relayed what he observed to his two lieutenants.

"Golf Mobile, Golf one actual, a semi-truck just pulled into the lot. It looks like you've got two armed men wearing black masks in the northeast corner and a lone semi-truck driver who got out of his truck in the southeast corner," squawked the radio transmission to the forward lieutenants.

"Roger, Golf one copies all," squawked back the radio in the command post.

In back of a seven-ton Bama yelled the information to his men as it rumbled down the road.

"We have two armed Iraqis in masks in the northeast corner of the lot and one possible friendly."

Back in the command post the screen portrayed the image of the semi-truck lot. The two mortar men wearing masks seemed startled by the truck and ran behind another parked semi abandoning the mortar tube. The men moved out of sight of the camera.

"Fly the unmanned aerial vehicle down over top, so we can see what they're doing," ordered Heath.

The Marine controlled the plane with a joystick that resembled something a teenager would use to play a Playstation game. The unmanned aerial vehicle circled around, flying low behind the semi-truck. On the screen the two insurgents crouched behind the stationary vehicle.

The insurgents suddenly looked up at the plane. They pointed their AK-47s up and fired into the air.

The image on the plasma screen started to wobble. The display flashed the image getting closer and closer to the ground. Suddenly, the screen went black. Heath stared at the blank screen.

Those sons of bitches shot down the plane.

"Golf One, Golf Mobile, the insurgents shot down the unmanned aerial vehicle…"

45

Outside of the semi-truck lot, Rogue and Bama executed their hasty plan.

Rogue's vehicles cordoned off the area. The intellectual lieutenant snapped his first two gun trucks on the backside of the walled lot to secure the far side. His third and fourth trucks rolled up on the nearside diagonal corner. His vehicles secured the area around the acre lot and covered the dismounts as they jumped off of the seven-ton.

"Gents, conduct the RPG roll," ordered Rogue to his section leaders.

The rocket propelled grenade roll, a technique the Marines used, constantly kept their vehicles moving to disrupt a rocket propelled grenade shot. Rogue came up with the technique after hearing how the Australian soldiers used a similar technique called warbling to avoid sniper fire. The Aussies said they wobbled back and forth in the open to disrupt the enemy sniper fire.

Bama sent one squad to the nearest building to overwatch the lot, his other two squads climbed over the wall into the semi-truck lot. The squads swiftly swept through the area. They methodically moved from truck to truck bounding around the large vehicles.

In the center of the semi-truck lot was a large open area. The squad leader in the overwatch position called down to Bama over the radio.

"Golf one actual, I see three men unarmed in the middle of the lot in the open area."

Bama maneuvered his squads to the area taking cover behind the large trucks. He kneeled behind a tire and turkey peeked around the corner. Sure enough three Iraqis stood with their hands in the air. None of them wore masks, and there were no weapons. Bama ordered one squad to continue to search the lot while he stayed with the squad covering the open area.

The lieutenant and a fireteam aimed in at the men and slowly walked to the open area. The men dropped down to their knees.

"Moody, ask the men who's the semi truck driver," ordered Bama.

"Sir, they all say they are the truck driver."

Bama sighed. *Of course, they are all the truck driver.* He pulled his translator away from the three Iraqis.

"Bring them back to me one at a time, I wanna talk with them one on one."

He walked behind the nearest semi-truck.

The first Iraqi came back with the translator. Bama studied his eyes. They excitedly moved back and forth rapidly.

"Ask this Iraqi if he's the truck driver?"

"Sir, he says he is the truck driver and that he loves America and appreciates what we're doing in Iraq. He says the people are standing up to fight *al Qaeda* and he wishes to join them."

"All right, take him back," ordered Bama

The interpreter walked back the first Iraqi and grabbed the second man. Bama looked at the second Iraqi's eyes. They looked calm and resolute. The Iraqi stared back at the Marine lieutenant with a confident look filled with hate. He asked again.

"Sir, he says he is the truck driver and that he knows the other two men are the insurgents. He says they were shooting the weapons from over there," explained the translator pointing to the northeast corner of the lot.

The radio chirped that the other squad found two mortar tubes and two AK47's behind a semi in the northeast corner of the lot.

"Is he *al Qaeda*?" asked Bama.

"He says he hates *al Qaeda* and that he fought against them for years; he was one of the first people to stand up against them."

"All right, take him back and bring me the third man."

The interpreter walked back and grabbed the third Iraqi. Bama studied the third man's eyes. He looked tired. His eyes told the story of a man who was the former shell of the better man he once was.

"This man says his father was killed by a U.S. air strike in the nineties by Bill Clin-town. His brothers were killed by *al Qaeda* during the beginning of the war."

Bama looked at the Iraqi whose face filled with anguish as he told his plea.

"He says he hopes you don't think he is the truck driver. He says to be arrested by the Marines is a good thing. They will feed him and pay him when he gets released. The U.S. detained his cousin in '04 and brought him to Abu Ghraib. They treated him well."

The translator asked another question.

"He is asking that you arrest him because the insurgents will kill him or worse if they know he has helped the Americans."

The Iraqi man looked defeated, but something in his eyes spoke to Bama. The man carried a slight look of hope that reminded him of Little Camper.

"The man says he prays to *Allah* for the day when the Americans and *al Qaeda* leave the country of Iraq so it can be pure again. His grandfather told him stories of when the tribes lived simply as farmers. He hopes Iraq can one day return to this simple state."

Bama studied the man's face as he spoke.

"Tell the truck driver that things are getting better," said Bama. "Tell him that *Malik* of the *Alwani* tribe has mobilized the city against *al Qaeda.*"

The translator relayed the message.

"Sir, he does not believe you; he thinks *al Qaeda* will kill him"

"Tell him to trust me; things are changing. The city will get better."

The southerner looked at the Iraqi truck driver and reached out to him.

"I'm sorry."

* * *

"All right, let this Iraqi go and we're gonna take them other shitheads," ordered Bama.

The truck driver stood next to the semi looking confused.

The Marines flex cuffed the other two Iraqis and escorted them out to a highback humvee. Bama stood beside the back of the truck as they loaded up the two *al Qaeda* mortar-men.

Before the second man got in the truck, he looked at the lieutenant.

"Fuck you," said the Arab in perfect English.

"What'd you say to me?"

He puffed his chest up on the Iraqi.

"I said fuck you; I've been to Texas in '95. I'll go back and kill your mother. You have already lost," said the insurgent.

"Now hold on a damn minute. This Iraqi must be drunker than cooter brown."

He turned from his Marines to the man.

"Were going to win," said Bama. "We wiped your ass across town today. *Malik* and the Marines said they killed 60 of you shitheads at the mosque less than an hour ago. Your countrymen are sick of your *al Qaeda* bullshit and the good Iraqis are standing up."

"Iraqis ha," laughed the man. "Iraqis are dogs; they are weakest of the Arab people. The *jihad* comes to Iraq to kill *infidels*. We will fuck you. We will come to you."

Bama's blood boiled; his instinct was to punch the man but he restrained himself. He looked at his Marines and walked away slowly breathing and counting to himself. He turned around.

"Gag this woman," ordered Bama. "We won't fuck you, but I reckon your insurgent buddies will in Abu Ghraib."

The Marines stuffed a bandanna inside the man's mouth and roughly put him in the truck blindfolded.

Bama walked away from the highback and turned back. He leaned in close and whispered something in the insurgent's ear.

"If you try to get in the states, I'll kill you myself, you son of a bitch, and don't go to Texas," said Bama in the trembling man's ear. His whisper escalated to a yell, "Come to TUSCALOOSA, ALABAMA!"

46

The Marines of Golf Company filled the *Sabatash* chow hall for Isaac's memorial. After two nights in intensive care, Isaac passed in a hospital in Germany. His mother flew to Europe and sat at his bedside when he died.

At the front of the chow hall sat the make-shift memorial for the first lieutenant. Cash, Rogue and Bama stood at the back of the chow hall with *Malik*. The chief held Bama's hand.

Heath stood behind a makeshift podium.

"... He was the glue that held the company together... On September 11 the country was aghast that terrorists attacked us in our own country. On September 12 the whole country said they were going to stand up against the terrorists. Six years later that number has become damn near nonexistent. Isaac Trimble stood up when others would not. Isaac Trimble fought when others would not. He will be remembered as the best of us all."

Heath was the only person who spoke that day. He despised the fat chaplain and refused to let the proclaimed man of God belittle another one of his Marine's deaths. The lieutenants declined to talk, saving their words of remembrance for the privacy of their room.

After the memorial the lieutenants, Heath and *Malik* sat in the Hooka Room. They smoked cigarettes and reminisced about their lost friends. After some time, the chief stood up.

"I must go," said *Malik*, "I have a meeting with the brigade commander."

The Iraqi leader looked down and pointed at his watch.

"There isn't much time."

Malik and his entourage filed out of *Sabatash* and drove away.

* * *

In the Hooka Room, Heath sat with his lieutenants. The men were exhausted from the last few days. Something new dangled in front of them. That week a light appeared at the end of the tunnel. That week they saw their journey through hell had the chance for a happy ending. After months of feeling like they were losing something changed. They were winning.

"Did I ever tell you about my national championship match?" asked Heath.

The lieutenants shook their heads no.

"I dislocated my left shoulder in the semi-finals but won. In the finals I wrestled a guy who placed first the year before. I was down 2-0 going into the third period. He chose the standing position, so I needed a take-down and something else to beat him. I refused to let this guy pull away from me and I continued to try and shoot in on him."

"So, did you take him down?" asked Cash, a fellow wrestler.

"No, he took me down with forty-five seconds left," explained Heath.

Cash knew the other wrestler secured the match making it near impossible for Heath to win.

"So what did you do?"

"It's hard to explain," replied Heath, "I remember thinking the whole match, this is it; I can beat this guy, he's only up by two, but I never let myself think it was going to be easy. Then in the last minute he got me, he finished it. I remember thinking this will take a miracle. So I was on the bottom and the ref blew the whistle; I exploded out of the kneeling and this man grabbed an iron grip on me and rode me back to the mat. I shot up again and broke away getting an escape. The score was now 1-4 and I immediately pivoted back and lunged at the guy and he met me square, locking my arms in the standing. We pushed against each other stuck in a standing Greco-Roman stance. With twenty seconds left, I lateral dropped him."

"So that's it? You took him down to his back and won?"

"No," answered Heath, "I was now up 6-4 but there was still fifteen seconds left and he managed to get off his back and get an escape. We went out of bounds and the score was now 6-5. We came back onto the mat again in the standing. I remember looking at the clock and thinking I only have to keep this guy from taking me down for ten seconds. The ref blew the whistle and he shot in on me and I blocked him. He shot in again and I blocked him."

"So, you rode it out not letting him shoot in on you?" asked Cash.

"No. After I blocked him twice, I saw an opening and shot in on him. He blocked it but there was still five seconds left. I shot in on him again. The referee blew the whistle. I had won the match by one point."

The lieutenants looked at their company commander and now knew where he discovered his steely resolve. Time and time again, he did not waver throughout the hard times of the deployment.

"The thing I remember most about that match," said Heath, "was the sound of the referee's last whistle blow."

BOOM.

An explosion rattled the room. The purple fabric covering the sand bag wall shot dust into the air. The blast exploded over a kilometer away from *Sabatash* but still shook the building.

The officers ran into the command post and waited for an explanation to come across the radio.

* * *

After *Malik* left *Sabatash,* his crew drove down Route Michigan. He sat in the passenger's seat of a Ford F-350 police truck.

In the bed of the truck, one of *Malik*'s security *shurta* stood with a PKC machine gun on a turret. As the truck drove down the street, *Malik* spoke into a loudspeaker and his words projected on to the street.

"Sons of Ramadi. We will defeat the *irhabin*. The *Alwani*s have pushed the *irhabin* from the city. Please join with us to defend our great city…"

Malik needed to stop at his house before his meeting with the brigade commander. His truck pulled off of Route Michigan north on to the street where he lived. One of his men in the back seat noticed a black Opel Sedan trailing the police truck.

"Sir, there is a car following us."

He pointed out the back window to the black car that also turned onto the side street, now 75 meters behind them.

Over the loudspeaker *Malik* gave a warning.

"Stop. If you come any closer we will engage with the machine gun."

The black Opel slowed down to a near stop. The policeman manning the machinegun in the bed of the truck aimed in at the vehicle. Suddenly, the car sped up and continued towards the police truck at max acceleration. At fifty meters distance, the policeman fired several machine gun bursts. The shots disabled the vehicle.

"What do you thi—?"

BOOM!

The car exploded. In an instant, *Malik* was decapitated from a piece of shrapnel that broke through the back window glass.

The leaders of *al Qaeda* fearing the *Alwani*'s uprising, successfully assassinated one of the most dynamic, charismatic revolutionary leaders the world had ever seen.

ACT IV

EXECUTION

When I was a young officer, I was taught if you have
air superiority, land superiority and sea superiority, you win.
Well in Vietnam we had air superiority,
land superiority and sea superiority, but we lost.
So I realized there is something more to it. — Colonel John Boyd, USAF

The senator went back into his personal office and continued to review reports. It was late when he received a call on a secure line.

"Sir, how are you doing?" asked Lieutenant Colonel Courtney Cash, Jr.

The call was being transmitted from an unknown location in the Pacific. Lieutenant Colonel Cash, Jr. commanded the Battalion Landing Team on a Marine Expeditionary Unit as part of an Expeditionary Strike Group.

If the call was made to take action, Lieutenant Colonel Cash, Jr. would be leading the initial troops into Malaysia and Brunei. The senator took great pride and comfort knowing Courtney would be leading America's sons and daughters if they were called to duty. He took no comfort in knowing Courtney may have to venture into the horrors of war.

"Son, I'm doing well; it's good to hear your voice," replied the senator.

The small talk faded away and Lieutenant Colonel Cash Jr. explained his recent meeting with the leader of Pacific Command known as PACOM Commander. The Navy admiral had a detailed plan for the initial intervention and Lieutenant Colonel Cash, Jr. sounded confident in the preparation that had been made. The conversation was brief and the senator stared at the phone after the call had been disconnected.

The PACOM Commander, Admiral Scott Johnson, attended the Naval Academy with Lieutenant Isaac Trimble four decades earlier. The Senator considered Scott Johnson a close friend. The two men had drunk whiskey in every major city on the Eastern Seaboard over the last 40 years.

The admiral only answered to two people; the President of the United States and the Secretary of Defense. He was advised by the Joint Chiefs of Staff, but for operational military matters his chain of command was quite direct.

In military and high political circles the admiral had voiced his opposition against military intervention. He argued the problem needed a softer broader focus. The country had failed diplomatically when they allowed China to persuade Malaysia to leave the U.S. allied organization of ASEAN. When this act occurred they should have immediately deployed Peacekeeping and Nation Building Assets to other smaller South East Asian Countries to reinforce the U.S.'s commitment to them. This action would be a pre-emptive move that would be as much a military as it was diplomatic.

The admiral argued that by taking military action the U.S. would open a division that either would cast the country into a world war or commit the country to a thirty-year military occupation that would require extensive man power and constant Naval logistical support to a questionable region. The admiral wanted neither. If the U.S. could contain the act and supplement the surrounding countries; he argued that in a shorter amount of time they would see more positive results through this than a direct intervention. Ultimately, the admiral saw that direct action would diminish American influence in other parts of the world. He argued that this was exactly what China wanted.

The politicians largely dismissed the admiral as unqualified to make such foreign policy arguments and they listened to other appeals that supported immediate military intervention.

Although still night in D.C., the screen showed a CNN reporter standing in daylight at an Indonesian shipyard with several Indonesian and Asian reporters.

"Reporting live from the Indonesian side of the Island of Borneo. Early this morning a Malaysian Ship bumped into a U.S. Naval Ship in the South China Sea..."

The reporter faded away and footage of a Malaysian Ship nudging the U.S. Ship was shown. The senator did not need to hear CNN's spin on the situation. By airing the footage they just multiplied its effect a billion fold, forecasting it to the entire world. This was easily the goal of the nudge and the media had just played into the plan.

The senator went back into his office and sunk his head into his hands. The act was just enough to pique the interest of every media watcher in the world. It was subtle enough to deliver this message and reinforce the U.S.'s convictions about intervening in the situation. It in itself was not a bold enough act for the U.S. to declare war.

"Sir, we just received a message from the Office of the President. They will wait for the vote tomorrow..."

Essentially, the president had just shirked his responsibility off to the senator. The decision still remained almost entirely up to him. He would cast his vote tomorrow. He looked at a picture of Courtney on the wall in his dress blues and remembered holding him as a child. It would be a long night.

47

"Courtney, it's so good to hear from you," said Jill, "I'm sorry about Isaac I have something to tell you."

"Jill, you won't believe it. The violence has stopped."

"Overnight the city has ... Iraqi people walk the streets... ice is sold at every corner."

"Courtney, what are you talking about? Ice is being sold?"

"Listen to me, honey!" replied Cash. "Shop owners place cucumbers next to tomatoes. The Iraqi women dropped their veils. We've had no contact for two weeks. Ramadi is—"

"Cucumbers? Courtney will you shut up for a minute; I need to tell you something."

"Oh, I forgot. I need to tell you something too. Heath made me the XO."

"Courtney, I'M PREGNANT!"

Cash looked into the phone confused. *She's pregnant? I've been gone seven months.*

"Honey?"

"Courtney, I'm seven and a half months pregnant."

Cash exhaled in relief.

"Why didn't you tell me?"

"I tried, but you never call and the time was never right."

Heath walked into the room.

"Cash, sorry to interrupt, but I need to talk to you; it's important."

"Honey, I've got to go. That is great news; I'm so sorry you have to go through this by yourself. I'll call you tonight," said Cash.

"Courtney, I'm so happy that things are going better, you wouldn't know it by the news. All they say is the surge was a mistake," said Jill. "We'll talk names tonight."

"Take care of yourself and my baby. I'll see you in two months."

Cash hung up the phone.

"Baby— is your wife pregnant?" asked Heath hesitantly.

"Yes sir, seven and a half months. It's a boy and she's due right before we get back."

Heath exhaled in relief. He did not need a heartbroken executive officer.

"Well shit, Cash, I guess you did have it in you. I always figured you'd be the type of chap who shot blanks."

"Funny. What's up?"

"*Mulazim* Lieutenant Nate says he needs you to go over to *Jumuyah* Police Station," said Heath. "He might have that fifty-cal the Army lost."

"What are you talking about?"

"You remember at the beginning of the deployment, battalion sent out a guidons call asking if we had any extra fifty-cals because the Army lost one?"

"No shit. I do remember that. I think I was in an OP," answered Cash, "I'll grab Moody and head over."

* * *

Since *Malik's* assassination, *Abdullah* had taken over as the leader of the Iraqi Police. He continued to drive the people to fight the *irhabin*. Over three thousand Iraqis stood up against *al Qaeda* and joined the Iraqi Police. The other three big tribes and all of the smaller tribes throughout the city joined in the Awakening.

In addition to the people who joined the Iraqi Police, the entire city now used their information network that had previously been used against Americans, to report on *al Qaeda*. The death of *Malik* and *al Qaeda's* attack on Captain *Fuluh's* funeral served as a negative catalyst against the insurgents.

When *al Qaeda* committed those two actions, all of the citizens who were on the fence about whether they supported *al Qaeda* had their decision made for them.

The thousands of police now stood up in police stations across the city. The Marines did not have the manpower to place a single platoon at each site, but they knew to win they had to live and work with the police to make the situation work.

* * *

One week earlier Heath, Skinner and Cash sat in the Hooka Room and attempted to devise a plan to meet this new challenge. In honor of *Malik* they hung a large picture of the Iraqi martyr in a gold frame in their Arab room.

In the Hooka Room lay white boards, rosters of the company and multiple publications. The men spent three days with no sleep trying to figure out the best solution to the problem. There were empty energy drink cans and cigarette butts everywhere.

"We don't have enough lieutenants to put one at each station," said Heath.

Golf Company was responsible for five police stations.

On the table in the room the men looked at several documents highlighted and tabbed with Post-it notes. They wrote excerpts from the documents on the white boards. The three most important were; General Petraus's *Counterinsurgency Manual*, Victor Krulak's, *First to Fight*, and David Kilcullen's, *Twenty-Eight Articles; Fundamentals of Company-level Counterinsurgency*.

"I want to break the company down into ten-man teams similar to the Combined Action Platoons from Vietnam," explained Heath.

From Victor Krulak's book he highlighted the following passage:

Officers and those who had an interest in Marine Corps history knew the Combined Action idea had been applied with success before- in Haiti (1915-34), in Nicaragua (1926-33) and, probably most effectively, in Santo Domingo (1916-22). There the Marines organized, trained, and directed a new national police force, the Guardia National, later to become the Policia National. Formal training schools imbued the Policia Rank and file with a sense of discipline. Under Marine leadership, the Policia exercised their new knowledge of weapons and tactics in hundreds of antiguerrilla patrols.

But even more important, the Marines got to the heart of the security in the Dominican villages by organizing, equipping and training...residents who were willing to defend their own home and families. Led by a Marine Officer and including ten to fifteen Dominicans and two or three Marine enlisted men, these mixed groups successfully brought a measure of peace to their small communities. In Vietnam, half a century later, similar combined formations again validated the concept, proving their effectiveness far exceeded what might have been expected from their small numbers.

"What about Rock?" asked Heath. "Could he be our fifth lieutenant?"

"Sir, he's good. Tactically he is better than most lieutenants, but I don't know if he understands the COIN counterinsurgency piece working with the Iraqi people," replied Cash. "What about Nate? Nate's dad was a colonel. He's taken three years of school. He is open-minded and did a great job with the Iraqi Army."

"Nate's perfect," said Heath. "I want to frock him to lieutenant and put him at *Jumuyah* Police Station with Rock as his second in command."

"You can't frock him to lieutenant," interrupted Skinner.

The only reason first sergeant participated in solving the problem was because of his knowledge of the personnel numbers in the company. Heath realized long ago that his senior enlisted advisor worried more about his career than anything going on in Ramadi.

"First Sergeant, does Chesty Puller embody everything about the Marine Corps," asked Heath.

"Yes, sir, Chesty is the Marine Corps."

"Well, did you know that when Chesty was a sergeant in Nicaragua, he was frocked to captain in order to become a CAP platoon commander?"

"No, I didn't know that, but you can't frock a sergeant to lieutenant. I'll go to the sergeant major."

"First sergeant, you go to the sergeant major, I go to the battalion commander. Who do you think is going to win that?"

Skinner looked at Heath knowing the outcome.

On one of the white boards, Cash wrote 'Rank is Nothing, Talent is Everything' from David Killcullen's *Twenty-Eight Articles*.

"I'm not doing this for the hell of it. It is important that the Lieutenant Colonel Iraqi Police Chief at *Jumuyah* thinks he is getting an officer. In the Marine Corps, the good guys know rank is far less important than talent, but the Iraqis don't think this way. If you aren't an officer, you aren't shit to them; so in order to make the relationship work we need an officer there."

"All right, but I'm not calling him sir."

"Fair enough," replied Heath in a stern tone, "but you will call him *Mulazim* and if you undermine him I swear to God, I will fuck over that career you are so God damn interested in."

"So it's settled," interrupted Cash remembering Isaac's ability to be the voice of reason between the first sergeant and the company commander. "Nate will run *Jumuyah*."

48

"*As-Salāmu `Alaykum Mulazim Cashee*," said *Abdullah*, the police chief of the *Jumuyah* police station.

Abdullah, an *Alwani* cousin of *Malik*, had been promoted from a captain to lieutenant colonel. The *Alwanis* who stood up initially were rewarded with the prestigious billet of station commander.

"Hello sir, for its eighth day the station looks good," replied Cash.

"Thank you. Let's go back to my office," said *Abdullah* through the interpreter.

Abdullah's office was a large room. The lower halves of the walls were painted pink. The upper-half of the room was painted a light cream color. Lining two of the walls were two black leather Arab seating couches. On the front end of the room was an entertainment center with a small television. Behind his desk, an Iraqi flag hung with a framed picture of *Malik*. *Mulasim* Nate sat on one of the low leather couches with another Iraqi.

"Ahh *Mulazim* Nate, hello," said Cash.

Nate stood up and the two men hug and kissed like Iraqis. The man sitting next to Nate stood up and gave the same greeting. In the wall next to the Iraqi flag three incense sticks burned emitting a light grey smoke and the smell of jasmine.

"Would you like some chai tea?" asked *Abdullah* signaling Gonzo, now an Iraqi Policeman at *Jumuyah*.

Gonzo brought back a silver tray with several small clear glasses filled with chai. Cash looked at the glass and saw that the bottom half was solid sugar. He took a miniature spoon out of the glass and sipped the steaming sugary tea.

"What's up with the fifty-cal," whispered Cash.

Nate wrote on his green book.

191

I'LL TELL YOU LATER

"I want to tell you a joke," said *Abdullah* who portrayed a welcoming and friendly posture.

The chief knew the international language of humor strengthened bonds. The Marines now expected chit chat. The Iraqi sitting on the couch offered them a French Gallois Blonde cigarette. It was not quite as classy as Dunhill, but still a nice gesture. Cash and Nate lit up the French smokes.

"Prime Minister Maliki is walking through the streets of *Baghdad*," said *Abdullah*, "and as he is walking through the streets, he comes along a drunken bum laying in the gutter."

The Marines listened intently to the chief's joke.

"The Iraqi leader usually has people stand up and acknowledge his position, but the bum still lies in the street. The prime minister will not be disrespected and he kicks the bum. The bum shakes off his drunken stooper and looks up at the prime minister and says, 'Who are you?' Maliki looks at the bum and says, 'Who am I? You don't know who I am?' The bum shakes his head no. The prime minister replies, I'm Prime Minister Maliki. I'm the leader of all of Iraq. The bum looks at the leader in disbelief and replies, 'Yeah right, if you're Maliki I'm George Bush'."

The lieutenants laughed.

* * *

"Sir, can I ask you a serious question?" asked Cash breaking the code of the Arab formality.

"We are brothers," said *Abdullah*, "of course."

"Sir, what happened to *Khalid Alwani*? I'm assuming he is your cousin?"

The Iraqi leader's face went from a pleasant smile to a solemn look. He looked through the Marines with a thousand-yard stare.

"Ahh *Khalid,* yes, he went astray. If you want to know what happened to *Khalid,* you need to have some perspective on Iraq."

"Yes, please tell me sir, I want to understand."

"You see when the U.S. first invaded Iraq we expected that you would bring us red sports cars and Pepsi. Before the U.S. invaded, *Saddam* ordered all of the school children to memorize the following saying in English, 'America Bad *Saddam* Good.' Well, shortly after the invasion, the commerce did open up and we got satellite television and Pepsi was being sold in the market. When my grandmother tasted Pepsi for the first time she said, 'Pepsi Good, *Saddam* Bad'."

Cash nodded his head and laughed.

"After the invasion we were waiting for more. We were waiting for the better lives we thought the U.S. could bring us and seven months later nothing happened. Getting a cold Pepsi every now and then wasn't enough to justify the total upheaval of our lives. So the Iraqis stood up with *al Qaeda* to fight the American occupiers. *Khalid* was in the Iraqi Army during the Iraq-Iran War. He was a war hero. He was a dynamic leader even more than *Malik*. He mobilized the people to fight with *al Qaeda* and the *irhabin* recognized his leadership. Soon he was sucked into *al Qaeda* deeper than he wanted and they anointed him the Prince of Ramadi for *al Qaeda*."

"So, *Khalid* was a good leader like *Malik* before *al Qaeda*?" asked Nate.

"*Malik* and *Khalid* were brothers."

Nate and Cash looked at each other. *The head insurgent leader and the first Iraqi Police chief were brothers?*

"I don't understand."

"When the breadmaker's son was killed, *Khalid* became upset with *al Qaeda* and he curbed the violence for a few days. The *al Qaeda* operatives, not from Ramadi, went to the prince and asked him what was going on and *Khalid* told them they inflicted too much damage on the people."

"So *Malik* fought his own brother?" asked Nate.

"No. After *Khalid* tried to curb the violence," said *Abdullah*, "*al Qaeda* killed him."

The police chief looked down at the ground and paused.

"After his brother's death, *Malik* vowed to rid the city of *al Qaeda* and *Sheik Ali* delivered him to the Marines."

The incense burned out and a thin stick of ash glowed on the wall. Gonzo brought in the next round of chai. The men in the room sparked up another Gallois.

"We are in a similar time now," said *Abdullah*.

"Similar time to what?" asked Nate.

"This is very similar to after the invasion. There is a lull in violence, we've ridded the streets of *al Qaeda* for now but they will try to come back in. If you can't offer more than a cold Pepsi to the people, I fear in a few months they will align with *al Qaeda* again."

"Sir, I agree," replied Cash. "What needs to be done to keep this from happening?"

"Show us. Show us you are truly here to help. Pay the police. These are the bravest men in the city they risked their lives to fight *al Qaeda* and now they sit on post defending the city against the *irhabin* and their families go without food because they are not getting paid. Pay the police first and then help the people fix the city that you destroyed."

Cash looked at Nate. *The police aren't getting paid. How is this possible?*

"We will do everything we can, sir," said Cash.

"Thank you. Ahh I have something for you, *Mulazim Cashee*," said *Abdullah*. "I have a fifty-cal that I believe belongs to you."

"Oh great, I'll have a mobile section come pick it up today."

Nate, *Abdullah,* and Moody all looked at Cash with astonished looks.

"Sir, if an Arab offers you something, he wants something in return," explained Moody. "He's negotiating."

Cash looked at Nate and Moody.

"He's not going to give it to us?"

"No," responded the translator and Nate simultaneously.

"Excuse us for a second, sir," said Nate.

49

In the hallway two Iraqis stood on security outside of the door.

"He wants us to buy back the weapon," explained Nate.

"No, we're not paying for a weapon that belongs to us," said Cash. "Also where are we going to get money for that?"

The two men walked from the hallway to the Marines' small area located in the back of the police station.

"Sir, he's not asking for us to pay him for the weapon so he can buy a Lexus. He wants the money so he can pay the police," said Nate. "*Abdullah* is a good man."

"Well, Nate, even if I wanted to, I don't have money to pay for that weapon."

"Sir, what about the weapons buyback plan?"

Earlier in the deployment the Marines paid Iraqis who turned in weapons.

"Hmm, I'll look into that, but I don't know if battalion is going to buy off on it."

"Sir, I already checked with the command post; they said the battalion still has the funds for the weapons buy back; I only need you to sell it to Heath."

Nate's leadership alone held the fragile alliance together at *Jumuyah* police station. In a few short days he made a bond with *Abdullah* and promised to do everything within his power to help the Iraqis. His pledge and *Abdullah*'s faith in the pledge were the only reason the Marines were still alive.

"We need to make this happen now," said Nate. "We're out here living ten men with one hundred Iraqis. The Marines are scared. On post, some of the Iraqis are saying if they don't get paid they are going to quit or worse."

Cash looked at the three Marines in the command post. *We're sending them to their deaths if we can't get the Iraqis paid.*

The lieutenant thought there may be negative effects on the other police stations if they found out *Jumuyah* received pay. He could not wait though; he would work out a deal and do everything he could do to get the rest paid as well. He couldn't afford resentment between stations.

"Okay, let me call Heath and see if we can work something out, but we need to be careful how we proceed."

* * *

In *Abdullah*'s office the Marines re-entered the room. Before they re-entered, Cash called Heath who backed whatever decision was made and said he would pay the money out of pocket if needed.

The Golf Company's weapons buy back fund consisted of $3,000 intended to last them the rest of the deployment.

"Sir, how much do want for the fifty-cal?"

"Whatever you think," responded *Abdullah*.

"Sir, don't tell him the first price," whispered Moody, "Make him give you the first price and go lower from there. If you say the first price, he will spin it on you."

"Whatever you think, sir."

Abdullah laughed when he saw the interpreter coaching the Marines.

"Well, I think $5,000 would be a good start."

"$5,000? We don't have that kind of money!"

"America has all the money in the world," said *Abdullah*. "Remember these police need more than enough to buy a few cold Pepsis."

"Sir, say $2,500," suggested Moody.

"Sir, I'm serious; we don't have that kind of money. What about $2,500?"

The police chief looked at the Marines. They each were wearing at least $5,000 worth of gear. They have the money, thought *Abdullah*.

"Five thousand," said the police chief.

"Sir, we just don't have it, I think $2,500 is the best we can do."

"Five thousand," said the police chief.

"Sir, we don't have five thousand."

"What do you have?"

"Sir, $3,000 is all we have."

196

The translator's face looked like he had been betrayed by the lieutenant. He knew nothing of negotiating.

Abdullah read the facial expressions of Nate, Cash, and the translator and knew $3,000 was all they had. He could have easily made it to the World Series of Poker.

"Okay, $3,000 it is," said *Abdullah*, "but *Mulazim Cashee,* that is barely enough for one month, let alone next month."

"Sir, we will do everything we can to get you paid," said Nate.

The talk turned casual again and the men spoke for some time before they said goodbye. Nate walked Cash out to the exit of *Jumuyah* police station. While they were talking Gonzo came up to the Marines.

"*Enteenee Fluus,*" said Gonzo.

"That means give me money," said Nate

"You must get the police paid sir. I beg you. The *shurta* have given their lives to stand up with the Awakening. They need the money to provide for their families."

Something about the young Iraqi's courage impressed Cash. The young man saw his opportunity to influence events above his means and tried to make a difference the same way he had at the elections.

"How old are you Gonzo?" asked Cash.

"I'm eighteen-years-old," said Gonzo though the interpreter. "I'm married and my wife is eight months pregnant."

"So, you need money to provide for your wife?" asked Cash.

"Yes, we have nothing; if we don't get paid, the insurgents will find a way back into the city. They are evil men. The *shurta* are only victims. Imagine the choice between feeding my family and not feeding my family."

"We'll do everything we can do get you paid," said Cash. "You are a brave man, Gonzo. I wish your family the best of luck. My wife Jill is pregnant too. Seven months."

"So you know that it is no choice at all."

50

Rock despised the idea of another sergeant taking over his squad. He was, after all, a small legend in Golf Company.

How are they going to frock this boot sergeant and give him my squad? In the two weeks he lived at *Jumuyah,* he changed his mind and now agreed the company made the right decision. *Nate's better working with the Iraqis.* He had all of the confidence and force of will that most sergeants have, but he had something else that Rock knew he did not.

When they received the word they were moving to *Jumuyah* and that Nate would be in charge, the two sergeants sat down together. They planned out how they would execute the daunting task of embedding ten men with one hundred Iraqis. The first thing Nate wanted to do was get rid of Rock's fireteam leaders.

"They're not right for this mission," explained Nate.

"My fireteam leader is the best damn corporal in the company!" yelled Rock. "I'm not trading him."

Nate wanted to trade the two fireteam leaders for two lance corporals. The first was married to a Brazilian woman and spoke some Portuguese. The second was born in Amursk, Russia, and immigrated to the U.S. in the nineties.

"Why would you trade two solid corporals for some unknowns who've barely been tested?" asked Rock.

"Because they have open minds and don't think like Americans," replied Nate. "If your fireteam leader comes to *Jumuyah* and has all of the Marines on edge about the *shurta,* he is going to do us more harm than good. We need the men to become boys with the Iraqis; that is what will keep us secure at night, not the weapons on the roof."

After an hour of going back and forth, Rock finally submitted to Nate's request.

Two weeks after their meeting, Rock studied *Mulazim* Nate as he briefed four Marines preparing for an Iraqi Police patrol. Rock looked at how many bodies he had left at the station.

We have four going on that patrol and three sleeping on their rest cycle. That leaves me, the radio watch, and the rover. He counted the number on his fingers. *Three dudes. Nate was right, we are not doing much with three dudes.*

The rover Marine, Almetsyecsk, nicknamed "Russian" was one of the Marines Nate traded for Rock's fireteam leaders.

Rock sat next to the radio watch and observed the Russian. The Marine always received large care packages full of food from the states. He sat in an open area surrounded by twenty Iraqis and handed out the food from his care packages. He walked over to Rock.

"What are you doing over there, Russian?" asked Rock.

"Buying us some time, sergeant."

51

On patrol in *Jumuyah* Nate walked with *Abdullah*. The forty-year old Iraqi held the twenty-three-year old Marine's hand. Spread out in front of them, one marine and five Iraqis patrolled. Behind them, two Marines and seven Iraqi Police patrolled. They did not bump and bound but strolled as if they were going on a walk in a park.

"We need a lot of things," explained *Abdullah* pointing to the streets filled with sewage and trash. "This city used to be a nice place."

Nate took several pictures of the streets with his digital camera. As they walked, the chief held his arm in front of the makeshift lieutenant while the Iraqi Police searched the cars.

"Hey, where are they going, sir?" asked Nate.

He pointed to two Iraqi Policemen going into two separate homes. He worried the Iraqi Police were going to abuse their new power. The Iraqi Army notoriously looted civilians' houses.

"Those are their houses," explained the chief.

That's what's different. These people are protecting their own homes. For the first time, he looked at the streets. Months earlier the tension of near death was so great that it was almost as if he had been looking through static. The heavy anxiety made the city appear to be a large battlefield with several obstacles. Buildings were not for anything other than cover. Houses were not for living, they were enemy strong points. Shops were obstacles; roads were pathways to move troops.

With the violence stopped, he saw the people living in the city. All of a sudden children played in the streets. Donkeys pulled carts of goods to the markets. The battlefield started to appear like an actual city with the actions of everyday life starting to reappear.

Behind the donkey carts and fruit stands the city remained in ruins though. In *Jumuyah,* it was the unusual building that did not have bullet holes in the side of the outer walls.

With the new Iraqi Police standing two man checkpoints on every block, the threat of death seemed to disappear. The bullets stopped flying and the IEDs quit exploding, but the city of Ramadi looked like Stalingrad during the mid-1940s. Nate looked at the former battlefield.

We have to fix this.

52

Blaine looked up at the hanging, silver, cylindrical bars. Wind chimes clanged against the center object of the ornament in the D.C. night. John's future father-in-law sat with him in the outside seating of a D.C. restaurant. Amy attended a parent teacher conference and asked her father to take John out to dinner.

Blaine Wilson was a political science professor at George Washington University. He was raised in New York City and although he lived in Alexandria for 13 years he still felt like a tourist. He didn't understand why his daughter fell for the Marine and felt he had nothing in common with John.

"Would you like any appetizers?" asked the server.

"Yes, we'll have some lettuce wraps, and I'd like to see your wine list," said Blaine.

He worried about his daughter's relationship with the Marine officer and felt he might have psychological damage from his ordeal. Blaine was a good man and cared about Amy's well-being. He wanted to connect with his daughter's fiancé.

"So John, Amy tells me you're recovering well?"

"Amy has been a big support to me," replied John. "She said you recommended that I see a Doctor Kerry."

"Yes, Doctor Kerry's excellent. I think Doctor Kerry, albeit young, is on the way to being one of the best in that field some day."

The server brought out the wine list. Blaine barely glanced at it and handed it back.

"We'll have a bottle of something red from the Russian River."

"So, John, Amy tells me you've been reading a lot with all of your free time," said Blaine, "Anything good?"

"Yeah, I recently finished reading Charlie Wilson's War."

"I heard that was a good perspective on Afghanistan and U.S Foreign Policy from Charlie Wilson's point of view," said Blaine. "I like the truth-as-I-see-it style; it usually broadens a person's perspective."

Blaine handed John a green Barnes and Noble bag. The lieutenant pulled out Howard Zinn's *A People's History of the United States* and Kurt Vonnegut's *Bluebeard*. John never heard of either book.

"The Zinn book is a history book you might like. It has some interesting ideas on Vietnam that you might relate to today's situation in Iraq," said Blaine. "And the Vonnegut book has a great perspective on some survivor's syndrome issues."

The first act of kindness by his fiancé's father surprised him.

"John, Amy says you're interested in grad school. When you're feeling better maybe you could come down to the campus."

John nodded his head.

"So, John, you don't have to answer this, but how do you feel about everything going on over there?" cautiously asked the political science professor.

John never liked Blaine. He knew Blaine told Amy that he was not good enough for her. His over-confidence in his beliefs offended the Marine officer. Since his abrupt homecoming, John could not explain it, but something changed. Maybe in Blaine, maybe in him— he couldn't tell— but now he felt the kindness of Amy in her father. John opened up.

"Well, I don't know, the more I think about it, I don't even know if we should have invaded Iraq," said John. "I think we should, I don't know, cut our losses. I am not sure if there is anything worth dying for over there. I know Flynn's parents probably don't think so."

John immediately felt dirty for saying those words. He thought he had an affair against everything he once believed in. He went back and forth— wavering what he believed. He felt mixed emotions.

"Hmm, intriguing," replied Blaine.

The server brought out their dinners. John enjoyed a medium-well steak and Blaine nibbled on a rare filet mignon. Blaine took pleasure in a glass of fine merlot.

53

"We need to get the Iraqis paid!" yelled Bama.

"I feel like an idiot," replied Cash. "The Iraqis aren't getting paid? I'll do everything I can, Bama."

"Man, you better do something. You don't know what it's like living out there. I can't sleep. I know these fuckers were shooting at me and my boys two months ago."

"I don't understand, the Iraqis here at *Sabatash* are getting paid," said Cash.

"Ain't that the irony of it," said Bama. "You got sixty Marines here at *Sabatash* and you're the only station getting paid."

Suddenly Heath walked into the Hooka Room with multiple unexpected guests. The two lieutenants stood up out of respect for the unannounced visitors.

"At ease, at ease, gentlemen," said General Mattis. "Your battalion commander tells me out here in Ramadi, Golf is leading the way."

"We're trying, sir. There is a lot of dynamic stuff happening in Ramadi right now. The last few days have been good," replied Heath.

"I'm sorry to hear about your executive officer," said General Mattis, "He sounds like a real hero."

"He was, sir," replied the lieutenants.

"I know," said General Mattis. He cut the niceties, "Well, gentlemen, I don't have a whole lot of time, so let's do this."

He looked at the battalion commander and sergeant major that followed him in the room.

"Attention to orders," said the sergeant major.

He read a citation for a Silver Star medal. He called forth Second Lieutenant William Whiting. The men in the room stood at attention while General Mattis pinned the medal on Bama's cammies.

"You know these things usually take a while to get through the system," explained General Mattis, "but when I heard of what you've done, I thought, 'I've got to come reward this lieutenant.' Men like you are why we're winning the war."

The gray general shook Bama's hand. He was not an imposing man and portrayed a grandfatherly appeal. Something about General Mattis resonated with Marines. He seemed to get it. All of the politics and bureaucracy did not seem to slow his ability to make the right things happen.

"Well, gentlemen, I've got to get going. I appreciate all of your hard work and am in awe of what you men in Golf have accomplished here in Ramadi. Shit, I got blown up rolling through here in '05 and your battalion commander told me that the streets are safe enough to buy ice cream now. Truly amazing. Do you have any questions an old bachelor might be able to shed some light on before I leave?"

Cash looked at the general. *Well, fuck it. Here is my chance; I might as well go for it.*

"Sir, why can't we get the Iraqi Police paid?"

Everyone in the room looked at the lieutenant. He was unsure if what he said was going to be viewed as inappropriate, but he did not care; he wanted an answer. *General Mattis as good as he is, isn't the one out there living every night.*

"Well, lieutenant, that's a great question. I wish I could give you a better answer than what I'm going to tell you, but I refuse to tell a man risking his neck a lie."

The battalion commander and Heath turned their look from Cash to General Mattis. They too wanted to know the answer to the question.

"Right now the Iraqi Government is mainly run by *Shī'ah* Iraqis," explained General Mattis. "The Ministry of Interior only voted to sanction three hundred Iraqi Police to be paid in Ramadi."

"But, sir, we have almost three thousand Iraqi Police that have stood up in Ramadi," said Cash.

"I know," said the General, "and so does the *Shī'ah*-run Ministry of Interior. The last thing the *Shī'ah* wants to do is arm a bunch of *Sunni*s who have oppressed them for the last fifty years. They feel if they fully fund the *Sunni* police in *Al Anbar,* they will be arming a militia that will try and attack them when the U.S. leaves."

All of the men in the room stared at the general. He looked at the men with apologetic eyes knowing he gave them a near impossible mission.

"Gents, I'm working on this problem. I hope I can give you some comfort in knowing that everyone, up to the president knows about this problem and we are working around the clock to get it fixed. Keep hanging on, gents, what you've accomplished up to this point is amazing."

He turned and walked out of the room followed by the battalion commander, sergeant major, and Heath. Cash and Bama sat back on the gold plush couches. Bama took the Silver Star off his cammies and tucked it in his pocket.

"I don't take any comfort in knowing he's working on it," said Bama. "I'll take comfort when the Iraqis have been paid. I just don't understand."

"He could have lied to us and we wouldn't have known. Congrats on your medal, man, that's awesome. You deserve it."

"Don't go and tell nobody about this medal," said Bama. "I don't want my Marines thinking I'm chasing this shit like Skinner."

"I won't but you should be proud," said Cash, "you're the protector."

"Well, I'll need someone protecting me here shortly if we can't get them Iraqis paid."

54

Cash and Skinner sat in the brigade briefing with several other lieutenants and senior enlisted personal. It was only the second time in the whole deployment that Cash had been to the big base. In the room a half dozen military personal took notes on a subject none of them ever expected.

An unattractive Army female lieutenant aimed a laser pointer at the projected bullets on a PowerPoint presentation.

The slide read:

HOW TO CONDUCT CERP WITHOUT GOING TO JAIL

WHAT IS CERP?

• COMMANDERS EMERGENCY RESPONSE PROGRAM

• ALLOW COMMANDERS TO RESPOND TO URGENT HUMANITARIAN RELIEF AND RECONSTRUCTION ASSISTANCE.

• IMMEDIATELY ASSIST THE IRAQI PEOPLE.

• ALLOW COMMANDERS TO MAKE IMMEDIATE, POSITIVE IMPACT IN THEIR AREAS OF RESPONSIBILITY / OPERATIONS.

"You're here today because you've been chosen as a project manager or a paying agent for reconstruction projects," explained the female lieutenant.

Cash wrote the bullets down in his notebook.

"You will be responsible for hiring out Iraqi contractors to conduct projects that the commands deem necessary to keeping the stability in and around Ramadi."

"What is the process?" asked an Army captain.

"The process is fairly simple," said the instructor. "The project manager fills out a justification letter for a project that you wish to do and then you submit it to the comptroller. If the paperwork is in order and it falls in line with a sewer, water, electricity, or trash project; it will be approved."

Everyone in the room took notes and listened attentively to the Army lieutenant.

"Let me tell you a story about two Army captains who embezzled $2.1 million dollars in *Baghdad*," said the Army lieutenant. "They figured it out, but they got caught. They conducted projects and the Iraqi gave them a kickback. Kickbacks are almost impossible to trace because all of the paperwork is correct. The only discrepancy is at the end of the deal, the Arab pays back the project manager. This is standard practice for Arabs, so they have no problem doing this. I MUST REITERATE, THIS IS COMPLETELY ILLEGAL!"

Cash wrote down what he perceived to be the most important line:

KICKBACKS ARE IMPOSSIBLE TO TRACE

Everyone in the room felt dirty hearing the story. They were not supposed to be project managers and paying agents; they were supposed to be war fighters. They trained to shoot, move, and communicate not spend money and conduct reconstruction projects. Nobody in the room wanted the responsibility of working with the money, nobody except Cash. His head spun rapidly as the lieutenant outlined how easy to was to embezzle money from the projects. The requirement to get the money to the men on the frontlines as quickly as possible made it near impossible to track. The Army lieutenant reiterated her point.

"If you try to steal, you will be caught."

55

Rogue, Skinner, Bama, and Nate sat in the Hookah Room.

"Gents, I think we need to evaluate where we are at now and what we need to accomplish during our last push before the next unit gets here," explained Heath. "Before I start do you have any questions?"

"Sir, how we going to get the Iraqis paid?" asked Bama.

Nate and Rogue leaned in, very interested in the company commander's response. Things were getting edgy at their police stations.

"I have a meeting in three days where battalion says they have the plan for the Iraqi pay issue," answered Heath. "In the meantime, we will continue to give them stuff out of our care packages and bags of rice that the gunny is getting from the civil affairs team."

"Sir, I think we need to have a backup plan in case they don't get paid," said Cash.

"I said battalion is working on it!" yelled Heath. "I don't want to talk about the damn Iraqis not getting paid until I get back from this meeting. That's final."

He had not slept in several days. Although the violence had stopped, Heath realized he needed to exploit the opportunity before the insurgency crept back into the city. In the Hookah Room, three large white boards displayed three diagrams.

"Gents, we are in a race against time, against the insurgents."

He spoke with a sense of urgency. The lieutenants listened intently.

"We need to start fighting the counterinsurgency the way they fight us or things will return to the way they were. It took us being bruised for four fucking years to figure out this shit."

He pointed to the FM 3-24, General Petraeus' Counterinsurgency Manual.

"Sir, what do you mean?" asked Nate.

"The whole military was fucked up and our own arrogance is why we were losing," said Heath. "It took me losing Isaac to take a hard look at myself and ask if we're doing the right thing and we weren't. We need to stop focusing on the enemy."

The staff looked at the company commander, surprised by what he said. Marines are taught from day one of boot camp and officer candidate school to focus on the enemy. They had all been trained that focusing on the enemy is how to win.

"We need to focus on the people."

He pointed to the first white board.

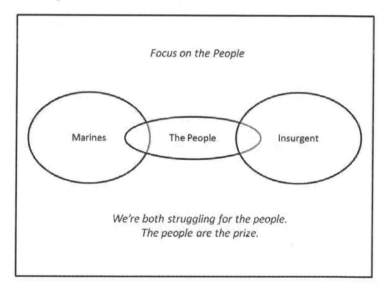

Focus on the People

Marines   The People   Insurgent

We're both struggling for the people.
The people are the prize.

"Both the insurgents and the Marines are struggling for the will of the people," said Heath. "If we focus on the people, they will provide us security against the insurgents. If we focus on the enemy and continue to treat the people like shit, well, we're fucked, because the people will go back to supporting the insurgency."

Bama shook his head with doubt.

"Sir, I don't understand what you mean. Why would we focus on the people?"

56

Heath lost Bama. The southerner thought about the deployment up to that point. *If we're not trying to kill al Qaeda, then what are we trying to do*? He was out of dip and did not feel like smoking. Suddenly he became uninterested and tired.

"Okay, I can see you all want to know how we are going to do this," explained Heath.

He pointed to the second white board as Bama's head started to bob.

"The way we fight in a conventional model is two dimensional," said Heath. "Picture conventional warfare as algebra and counterinsurgency warfare as calculus. This may be interpreted wrong, but in counterinsurgency I submit that there are more variables to worry about. In order to affect these variables, you have to be able to fight on more than one level. The new counterinsurgency, COIN, pub outlines this in five logical lines of operations. We'll call them the five LLOs."

Bama started to nod off and only halfway followed what Heath was saying. *Five LLOs? What the hell is a LLO?* As he nodded in an out, all he thought about was getting the police paid.

We need to get them paid. As Heath continued to talk about the five LLOs Bama started to daydream. In his illusion he saw a large pink elephant sitting next to Heath on the plush yellow couch. He barely saw the pink elephant, but he could tell that the pachyderm held something in his hands. As Bama slipped further and further out of consciousness, the elephant became clearer and clearer. Bama fell completely into his daydream and the object in the elephant's hands became clear. He held a sign that read:

BAMA,
YOU NEED TO PAY THE IPS...

OR YOU WILL DIE!

"BAMA!" screamed Heath.

* * *

Bama sat up straight, completely awake, ripped suddenly from his daydream.

"What am I talking about?" demanded Heath.

"The five LLOs," answered Bama who sweated profusely.

"You better pay attention. That goes for all of you."

"The Five LLOs are Security, Training the IPs, Essential Services, Economic Development, and Governance," explained Heath. "In order to beat the insurgents we need to focus on all of these LLOs."

"I don't understand, sir. How are we supposed to do all of these things at the company level?" asked Skinner. "It seems impossible for a rifle company to do more than security. Maybe we can train the police, but this isn't what we were trained for, especially you grunts."

Heath pointed to the second white board.

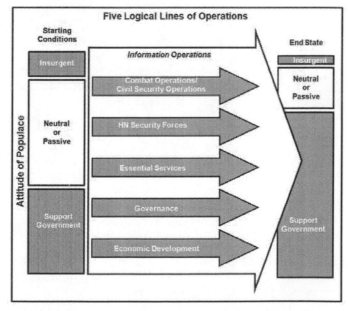

"Gents, that's why we are having this meeting," said Heath. "I don't know how we are going to do it, but we need to figure out a way. The way I see it; you all focus on all five LLOs at your stations and Cash and I will shift assets and resources to you to help support."

"In *Jumuyah* I took a bunch of pictures of streets that were ankle deep in sewage, can I do a reconstruction project to—"

"Yes, that's perfect, Nate."

"Sir, what if I go around to each station and have a meeting with the local leaders from the area? We'll have the Marine lieutenants, who are now mini-governors, the Iraqi Police station chief, and a local leader to discuss what problems—"

"That'd be awesome, Cash," said Heath. "A mini-governance meeting at the local level."

"Sir, up in *Thaylet* they are located right next to the *Euphrates* River, but they have to travel all the way into the *souk* to buy food. I want to create a mini-*souk* up there to stimulate economic development," said Rogue.

"That's the right mentality," said Heath, "but I want to show you this chart on how I think we should prioritize our objectives."

The company commander pointed to the third white board:

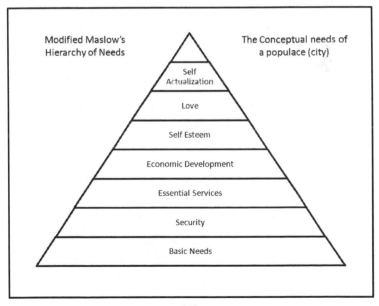

"This is what I think are the conceptual needs of a populace," said Heath. "This is a modified example Maslow's Hierarchy of Human Needs. The thought is that if you can provide these things to people, they will be satisfied and you can cover these gaps therefore denying the insurgents the ability to win the will of the populace."

"So, you want us to start with basic needs?" asked Nate.

"No, not at all," said Heath. "At your level, in your area, I want you to conduct a mission analysis to see what needs to be done. People instinctively will take care of their own basic needs such as food, water, and shelter. If they can't, we'll help them, but most people in Ramadi already have these things."

"So, for example, the security is good right now," said Bama, "but if we can't get them Iraqis paid, then we'll all die, or at least those of us living out in the ville—"

"God damn it, BAMA! Enough with the police pay. I will fix this at the battalion meeting."

57

Heath sat in the battalion briefing room for a meeting he thought was supposed to be about police pay. He looked down at his watch. Four hours passed and nobody mentioned what he considered the most important item on the agenda. He listened to the battalion adjutant explain FITREPs were due at the end of the month.

The operations officer spoke next.

"Gents, we need to focus— on our force protection," said Powers. "Our men's security is at stake. If we don't tighten up our— own perimeters, we could be over run— especially with our men living with 100 Iraqis…"

Heath hated Powers. He blamed the operations officers for Flynn's death. *His inability to adapt to the fight has cost Marines their lives.*

"With that being said, I think we need to turn the map around and refocus on the enemy…" said Powers.

This guy is a bumbling fucking idiot. He sounds like the cook from the Muppets show. He dealt with his speech impediment. What he despised was Powers' total lack of understanding about what occurred in the ville. *Our force protection of the police stations is not keeping the ten Marines living out there alive, it is their relationships.*

Next, Duncan the battalion executive officer spoke.

"Heath, next week, you have to meet with *Sheik Ali*. The battalion is awarding him a $450,000 project to repave a half mile stretch of road on Route Michigan that was destroyed by several IEDs. Especially CP 295," explained Duncan. "If you or your XO have any questions, give me a call. I spoke with *Sheik Ali* today and he has heard of Golf's Hookah Room, so he knows where to go."

Heath liked the battalion executive officer. He was Irish and he had been a company commander earlier in the war. He was open-minded and never held his rank or billet over the other officers in the battalion. The biggest reason Heath liked Duncan was because unlike the operations officer, the battalion executive officer understood counterinsurgency. Duncan would not hesitate to throw out the rules to win. He would not disobey the moral ones, only the non-essential bureaucratic ones that hindered progress.

Next, Powers was awarded the Bronze Star with 'V' for his actions during the elections. Heath clenched his fists as he stood at attention while the major received his award. He was not mad that the operations officer was getting an award. *He should get an award. He definitely deserves it, but it shouldn't have a 'V' on it.* Several weeks earlier some of his squad leader's lower awards were approved, but without the combat distinguishing device. After the ceremony, everyone milled about the room congratulating Powers.

"What about the police pay, sir?" asked Heath to Powers.

"What about the police pay, Heath? We're working as hard as we can."

"Sir, that's not good enough. We need to get the police paid. This is the single biggest issue we're facing right now. I believe if we don't resolve it, that it will unravel our fragile alliance with the newly founded Iraqi Police."

"You don't think I know how important this is!" yelled Powers. "We're waiting for higher to get an increased budget for the Iraqi Security Forces. Until then, our hands are tied until they reallocate the money."

"THAT'S YOUR ANSWER!" replied Heath. "To wait. Sir, we don't have time; we need to get them paid."

"I don't know what else to tell you."

Heath saw Powers was a victim of his environment and would not force his will to help solve the problem. He politely ended the conversation embarrassed for his outburst. He gathered himself and did something he vowed he would never do. He started politicking. He walked over to Duncan.

"Sir, how's it going?" asked Heath.

"Good, Heath," replied Duncan. "What's on your mind?"

"What are we going to do about police pay sir?"

"I overheard your conversation with Powers— I think everyone did. Let's go outside."

Duncan put his arm around Heath as they walked into the night.

"Care for a cigar?" asked the major.

"No thanks, sir."

The battalion executive officer sparked up a Cohiba Cuban cigar. One of the benefits of being in Iraq was there were Cuban cigars available.

Duncan learned this simple pleasure during his first pump to Iraq in 2004 as a company commander.

"I know what you're going to ask," said Duncan. "We can't use the reconstruction funds to pay the Iraqi Police. In the wording of the CERP order it specifically says that the money can't benefit Iraqi programs that fall under the ministries. Unfortunately for us a senator's aide on the budget committee added that verbiage in D.C. It is this bureaucratic formality that keeps you and the men in the arena from sleeping at night."

"No disrespect sir, but what the fuck? I feel like they are putting us in a situation we can't possibly win. It is almost like higher is actively trying to kill us."

Duncan laughed.

"Yes, sometimes it feels that way."

He took a deep drag off of his Cuban and the cherry glowed bright red in the dark night.

"There is a way to temporarily fix this problem," explained Duncan. "Do you think it costs half a million dollars to pave a half mile of road when it only needs some patches?"

"What are you saying, sir?" asked Heath.

"I'm not saying anything," said Duncan. "If you recommended to *Sheik Ali* that we were giving him a generous contract, and that it would be benevolent of him to help out the Iraqi Police in their time of need— well, hey, that's just people helping people right?"

"Sir, say no more."

He did not want to do business like this, but at this point in the deployment, he would do worse to keep the rest of his Marines alive.

"Wait," said Duncan exhaling his cigar smoke slowly.

"You have to make sure your paying agent and project manager are on board with this or you can't do it," explained the executive officer. "They are the ones who sign for the money. If this thing goes south, it will be them in Leavenworth, not you or me."

58

"Cash, give me a cigarette."

Heath sighed and plopped down on one of the gold couches. He looked defeated. In the Hookah Room, Cash and Skinner awaited the news from the battalion meeting.

"So, what did they say sir?" asked Cash.

"They said we were on our own. They said to keep living with them and make it go with leadership."

"THAT'S THEIR ANSWER!"

"That's what I said. Hey, my men are waiting to die unless we come up with something and we get nothing."

Heath stood up and walked over to the fridge. He pulled out three ice cold Cokes. He handed one to each of his men.

"Well, what do you think?" asked Heath.

They sat in silence while they each cracked open the drinks. Cash took several drags off of his cigarette. Finally he spoke.

"Sir, I think we need to take the CERP money and pay the Iraqi Police with it."

Skinner stared at Cash.

"You can't be serious."

"I'm dead fucking serious! What's the alternative, not pay them? We're leaving these Marines out to dry if we can't get the police paid. It's only a matter of—"

"Cash, enough," said Heath "I have a solution that might work."

Cash and Skinner stared at the company commander. Heath gave Cash a weird look before he spoke.

"Golf Company is going to award *Sheik Ali* a $450,000 contract to repave or repair the road from checkpoint 295 to the *Souk*. It is about a half-mile job. We're meeting with him next week."

Cash thought about what Heath said. *A half million dollars to do a patch job. That is way too much.* He looked at the company commander who nodded his head sideways tilted at an angle. *Aha! He must have a deal worked out with Sheik Ali to pay the police. Brilliant!*

"No problem, sir, that sounds like an excellent project."

He had worked with Heath long enough to know what he was trying to do.

Skinner had also worked with Heath for some time now and was not born yesterday. He saw the two officers nodding their heads at each other with weird glances.

"There is no way that contract is worth $450,000," said Skinner. "I can't in good conscience sign off on that project."

"You're going to sign off on it. We were assigned it by battalion."

"I'm not doing it," said Skinner. "For that amount of money, they are going to look into what was done and I'm not putting my name on—"

"God damn it, first sergeant!"

He slammed his Coke on the table.

"*Sheik Ali* has agreed to pay the police with some of the money from the contract. You're signing it!"

"I'll go to the sergeant major!"

"The battalion has blessed this," said Heath.

Heath did not intimidate Skinner. Sixteen years in the Marine Corps taught him how to get around company grade officers. He weighed his possibilities.

"I'll go to the colonel."

"First sergeant, this isn't a matter of legal or illegal," interjected Cash. "If your wife was pregnant and needed to get to the hospital, you wouldn't speed to get her there? We have a moral obligation to do the right thing here for the Iraqi Police and the Marines; don't let some admin rules cloud your judgment of what is actually important..."

"Lieutenant, we have rules for a reason," replied the first sergeant.

He looked at Cash and then turned his head towards Heath. "And, sir, I expected more out of—"

Heath leapt out of his gold chair and lunged at Skinner knocking over his soda. He crouched down low and exploded up into a wrestler's shot. He held out his right arm and grabbed the first sergeant's throat, pinning him against the purple walls, lifting him out of his chair.

"Listen, you careerist piece of shit!" shouted Heath. "I will not let you get another Golf Marine killed or dismembered because of some admin fucking rule."

Cash got out of his chair and moved towards Heath. Coke spilled over the table and ran onto the floor.

"Sir."

Cash reached to pull Heath's arm from Skinner's throat, but Heath pushed him away with his free hand.

"Remember December Seventh!" yelled Heath. "You son of a bitch, remember those Marines who lost their legs?"

Skinner tried to pry off Heath's hold. The national championship wrestler's iron grip clenched even tighter on his senior enlisted man's throat.

"Remember, you gave the order behind my back to have the Marines wear cammies and now some poor kid is burned."

He released his grip and the first sergeant dropped back into a gold chair holding his throat gasping for air.

"Give me a cigarette, Cash," said Heath.

Cash handed him a smoke. He fumbled one out for himself. The three men sat in silence while the two officers smoked.

Thirty minutes passed in silence. Finally Skinner spoke.

"Give me a cigarette, lieutenant."

He took a deep breath and winced holding the cigarette. He lit up the Dunhill. Cash had never seen the first sergeant smoke. Golf Company's senior enlisted man took four drags off of the cigarette then looked up at Heath.

"I'll do it."

59

John sat in the waiting room of Doctor Kerry's office. He picked up *The Economist* and read about how the war effort was floundering in Iraq. He set the magazine down. John looked at the people coming in and out of the waiting room. They all looked normal to him. *I wonder what problems these people have. I can't believe anyone would pay someone for therapy, but here I am.*

He looked up on the wall and saw a picture of an attractive lady in her mid-thirties wearing a suit. Under the cherry wood frame a small gold plate read "Doctor Kerry" in stamped letters.

Great, at least I'll get to talk to an attractive woman. I don't know how she'll help me get over an IED blast but it's worth a shot.

"John Magruder, John Magruder," said the receptionist. "Doctor Kerry will see you now. It's the second door on the left."

John grabbed his walker and slowly moved to the second door. He opened it and sat down on a Freudian leather couch in an empty room. *I can't believe this office actually looks like this.* He had an image in his head of what a therapist's office looked like and that is exactly what the room looked like.

On the corner of the desk sat a glass pyramid trophy that read Keeler Award, for distinction in cognitive care sciences. A picture frame on the desk showed Doctor Kerry and an extremely ugly man, who he presumed to be her husband. On the wall hung several framed diplomas. University of North Carolina, Bachelor of Art's Psychology 1996. Duke University PhD Psychology and Counseling 2002.

John did the mental math. *She can't be older than thirty-one or thirty-two. She's only five or six years older than me.*

At that moment, the ugly man from the picture entered the room. He wore a dark blue two piece suit with light blue pin stripes.

"Hello John, I'm Doctor Kerry. It's nice to meet you," said the ugly man.

What?

"I've heard a lot about you," said Doctor Kerry.

"It's good to meet you," said John.

He dreaded the next hour.

"Now, John, I want to talk to you about three things today," said Doctor Kerry. "First I'm concerned about your use of drugs to mask psychological problems that you may have. Second I want to talk to you about post-traumatic stress disorder and then if we have time I want to talk to you about survivor's guilt."

John liked the ugly man's assertive get-to-the-point attitude. *Maybe this won't be that bad he thought.*

"That sounds good, Doctor Kerry," said John. "I have been having trouble with getting off the meds."

"The opiate type drugs are addicting," said Doctor Kerry. "I'm going to prescribe Xyenatac. This should still help you with the pain. It's not as powerful as the other stuff and it shouldn't be addictive."

"I want you to take a conscious look at when you are taking the pills though; if it's for physical pain, that's all right. That's perfectly normal and actually needed for the healing process.

"If you are taking them for emotional or mental reasons, I must strongly caution against this. Drugging away your mental problems especially caused by a terrifying event will only turn them into a ticking time bomb. We must deal with them in the real world."

"Yes, I agree with you, doctor."

"Now, I want to discuss post-traumatic stress disorder. Have you ever heard of it?" questioned the doctor.

"Yes, we received some classes before we went to Iraq, but I don't remember much of them."

"John, when a person experiences or witnesses an event that involved actual or threatened death and or serious injury, there is potential for that person to have a natural response which involves intense fear, helplessness, or horror. This is a classic case of PTSD. The best way to cope with this is to talk about it."

"You want me to talk about it?"

"You don't have to talk about it with me, but I'm here to listen if you want to talk. I want to shape your expectations about discussing it with intimate people in your life though, such as a sibling or spouse.

"A common problem that I've seen is veterans will try to talk with their spouse about horrific things that have happened to them. When their spouse doesn't understand, they feel isolated and alone because they sense the person doesn't understand. Truly the best people to talk to are other Marines who have experienced the same thing."

* * *

John felt comfortable with the ugly man. What he said made sense. He normally, only felt comfortable talking to other people who experienced the same thing. He didn't want to discuss it with the doctor, but he worried about some of the things he felt and wanted to know if they would ever go away.

"Doctor, I'm consumed by the event," said John. "The magnitude of how much I think about it scares me. Every day, every second. The only thing I can equate it to is sex. Before, or even now, I can't go through the day without thinking about sex, literally all the time. I think this is normal for a dude, every man I've ever talked to says the same thing. What scares me is that I feel the same way about this event. I can't get it out of my head.

"I'm driving on the way over here and every song makes me think of it, I'm shaving in the morning and I look in the mirror and I think of it. I can't hide from it. It dominates my life right now. Will that ever go away?"

"I'm going to be honest with you, John. I think you will carry this with you, to some extent, for the rest of your life. Over time, prolonged exposure to therapy reduces the debilitating anxiety and avoidance, centered on the feared memories and situations, which may allow you to lead a more normal life."

"By therapy, that includes talking to your buddies or even writing about the event to yourself. It's hard to do, but the best thing for you is to revisit the event and try to accept it for what it is. If you can do this, it will help with the event and not consume your entire life."

The ugly man's honesty and empathetic approach impressed John.

"Doctor, you are explaining this all in a way that is making a lot of sense to me," said John. "Have you worked a lot with veterans?"

"No, not really," replied the doctor. "I've studied a lot about the subject and I'm very interested in it. John, this actually is a textbook type case. I'm actually excited that I might use some of these themes in a lecture I'm giving next week. Of course nothing personal, all general."

The doctor's comments had been making sense helping John up until that point. *Textbook type case, giving a lecture, this asshole. How can he equate my experience to a textbook type case?*

223

"Let me tell you more," said John in a stern tone. "I hope you don't take offense to this, but I want to explain this in a way so you can have some perspective on how much you don't understand."

The doctor looked at John puzzled.

"Have you ever been in a life threatening situation?"

"John, this isn't about me. I apologize if I've insulted you," answered the ugly man, aware of his faux pas.

"Well, let's say you have just one time, just for the sake of my argument. Now take that feeling that you felt for maybe one second, maybe one. Now imagine having that choking feeling for sixty seconds, sixty seconds of knowing you might be killed at any moment."

"John, I see where you are going with this— really I'm sorry if—"

"Let me finish. You see I'm trying to help you out doctor. I see your diplomas, but with all of your 'experience' in academia world, I think you will still benefit from this. You do want to give a good lecture don't you? Now take that one minute of the choking feeling if you can possibly fathom that, and make it sixty minutes. One hour, can you handle that?"

"John, please is this necessary?"

"LET ME FINISH," demanded John. "So, you have the constant threat of death for one hour, let's make it twenty four hours, hell, why don't we make it one day."

"John, I will never understand what you went through."

"You're right, you arrogant fuck! Try thirty days of that choking feeling; try thirty days of touching the devil. I don't sit in here and try to tell you how it feels being fucking ugly!"

He let out a sigh of relief, and immediately felt embarrassed for yelling at the doctor. He also felt guilty because he only endured thirty days of hell and his men were still over in Iraq. For some reason he felt great. A weight was lifted off of his shoulders. *That was helpful.* The doctor sat looking at the ground unsure of what to do or say next. John grabbed his walker and started towards the door.

"John, I'm sorry I offended you. I think the beginning of the session was productive and I do want to help you. Would you consider putting this aside and seeing me again? I am concerned about you and I want to talk to you about survivor's guilt."

"I'll think about it," replied John.

He knew he needed to come back and see Doctor Kerry, or at least somebody about his issues.

60

Rogue reached his hand into a pile of rice and mushed it together. He squeezed it into a ball and shoveled it into his mouth with his right thumb. The unorthodox lieutenant's hair grew even further out of Marine regulations than before and his full mustache spilled over his upper lip.

"You've got to ball it up like this," explained Rogue.

He opened his arm and showed his guest the proper way to eat Iraqi food.

The two Americans stood in the *Thaylet* Iraqi Police chief's office where the *mukadem* lieutenant colonel treated them to an Iraqi lunch. Rogue's mind was somewhat at ease for the first time during his deployment. Cash and Heath had worked some kind of drug deal and the Iraqi Police were no longer complaining about being paid.

Since moving from mobile to becoming the leader of a ten-man augmentation team, he released all of his inhibitions and truly embraced the Iraqi culture. When Rogue moved into his police station next to the *Euphrates* River he swore off American food. He had only consumed Iraqi food for several weeks.

Rogue started implementing new counterinsurgency tactics and they seemed to be working. Having touched the devil, he knew they were in a race against time to do everything in their power to win the war in Iraq.

"Ah, I see," said Breedlove.

The civilian who visited Rogue at the *Thaylet* Police Station took note of the lieutenant's Arab eating lesson.

Rogue studied the man. The diplomat wore charcoal slacks and a starched blue button down with a white collar and navy blue suspenders. He looked proper as if he had worn a suit his entire life. Under the proper exterior, the man displayed a hint of roughness in his eyes; the lieutenant also noted his guest's firm handshake. The diplomat was unusually tan for a middle-aged man and his hair was a bold white. The minor wrinkles on his face made Rogue think he could not be younger than fifty-five.

Breedlove flicked his hands trying to get the sticky rice off of his finger tips. He reached over and picked up a piece of flat bread and wiped the rice residue off of his hands. He adjusted his suspenders and straightened his button-down shirt.

The two men stood around a table inside of a meeting room with a few Iraqis.

"So, what exactly is the role of the State Department here in Iraq?"

Breedlove was a member of the Provincial Reconstruction Team which was intended to be a State Department team that built political and economic successes at the provincial level and below.

Today was Breedlove's twenty-eighth day in Iraq.

The diplomat came to *Thaylet* to see some of the techniques Rogue implemented to fight the insurgency: they were creating a buzz all the way to Washington D.C.

Breedlove requested, against his higher's wishes, to come live out in the ville for a week to see what was actually going on in the city. After hours of arguing, his State Department superior finally agreed to let him go, on one condition. His boss needed to give a recommendation at the end of the week to the Ambassador on whether or not to pull the CERP funds which the Marines were using. He tasked Breedlove to find evidence to cut off the money the Marines were spending.

In the police chief's office the two Americans spoke in English largely ignoring the Iraqi men. The Iraqis in turn were having a conversation in Arabic equally content to have two sidebars with no interpreting.

"Well, they say they are here to advise, not to do nation building," replied Breedlove answering the lieutenant's question.

"What do you mean, they?"

The lieutenant stared at the clean-cut man across the table of Iraqi food.

"Oh, I'm not actually part of the State Department." answered Breedlove. "I'm a Department of Defense civilian that volunteered to join a PRT when they couldn't fill all of the slots required in Iraq. It was actually a big deal; several State Department Foreign Service officers basically refused to come to Iraq."

"Are you serious?" said Rogue. "That's ridiculous."

"Oh, yes, there were several reports on the news about the Foreign Service officers who refused to come," said Breedlove. "They were short on people willing to come and I got an email asking for volunteers. I'm actually a reserve National Guard Army lieutenant colonel."

"Oh, sorry, sir," said Rogue. "I thought you were a civilian. So, what do you do in the real world?"

"I'm actually retired," said Breedlove. "I used to be the publisher for *The Bakersfield Californian*. It's the newspaper for a town you've probably never heard of it."

Rogue stared at the man, he had never heard of the newspaper or Bakersfield.

"In Ramadi I'm supposed to be in charge of the essential services progress such as sewer, water, electricity, and trash services, but it is hard for me to know what is going on because I've only been at the big base. Also, I don't know anything about any of those items. I give weekly status reports on them but, I don't even know what they really are."

"Sir, I want to show you something."

The men excused themselves from the Iraqi meal and walked into Rogue's room. The maverick lieutenant's library had doubled and he now increased his collection of books to include John A. Nagl's *Eating Soup with a Knife, Counterinsurgency Warfare: Theory and Practice* by David Galula and *The Ugly American*.

Breedlove looked up on the lieutenant's wall and saw a letter pinned up from Rogue's father. At the end of the letter a highlighted quote read, "SON, TEACH THEM TO FISH."

He opened his laptop and displayed a series of maps with overlays on them. The first showed a sewer diagram that portrayed all of the outlets in the city. He flipped through several similar slides outlying the electricity grid, the water treatment plant, the schools, and the medical facilities.

"Sir, you see the problem with Ramadi's sewer, is there is no sewer system at all," explained Rogue. "What they have here is an old storm drain system that was built by the Brits eighty years ago and revamped by *Saddam* in the 70s. The slope of these drainage—"

"How do you know all of this about the sewer systems?" asked Breedlove.

"We ask the people."

The diplomat looked at the Marine officer's set up. His miniature office looked more similar to that of a city-planner than a military man. Breedlove wrote notes in his black leather-bound portfolio.

"Can I get a copy of your briefs?" asked Breedlove.

He had been sent to the city to take away the Marines' money and now he questioned whether they were making better use of it than the State Department.

61

"*A*s-Salāmm `Alaykum*," said Rogue, waving and smiling to several Iraqis on the street as they leisurely walked passed them.

"Should we be walking this slowly?" asked the diplomat.

"Yes, sir," answered Cash, "we want people to know how safe it is. If we're running, bumping and bounding all over the place, it will work the people into a frenzy. It's amazing how much has changed. What's right today was not right three months ago."

Breedlove liked the confidence Cash portrayed when he made the statement. As they walked, Cash stopped every couple of hundred meters, to shake the hands of all of the Iraqi Police manning the checkpoints. At the posts, stood two young Iraqi Policemen. *If it's good enough for a U.S. Marine to walk, it's good enough for me.*

"By the way sir," said Cash, "if there are snipers out there they usually aim at the one who doesn't look like the rest of us."

Breedlove looked down at his black vest and charcoal slacks in horror.

"He's joking, sir," replied Rogue. "Look here, we have three reconstruction projects going on."

The diplomat looked at the street and saw several Iraqis wearing blue jump suits fixing the power lines. Iraqi people came onto the streets and gave the workers cold glasses of water.

"They have more power now than during *Saddam's* time," explained Rogue. "We were giving locals who owned large generators free fuel to power several thousand homes, but now that the majority of the city grid is up we've stopped with the fuel distribution."

Breedlove looked down the street further and saw a group of Iraqis cleaning the street and painting the curbs yellow and white with a fresh coat of paint.

"We were paying people to pick up the trash. Now when we give them a project we tell them they have to fix the entire road. They have to patch all of the holes and fix the concrete. We've even painted the curbs and the surrounding courtyard walls. Our theory is if things look like they are getting better, the people will perceive them to be getting better and it will have a force multiplying effect," said Rogue.

"Like Rudy Giuliani's broken window theory in New York during the '90s," said Breedlove.

"Yes, exactly" said Cash. "Perception is reality; if the people perceive the city to be safe, it will tighten the gaps that are open to the insurgents, also research shows if businesses start to open it usually has a ripple effect."

"Well, it's not exactly the broken windows theory," said Rogue. "We're not trying to raise the value of property so the poor can't live here and they are forced to move to Jersey."

Breedlove laughed. *At least they're thinking.* Next they patrolled up to the farmlands of *Thaylet* near the *Euphrates* River.

"It's beautiful up here," said Breedlove.

The lush area burst with green date palms and bougainvilleas. Several large farms divided the area into two-acre lots. On the tilled soil, hundreds of Iraqis dug along an irrigation ditch.

"They say the Garden of Eden might have been where the *Euphrates* meets the *Tigris* a couple hundred miles southeast from here," said Rogue.

"These are my favorite projects," said Cash. "We call them John Deere projects. Out here on these small farms we bought all of the local farmer's pumps that will push water into the irrigation ditches."

Breedlove looked at the hundreds of Iraqis working next to the water from the *Euphrates* River flowing into the irrigation ditch.

"The *irhabin* insurgents blew up all of the pumps when the violence started to force the people to be dependent on them," said Rogue. "Now these people will take this locally grown produce and sell it in the *souk*."

* * *

That night the three men sat in the *Thaylet* Hookah Room. Cash routinely stayed at each station for a day or two before moving on to the next police station. The only time the lieutenants ever saw each other was during meetings and on Cash's visits.

Breedlove told them what happened in the states and the two lieutenants tried to explain how dramatic the turnaround in Ramadi had been. The guest looked down at his watch which read 0130. The lieutenants still seemed excited to be talking with the Bakersfield editor turned diplomat.

"I can't believe what you Marines are doing out here in the ville," said Breedlove.

"Sir, this is a new war," said Rogue. "I trained to shoot, move, and communicate and here I am practically the mayor of the *Thaylet*."

"Do you know what DIME stands for?" asked Breedlove.

"No," replied the two lieutenants.

"DIME means Diplomacy, Intelligence, Military and Economics," said Breedlove. "This is essentially our foreign policy approach. You gentlemen are conducting foreign policy at the company level, the decisions you are making at your level were reserved for colonels and generals when I was in the Army."

The lieutenants looked at the man and nodded.

"As a junior officer the line between the military and diplomats was distinct. I guess you have an image of senior ranking officers at parties in embassies and what not. My entire perception is changed by seeing what you men are doing. I have to ask myself, where does the military end and the State Department start?"

"I think this should be the State Department out here doing exactly what we're doing," said Cash. "Rogue and I have a unique perspective because we saw the bad times so we're willing to let go and be diplomats, but the military should not be the nation builders, and even if they aren't it shouldn't be the Marines, we're the —"

"Do you know what the State Department's budget is?" asked Breedlove.

"No, sir."

"It's around $30 billion," said the diplomat. "The Department of Defense's budget is $439 billion."

"So you're saying it's our job to do this?" asked Rogue.

"Well, I think you should be able to do it and it looks like you are doing more here than I've seen or heard about anywhere else," said Breedlove. "That's why I hate to tell you that I think they are going to pull the military's CERP money."

The two lieutenants looked at each other.

"I don't get it. A tank cost 12 million and they don't do shit in this war," said Rogue. "If they gave me 12 million to put into the economy and provided jobs to the people, the safety would follow."

He sighed.

"If they take that money away, the contractors will stop helping the Iraqi Police and we'll be fucked!" yelled Rogue.

"Sir, we need that money," said Cash.

"We'll continue to do reconstruction projects with the PRT and USAID," explained Breedlove.

"You don't understand, sir," said Rogue. "We need the *wasta* out here, or else it doesn't work putting ten Marines with one hundred Iraqis."

"What's *wasta*?" asked the diplomat.

"*Wasta* is Arab Social capital," said Cash. "If you redo a school, the Iraqis need to think Rogue's responsible for it. He's the American face living out in the ville. If it is some nameless entity, they will not grasp who is helping them."

"Sir, we have a theory that might help explain this." said Rogue. "Right now, we like to say there are five Iraqis sitting around drinking chai."

"Right now, at 0200 in the morning?" asked Breedlove.

"Not literally, okay, let's say today, five Arab men were sitting around drinking chai," said Cash.

"And the first Iraqi says, 'today we must kill Cash the Marine lieutenant'," said Rogue. "And they know his name and they see him out and about all over town. Three of the Iraqis agree with the first, but the Fifth Iraqi says, 'no we can't kill Cash because he is rebuilding my school and I very much want my son to get an education'."

Breedlove was amused with the lieutenant's story.

"So, a few weeks go by and the five Iraqis get back together for chai," explained Cash.

"The school is built now and the fifth Iraqi stands up and says, 'ahh today we will kill Cash'," said Rogue.

The diplomat nodded his head following the dialogue. Rogue continued, "...but now the first Iraqi stands up and says, 'ehh we can't kill the Marine lieutenant yet, he is fixing the electricity in my neighborhood—'."

"And on and on the story goes with water, transportation, medical and all of the other essential services," said Cash.

"Essentially we are buying time by showing the people we are here to help," said Rogue. "But the Iraqis need to know it's the people living in town doing it or we gain no leverage and we're put at risk. The two have to be tied together to maximize their effects."

The diplomat looked at the two Marines filled with hope. *They're right, either the PRT needs to live out in town with the Marines, one representative at each site, or the Marines need the money.* He sighed. *I can't take their money.*

62

He heard rustling and the lights came on. The clock blinked 0700. *Where do they get their sense of urgency?*

"Sir, sorry, I've got to go train some Iraqi Police this morning," said Rogue. "We're going to try and get them to do some Crossfit workouts. I'll come get you later."

He flipped off the light and the diplomat lay in the darkness for a half an hour consumed by guilt before he got up and started looking through Rogue's city briefs.

* * *

Three days later the *Thaylet* Hookah Room filled with Iraqi Police waiting to see the Asian Cup Game. Breedlove sat on the couch next to Professor *Haythem* who wore his signature black suit and bow tie. The fat district councilman offered the diplomat a Dunhill; he accepted the offering and lit up the British smoke.

"The Lion of the two Rivers…the Iraqi Soccer Team will be playing the highly favored Saudi Arabian Team…" announced the television.

After three days of living in the ville, Breedlove's appearance looked different. He grew a two-day stubble of salt and pepper beard. He lost the suspenders and his sleeves were rolled up on his button-down shirt.

For thirty minutes, Breedlove and Rogue watched from the roof as thousands of Iraqis flooded the streets of Ramadi and celebrated their country's victory. Men, women, and children of all ages waved Iraqi flags over their heads as the masses jumped up and down.

After the excitement, they moved back to the *Thaylet* Hookah Room. In the room sat four large platters with huge pyramids of rice. On top of each pile of rice lay a baked lamb, largely still intact with only the head and hooves removed.

After the Iraqi feast, they moved out to a sandlot behind the *Thaylet* Police Station where forty Iraqi youths played each other in a game of soccer. One team wore bright blue soccer jerseys that said *Thaylet* in Arabic with the Iraqi flags on the back.

Following the game, the Iraqis started to do a line dance called, *Chobe.* All the men linked arms and started a chain. In the center of the group the *Thaylet* Police Chief jumped and danced solo holding his MP5 sub-machine gun in the air. An Iraqi singer sang in a high pitched song while Arab music twanged in the background.

Rogue explained to the diplomat that the center *Chobe* dancer was usually the eldest Iraqi and that the weapon was traditionally a saber, but evolved to any weapon in the modern days to include machine guns. The Iraqis pulled the diplomat into the dance and celebrated. The diplomat took a picture of Rogue dancing with the Iraqis.

* * *

That night, Rogue and the diplomat stayed up and talked during another late night. The diplomat had to return to the big base the next day. The tiny room filled with smoke from the cigarettes both men were enjoying.

"I've been thinking about everything you're doing out here," said Breedlove. "What you're missing is a public affairs strategy."

"What do you mean?" asked Rogue.

"Well, every picture that I see of Ramadi shows the city in ruins," explained the diplomat. "You need to maximize your efforts about showing people both in Ramadi and the states the amazing things you are doing here."

"You mean information operations," said Rogue.

"Yes, in every picture that comes out of this place, you should strive to either have an Iraqi Policeman, a soccer game, an Iraqi flag or a reconstruction project. Do you realize how big of a strategic success the Iraqis winning this soccer game is?"

"What do you recommend sir?" asked Rogue.

"You should put Iraqi flags everywhere. Put up billboards of all the good things you are doing for the people. Highlight their nationalism."

Rogue wrote everything down on a notepad. He intended to propose a nationalistic information operation campaign to Heath at the next meeting. The lieutenant looked at his watch, exhausted from the exciting day. He climbed in the rack.

Breedlove stayed awake and wrote his report to his superior recommending, not only that the Marines keep their money, but that their amounts should be increased. After he sent off his report, he stayed awake another hour typing an article about the Iraqi's victory in the Asian Cup. He typed with a sense of urgency. When he finished, he sent his article along with the picture he took of Rogue to the editor of the *Bakersfield Californian*.

Breedlove had drunk the Golf Kool-Aid.

63

"We can't tell him."

Powers and the battalion intelligence officer read the intelligence brief. They discussed whether to pass it down to the company level.

"It doesn't say his name," said the intel officer, "it only says that they are going to try to assassinate key leaders."

"But the report we got the day before says they will target the company leaders who are handing out the money and Heath's company has done the most reconstruction projects. They've done triple what the other companies have."

The major shook his head. He did not want to add unneeded stress to Heath, unless he was sure there was a threat, and there were still too many holes to verify.

"Let's wait a week to see if anything more solidifies before we tell him, we think it's him. Pass it along as is, but don't add anything else."

The captain nodded to the major and hit the send button on the secret brief.

* * *

Cash sat in the Golf Company intelligence room and read the latest report. The daily brief summarized that *al Qaeda* could not infiltrate the city due to the overwhelming presence of the Iraqi Police. His stomach rumbled. He knew that in a moment he would have to run to the bathroom. He quickly read the rest of the report.

"The insurgents, in an attempt to create a gap to reenter the city, will use a catastrophic event such as a car or suicide bomb."

The brief also read that they intended to assassinate key leaders; both Iraqi and American. Cash's stomach rumbled again and he ran to the bathroom area. *Fuck, all of the stalls are full.*

He looked in the broken triangular shaped piece of mirror, duct taped to the wall. *Come on, come on.* His reflection showed sunk-in eyes after months of pushing himself to the max. He wondered if Jill would recognize him. His cheeks were bony and thin. The stocky Marine now weighed 140 pounds. The lieutenant resisted the urge to scratch himself. *My asshole has itched for weeks especially in the morning.* A Marine came out of one of the stalls.

The lieutenant ran into the open stall and sat down on the tent style plastic toilet. He exploded his insides into a bag. It had been several months since he produced anything solid. He got up and looked at his own waste trying to see if there was anything moving in the bag. The corpsman told Cash he might have worms from eating the local under-cooked meat.

He remembered the time his father shot a Canadian goose. When his father cut open the large bird's stomach, thousands of white slivery worms writhed inside the animal's belly. Cash stayed awake thinking of the wives' tale that if a person carried a tapeworm, the creature climbed from the intestines up into the mouth of the host and licked the back of the person's teeth while they slept.

He continued to examine the bag but saw no movement inside the salt-like substance that absorbed the waste. *Fuck it. I'll get cancer and kill this parasite.* He threw the bag in the burn can and lit up a smoke.

A young Marine ran up to him.

"Sir, they need you in the command post."

Cash walked quickly next to the Marine. He hadn't been called to the command post in a while.

"What's going on? Contact somewhere?"

Despite Ramadi being calm, in the back of his mind, he feared at any moment the city would erupt with violence again.

"I don't think so, sir," said the Marine. "It's about *Sheik Ali.*"

Since the start of the Awakening, *Sheik Ali* became an iconic figure for change not only in Ramadi, but also in all of *Al Anbar* and throughout Iraq. The Iraqi Police chiefs *Malik* and then *Abdullah* fought in the streets, but *Sheik Ali* was the figure who united all of the tribes to stand up. To the Iraqis he was equivalent to Martin Luther King, Jr. The *Sheik* knew that by speaking out against *al Qaeda,* he was making himself an assassination target.

In the command post, the watch officer told Cash that a car bomb killed *Sheik Ali.* Outside of the isolated incident, the city remained quiet. The lieutenant shook his head. *This was just in the intel-report; how did we not see this coming?*

* * *

A few days later, the Golf staff sat in *Sabatash*'s Hookah Room. In the center of the table lay two separate week-old national newspapers from the states. The front page of one paper read:

IRAQIS CLINCH ASIAN CUP, *WAR TORN COUNTRY CELEBRATES.*

The second more recent paper's headline read:

TOP *SUNNI* KILLED IN IRAQ, *Sheik Leading Revolt Against al Qaeda Assassinated.*

Underneath the soccer headline was a picture of Rogue cheering with the Iraqi Police in *Thaylet*. Rogue, Cash, and Bama all sat, waiting for Heath's message. Since the Iraqi soccer win, Golf Company pushed hard on Rogue's nationalistic campaign. They strung 20,000 Iraqi flags up across the streets of the city. They also focused their efforts on all of the highly trafficked business districts to renovate the faces of all the buildings.

Rogue contracted Iraqis to paint the tallest and largest water tower in the city like the Iraqi flag. He installed lights on the water tower and it glowed as a beacon of Iraqi Freedom throughout the city day and night. Despite *Sheik Ali*'s death, the city remained safe and the Iraqi Police and Marines were living in harmony. All throughout the northern half of the city, Golf Company posted billboards that showed pictures of the Iraq reconstruction projects. They also hung up thousands of posters of *Malik*. The Iraqi people soon added pictures of *Sheik Ali*.

"So, we've got a lot of great things going on in the city despite *Sheik Ali*'s death," explained Heath. "I've got to tell you a story first though."

He pointed to the picture of Rogue on the cover of the newspaper. Breedlove's story and photo ran in the *Bakersfield Californian* and was picked up by a national paper. Millions of people across the world saw the Marine lieutenant celebrating the game.

The photo did an excellent job portraying the Marine and the Iraqis hand-in-hand celebrating. Iraqi flags hung in the background. The picture easily told a thousand words. At least one hundred of the words described the lieutenant, well out of Marine regulations, centered in the photograph. His hair and mustache were too long. His flight suit was dirty and it was

239

extremely evident that the picture was taken outside of a Marine base. The Marine Corps' standing orders mandated that Marines, regardless of rank, wear their Kevlar helmet and clear eye protection. In the picture, Rogue wore neither.

"So, the Commandant is drinking his morning cup of coffee in the Pentagon," said Heath, "and he is happy because the Iraqis recently won this big soccer game that broadcasted as a huge 'FUCK YOU' to the insurgents across the world. He picks up the morning paper and sees Rogue."

The lieutenants all started laughing.

"Think this is fucking funny, gents? It's not. I know this sounds gay, but this shit matters, Rogue. The Commandant's pissed that some peace-going, free-loving lieutenant without his eye protection did not have his Kevlar on and was well out of grooming standards."

The lieutenants stopped laughing.

"So he calls in the sergeant major of the Marine Corps and down the chain the message goes to put your nuts on a chopping block."

"But, sir—"

"You messed up, period. Cut your hair and keep your mustache—"

At that moment, two men entered the room. Powers and Smith looked at the purple room puzzled by the décor.

"Gentlemen," said Heath to the battalion staff officers.

"Nice wallpaper," replied Smith.

"So, um, these are the gents behind all of the flags?" asked Powers.

"Yes, sir," replied Heath. "It was actually Rogue's idea."

The operations officer stared at the maverick lieutenant.

"You're lucky you're not posted lieutenant," said Powers. "The colonel wanted your head on a platter for that fucking picture."

He pointed at the paper.

"I don't know what you told Breedlove, but that's the only reason you're not back at the big base right now washing my cammies."

"Yes, sir, but—"

"Lieutenant," interrupted Powers, "the colonel, after cursing your name for that picture, told me you were the single reason our CERP money was not cut off from the State Department reps. I would not have let you off that easy."

The lieutenants felt awkward around the staff officers. Heath tried to say something in defense of his lieutenant, but was cut off by Smith. The intelligence officer spoke in a serious tone.

"We need to talk to you alone, Heath— it's important."

64

"Congratulations on your Silver Star, lieutenant," said Powers. "You know we're all talking about your heroism back at the big base. Lieutenants like you are why we're winning this war."

The major followed the lieutenants into the hallway. After slapping Bama on the back, Powers grabbed Rogue's arm.

"You know, you could learn a lot from Bama. Do you understand what I'm saying?"

Rogue nodded his head.

"I assure you I know something about the Marine Corps. I was awarded the Bronze Star for the elections," said Powers.

The field grade officer told the lieutenants about his career and how he intended to help them. He told them he only dreamt of seeing combat when he was a lieutenant. This generation of junior officers did not know how lucky they were, to have the opportunity to see a real war explained the major.

To have combat experience ensured promotions and medals and these were important for an officer's career. He was here to help and if either of them needed to say anything about Heath, they could go directly to him. Before he went back in the room he congratulated Bama again on his Silver Star and told him what a high honor it was for a Marine to be awarded the medal.

* * *

In the Hookah Room, the intelligence officer opened up his laptop and gave Heath a secret brief on the situation since the start of the Awakening. Powers re-entered the room and sat down on one of the plush yellow couches. Smith outlined how the *al Qaeda* insurgents fled from the city. He continually highlighted that several of the lower level operatives switched sides and became Iraqi Police.

"The current security status shows that the only way they can infiltrate with the overwhelming presence of the Iraqi Police is with a car bomb," explained Smith.

He knocked on the wooden table, "The insurgents almost can't attack us because they can't get close enough."

"Why does this warrant a trip out to see us?" asked Heath.

He already knew all of the information.

"Well, they also are going to try and infiltrate by assassinating key leaders. They have shown that they can do it with *Sheik Ali*," explained Smith. "You should look to protect your police chiefs like *Abdullah, Omar* and—"

"Do you have a specific report saying they are going to try and kill one of them?"

"Well, we have reports that they are going to try and kill all of the police chiefs, but they are real general," said Smith. "The reason we're here is—"

The intelligence officer paused and looked at Powers. Both staff officers stared at Heath.

"We have a detailed report that they are going to try and kill the Marine leaders who are conducting the reconstruction projects. Your company has done the most—"

Powers interrupted Smith.

"We think they are going to try and kill you, Heath."

* * *

In the other room, Rogue waited for Cash. Each week the lieutenants turned in project requests and he typed them up and forwarded them to higher to receive the money. After they turned in their projects, he opened up a footlocker with $500,000 cash stacked in $10,000 bundles of $100 bills.

He threw Rogue $20,000 for a small sewer project. The lieutenants joked that if they were hit with an IED, there would be $100 bills flying all over the air as they lay in a bloody mess.

"Bama, do you have one to turn in?"

The southerner shook his head no. Heath ordered all of the lieutenants to conduct reconstruction projects in their areas. Bama, despite now embracing the Iraqi Police, was still hesitant to work with the Iraqi civilians.

"You know, Heath—"

"I know, I know," replied Bama, "I'll get to it next week."

"You said that last week Bama. I need that turned in as soon as possible. You should be doing those in your area."

"I know. I said I'd turn it in next week."

Bama annoyed Cash. He couldn't tell if he was playing him along or if he intended to turn it in. Either way, he needed to put the past behind and embrace the Iraqi people.

"Powers is such a douche," interrupted Rogue breaking the tension. "Can you believe he said we are lucky to see combat? I can't believe he got the Bronze Star with V for the elections. He only sat on the big fucking base."

"The major does do a lot of work, but the 'V' should be reserved for the Marines who are actually out here day in and day out. Nate should get the fucking Bronze 'V' not him."

Bama sat embarrassed by the whole conversation.

"You know, Bama, I'm surprised by how humble you've been about your award," said Rogue.

"Yeah," chimed in Cash, "you're usually an arrogant fuck."

"It's no big deal," said Bama, "it's only a feather in my cap to people that don't know me. It actually bothers me that Powers even talked to me. I didn't even think he knew my name, but now that I have this piece of colored cloth, he thinks I'm a good Marine."

"It's as if he was congratulating himself. I'm still the same dude I was before."

The three lieutenants lit up smokes.

"Intellect, force of will, and character," said Cash. "Heath says these three things make a good officer, with character being the most important of the three."

"Yeah... yeah, he says that all the time."

"Did he tell you the rest?" asked Cash.

"No what do you mean?"

"He told me the one thing that defines being a good infantry officer."

Bama and Rogue waited in anticipation.

"He said— be perfect."

Rogue and Bama looked at each other in disappointment. They had heard the punch line before. They started talking.

243

"I'm not finished," said Cash. "When you say be perfect you are giving the lieutenants an impossible task. Since you can't be perfect, you must strive for perfection. That is the secret. Strive to be perfect because you will be put in situations that demand perfection. Situations where there is no right answer, but there are thousands of wrong answers that will get a Marine killed or dismembered."

The other two lieutenants had never heard this twist. They looked back up at Cash and stopped their side bar conversation.

"So the answer is to strive to be perfect?"

"Well, sort of," explained Cash. "On your quest to perfection, you will find some dangerous truths. The best people in the world strive to be perfect. All professional athletes, successful businessmen... The best ones all seek to be perfect."

"How's that dangerous?" asked Bama.

"The dangerous part is this," explained Cash. "On your quest to perfection, you will find that you are good at things, better than most. You know when you graduate the man school at Infantry Officer Course, they get your head so pumped up, you think you could make it rain if you had to."

Bama and Rogue nodded their heads.

"On your quest, when you find you are good, the dangerous part is that you will become arrogant. So, Heath told me that the secret in your quest for perfection is to seek humility. He said if you aspire to be humble, this will bridge the gaps in your shortcomings. You will never be perfect, but you can strive to be perfect. If you remain humble along the way, this is the secret to being a good leader."

65

That night Cash and Heath sat in the Hookah Room after the other lieutenants went back to their police stations. They often ended the night at 0300 with a twenty-minute bullshit session to clear their minds before they hit the rack.

"Do you think you could run Golf?" asked Heath. "You know, as the company commander."

Cash looked at Heath wondering where he was going with the question.

"Yes, sir. Probably not as good as you could, but I could run it the last month of the deployment. The next battalion should be on deck in three weeks right?"

Heath smiled. His favorite mentor, his first company commander, told him you know you've done your job when you've worked yourself out of a job. Despite all of the chaos and the turn of events, Golf Company had been amazing for Heath. *They've done everything I've asked and kept coming back for more.*

"Why do you ask sir?"

"Oh, it's an exercise a commander should have with his executive officer every so often." explained Heath. "You know you've done a good job when…"

He continued to give Cash some leadership mentoring and decided not tell him about the intelligence report. *We've only got a month left.* He thought about all Golf experienced. *Shit, if I can make it through that I can keep my head down for one more month.*

That night while Heath slept, Cash stayed up and tried to call Jill. He continued to do a horrible job calling her. After the phone cut out four times without him saying a word, he decided to write her a letter.

Dear Jill,

*It's only a month till I get to
see you! There are no words to describe
how much I love you and miss you...*

* * *

The following day at *Azzizziyah,* the interpreter heard yelling.

Cash and Bama argued in the lieutenants' room. The two Marines sat across from each other in plastic lawn chairs.

Bama's room at *Azzizziyah* was the size of a walk-in closet. The actual room was double that size, but he split the room in two with a white sheet, to give his interpreter a room. In the spartan room sat a bunk bed, two white chairs, a small table and a case of Redbull.

Bama was the only lieutenant in Golf avoiding governance operations. He refused to attend the mini-district council meetings at his own station. Cash had run the meetings at *Azzizziyah* for weeks.

"You've got to start participating in the district council meetings," said Cash. "First you don't turn in any reconstruction proposals and now this."

"I'm not doing it," replied Bama. "I'm sick of you being so damned..."

They continued to argue. Bama refused to go to the meeting.

"I dig the Iraqi Police, but I don't trust the Iraqi people; I refuse to work with them."

"You're going!"

On the other side of the sheet Moody, the terp listened to the Marine lieutenants yell at each other. In the room Cash, got out of his chair and walked towards the door. He reached down and pulled on Bama's sleeve.

"Let's go."

Cash pulled on his arm harder trying to pull him out of the chair.

"Let's go, redneck."

"What did you call me?" asked Bama.

"A fucking redneck!" yelled Cash. "Listen you've got to..."

The five-foot eight wrestler and the six foot four football player continued to argue.

"You're so God damn stupid!"

Bama pulled his arm back.

"Fuck you, Cash!"

He jumped out of his chair and threw Cash to the ground. As Cash tried to stand up, the large lieutenant punched him the face. He fell to the ground. Bama's rage immediately was replaced by a sense of guilt. *I punched Cash.*

He felt a grab on his left ankle. The next thing he knew his face slammed against the concrete. He tasted blood.

He felt Cash grabbing his arm and wrapping his legs around his waist.

Fucking wrestlers.

An arm started to choke the football player. He tried to break the grip. Blood from Cash's face dripped onto his own cheek as the wrestler pressed his head into Bama's temple and tightened his grip.

Bama now trapped, grabbed for something. He reached but grasped air.

He finally felt a Red Bull can. He slammed the can against Cash's face breaking the wrestler's grip, knocking him off.

The can exploded on impact. The energy drink shot everywhere and the can spun in circles on the concrete floor.

Bama stood in a defensive position waiting for Cash's re-attack. Cash crouched on the concrete dazed by the blow. The Red Bull can fizzed and sprayed both of the Marines.

Moody ran into the room.

"Gentlemen, enough, enough."

The two Marines stared at each other both breathing heavily.

"All right, enough," said Cash.

He stood up and and kicked the Red bull can. It slammed against the wall.

"I'm not going," said Bama.

Cash spit blood out of his mouth and walked out of the room.

* * *

At *Azzizziyah* there was no Hookah Room; Bama failed to create one. Cash sat on a low Arab couch in the *Azzizziyah* police chief's office. His eye swelled up and a cut underneath it bled. He held a napkin on his face, stopping the bleeding. A large goose egg swelled on his forehead.

In the room sat six Iraqis and Cash. The Marine lieutenant looked around the room at *Azzizziyah*'s police chief, Professor *Haythem* the district council man, Moody and an Iraqi man he had never seen.

247

"Mr. Cashee," said Professor *Haythem*, "what happened to you?"

"Don't worry about it, professor. Who is our guest?"

"Sir, this is *Rasheed*."

It was customary for the Iraqis to pitch the Marines every hare-brained scheme they thought up in order to get money. After all this was their shot to win the lottery.

Cash heard some good ones too:

-Start a cricket league that the Marines sponsor $1,000 per team
-Develop a freshwater fish hatchery
-Make a Ramadi version of *Who Wants to be a Millionaire*
-Build an enormous light arch into the city that said, "Welcome to Ramadi"
-Build an amusement park with a rollercoaster ride

Cash examined *Rasheed*. He looked like an ordinary Iraqi man. He was middle-aged, slightly hunched over, and shared the general beaten-down-by-life look that all Iraqis displayed. He wondered if it was the heat or being amidst the fighting for many years that made the Iraqis look so defeated. That day after fighting with Bama and enduring several months of Iraq, he felt the way *Rasheed* looked.

"Okay, let's hear it."

"Sir, he does not want money," replied Moody.

Rasheed grabbed both of Cash's hands. He stared him straight in the face and his tired look faded away. Cash saw something he missed before. A sparkle glimmered in his eye. *Rasheed* told the lieutenant something that captured his attention. After the meeting Cash left *Azzizziyah* without speaking to Bama.

That night back at *Sabatash*, Cash tried to describe to Heath what *Rasheed* told him. Since the Awakening the Iraqis celebrated lots of 'FIRSTS.' They declared everything after the violence stopped 'the first.'

They had more celebration dinners than Heath wanted to remember. They started several soccer leagues and each one had a 'first' game. Anything else the Iraqis thought of, they pinned the term 'first' on. The Golf company commander had heard 'the first' speech before. He waited for Cash's pitch.

"Sir, they want to have a race..."

248

66

"We're not letting them have a race," said Powers.

He sat in the battalion briefing room with Heath.

"But, sir, this could be a phenomenal event that will draw positive—"

"No," replied Powers.

Duncan walked in the room interrupting the conversation.

"What are you talking about?" asked the battalion executive officer.

"Heath wants to have a race, I don't think the cost-benefit works out," said Powers. "Let's say a suicide bomber infiltrates the crowd. We already know that they have you as a target, Heath. It's not worth the risk."

The topic peaked the battalion executive officer's interest. Heath looked at him for help.

"I think it's a great idea," said Duncan. "We'll tighten up security."

I knew he would go for it.

"Go ahead and start the planning," said Duncan.

Heath hedged his bets. After hearing Cash's proposal, he told him to run with it while he convinced battalion.

"This is insane," said Powers, "this is not what a Marine battalion should be talking about."

"This is exactly what a Marine battalion should be talking about..."

* * *

Two days later Cash sat in the *Sabatash* Hookah Room with Nate, Rogue, and several Iraqis as they planned the Ramadi 5k race. Bama was absent. The lieutenants listened intently as *Rasheed* explained why the race was so important. Every year the high schools in Ramadi ran from outside the city down Route Michigan, the main street the Iraqi's called "*Shara al*

Ohm." At the finish line, the governor handed out trophies to the top ten runners.

The races were big community events. They differed from high school races in the states because anybody could run, not only students. The winner was hailed a hero and crowned with bragging rights until the next race. The annual event had not occurred since the invasion.

"For five years from 1983 to 1988, the same man won the race. He still has legendary status as the ultimate running hero of Ramadi," explained the interpreter.

He said something about that man being in the Olympics. Nate whispered to Cash.

"Did he say that the same Iraqi took gold in the 1988 triple jump or that he liked watching the triple jump?"

Cash shook his head. Like so many other things, the Olympian question was lost in translation. Every time the Iraqis mentioned the race they called it the *mara'J'on.*

"It's not a marathon," said Rogue, "I think it is actually a 5k."

"Yes, a *mara'J'on,*" said the interpreter.

* * *

Over the next two weeks the Marines and the Iraqis included the *"mara'J'on"* in every meeting or conversation.

On post at *Sabatash* Mallard stood with an Iraqi Policeman. He looked out at Seventeenth Street. He remembered months earlier, it had been covered in sewage. In the past, each building looked abandoned and no one walked the streets. He remembered the tension of leaving the wire. He remembered the glares from the people. He remembered the smell. The smell of shit. He remembered it as a cold lifeless empty stage.

"*Mara'J on zien,*" said the Iraqi.

Mallard looked at him and smiled. They had stood post together for months and although neither spoke the other's language, they found a way to communicate. He looked back down on to Seventeenth Street, which was alive with color. The buildings shined with bright freshly colored paint. All of the windows showed new glass.

Thousands of Iraqi flags hung strung across the streets. Iraqi Police stood on every corner. Hundreds of people walked up and down the streets buying produce and goods from the market. He looked up at the water tower painted like the Iraqi flag then looked back at the Iraqi.

"You running in it?"

The Iraqi looked back with a blank stare.

"*Enta*, you?" asked the Mallard.

He pumped his arms back and forth as if running.

The Iraqi nodded.

"*In šā Allāh , enta*?" asked the Iraqi pumping his arms.

"What's going on up here?" asked the sergeant of the guard.

Mallard explained they were talking about the Ramadi 5k.

"I heard the lieutenants say that no Marines get to run in the race," said the sergeant. "They asked if they could run it and the battalion commander said no."

"If I ran, I'd wear no gear, I'd only take a pistol," replied the private.

"If you could run it, you'd better place first."

* * *

Inside an Iraqi house outside of the *Sabatash* neighborhood, a young Iraqi man sat holding his newborn child. His father told him a story.

"When I was in the Iraqi Army, we took a fitness test once a year," explained the father. "All of the soldiers ran 12 kilometers. They took us out into the middle of the desert on a marked course."

The Iraqi Policeman who the Marines called, "Gonzo," looked up at his father and nodded.

"All of the officers stood at the line," continued the father. "They started the test by shooting their 9mm pistols into the air. After we took off, they shot their pistols over our heads to make us run faster."

The fifty year old father laughed, thinking about the snap of the pistol rounds flying over his head all those years ago.

"You know, I placed first every time I ran the test," said the father. "The last time I ran it in 1972, I wore no shoes and still won."

He explained to his son a tale of Arab lore that if a person won a victory in a race it wiped away all of their shame. The father lied to his son. He knew that his son had been exposed to horrible things over the last three years. He felt shame that he could not protect his son against *al Qaeda* and the horrors of war. There are dark things fathers never want to think about their sons having to experience. He reached behind his chair and pulled out a gift. He smiled at his son.

"I want you to have this."

He handed Gonzo a red leather bound journal.

"To new beginnings."

251

He smiled as Gonzo took the book. Things were going better now, the city was safe. The entire city fought back against *al Qaeda*. His son had a baby and a job as an Iraqi Policeman. Hope was on the horizon. But the father could not shake the shame of the past. He knew his son could not shake it either. So he told him that if he won the race, *Allah* would forgive him of the shame. This was not exactly incorrect; if two warriors fought in a saber challenge, the winner took the spoils and no matter what the victory overshadowed his previous losses; this was the word of *Allah* straight from the *Qur'an*.

Gonzo looked up at his father rejuvenated by the challenge. He believed his father was a man of character. He tasted the possibility of pride that he lost long ago. If he won the race, he could lose the shame. Gonzo looked down at his new son and up at his father.

"I will win the race."

67

During the planning, *Rasheed* dedicated the race to *Malik*. With Iraqi Police integrated into the race, the buzz grew even bigger. The day of the *"mara'J'on"*, *Rasheed* hosted a huge feast in celebration of the event. There were five lambs killed for the fifty VIPs that were invited. The VIPs included all of the Iraqi Police chiefs, the martyr *Malik*'s son *Anwar*, who was now a lieutenant in the Iraqi Police, the three Arab news stations, along with several reputable sports authorities from *Baghdad* and a multitude of other local leaders. Cash looked at the Iraqi who he thought he heard somebody say was the 1988 Olympic triple jumper.

"Where is Heath?" asked one of the police chiefs.

"He said he's going to watch the race from the roof of *Sabatash* and meet everyone at the finish line," replied Cash.

At the dinner more stories of peoples' glory days surfaced. Several of the people told the story of *Saddam Hussein*'s birthday's in 2001. Thousands of people ran from *Tikrit* to *Saddam's* Palace in *Baghdad* holding a torch and the Iraqi flag. The Iraqis loved telling the stories and at one point, the 1988 triple jumper long-jumped across the room. His feat was met with five other people attempting to beat him. Each Iraqi fell short.

* * *

On Route Michigan, 2000 Iraqis stood in line to get their *mara'J'on* bibs. At the starting line crossing the main road a blue steel footbridge towered above the six lane highway. Atop the footbridge six Marines took pictures of the runners. Below the bridge on the road, Cash called up to the Marines.

"Where are the reporters?"

"Sir, battalion called and said no one is coming."

One of the only reasons they agreed to have the race was for the positive media coverage. Despite the lack of western coverage, three Arab news stations from *Baghdad*, Egypt and Lebanon all had reporters present.

He looked at the runners in awe. Behind them thousands of Iraqi flags hung in the street. For the Marines the event was as equally therapeutic as it was to the Iraqis. Cash asked several of the Marines if any of them thought this event was possible six months ago. All of them, with a wry smile replied, "There's no way this could have happened without the Awakening."

He looked up at the Marines on the bridge. *A few months ago you had the same odds as in a roulette game getting from the race start point to the government center without getting shot at or hit by an IED.*

Cash remembered the beginning of the deployment rolling down Route Michigan in the back of a seven-ton truck hunched over white-knuckling his weapon waiting to get blown up and torn to pieces. He thought for the Marines who fought in Ramadi the last three years, Route Michigan and checkpoint 295 will be remembered to Iraq veterans as the Hill 364s were to Vietnam veterans. He shook his head in amazement as the runners prepared to run down the once lethal strip.

"Excuse me, sir, where is Heath?" asked *Anwar*, *Malik*'s son. "I want to tell him I'm going to win the race for my father."

Heath had befriended *Anwar* and he often hung out in the Hookah Room at *Sabatash* with the Marines since his father's death.

"He'll meet us at the finish line," responded Cash.

The excitement of the moment almost grabbed the lieutenant, but Rock talked him out of it. They sat in the back of an Iraqi Police truck driven by *Abdullah* as they waited for the start of the race.

* * *

Rasheed announced over the loud speakers, "Go," and the "*mara'J'on*" was underway. Two runners burst ahead of the crowd. *Anwar* and Gonzo traded first place for the first one hundred meters.

Cash looked back at the hundreds of runners in awe of the flags and the Iraqi national anthem that played from the tops of the mosques and the firm bases. Rock looked at the lieutenant with a grin ear to ear on his face. He looked at the scenery and smiled as well.

As the runners reached the 400 meter mark, the pack started to separate and several of the runners stopped at the first water point obviously not interested in being heroes in the *"mara'J'on."* Along Route Michigan, the Marines stood in the street and handed out water cups to the Iraqi runners.

At this point a distinct group of hard chargers broke out and were pushing to be number one. The young Iraqi men at the lead displayed a solemn look on their face. They were pushing themselves harder than the Marines had ever seen athletes push. *To think what they are grasping for, to be the fastest Iraqi in the first 5k after the violence had stopped.* All the excitement from high school sports rushed back to Cash and he thought about jumping out of the truck to run with the young Iraqi men giving it their all for a chance at glory.

Cash looked out at *Anwar* who was now the lead runner as he ran through the notorious checkpoint 295. He looked down the street that ran from checkpoint 295 where his Marines shot the pregnant lady months earlier. Further, down the same street John had been hit with the IED. A few months ago any person who stayed in that area for more than 20 minutes would have surely died. On that day several Marines from the government center and *Sabatash* stood at checkpoint 295 to cheer on the runners.

The race pushed passed the *Al Boheim* Mosque where Captain *Falah's* funeral had been and where Isaac was killed by the mortar round. Cash looked out the truck at two ravens. The black birds sat atop the huge teal tiled domed minaret above the largest mosque in Ramadi and looked down on the runners as they rounded the corner closing on the last 800 meters.

"Sheik Ali and *Malik,"* laughed *Abdullah* pointing to the two birds perched above the mosque.

On the streets lining the route hundreds of Iraqi Police and thousands of civilians cheered the runners from each of their neighborhoods. The Iraqis cheered for *Jumuyah, Azzizziyah, Sabatash, Warar,* and *Thaylet.*

As they rounded the last corner of the half-octagon shape road the Marines called, "Racetrack," the runners saw the finish line less than 400 meters away.

Gonzo in second place tried to close on Anwar's fifty meter lead. Gonzo's father stood on the side of the road cheering for his son as he gained on the leader.

"Come on *Salah,"* said Gonzo's father holding his grandson, "don't give up."

As they closed on the last 100 meters the top five runners all ran within feet of each other. They each avoided the Marines from *Qatana* police station who cheered them on and offered them water.

Anwar still in the lead seemed to sense the runners coming up on him. He saw the finish line and began to pump his arms and speed up to kick out the last 75 meters.

Out of nowhere Gonzo came from behind, dominating every other competitor and pushed to be neck in neck with *Anwar*. In the final five feet Gonzo burst ahead of *Anwar* and broke the finish line.

Cash looked down at his watch which read 16:17. Gonzo's father ran to hug him as he crossed the finish line. Hundreds of people hoisted the winner up on their shoulders and started cheering. Several others massed at the finish line. The crowds chanted, "*Salah Mabrook, Salah Mabrook* Congrats, Congrats."

While the rest of the finishers came in, the crowd celebrated waving Iraqi flags. Before all of the runners finished *Rasheed* started handing out trophies to the top six placers. The three Arab news stations filmed the event with reporters questioning the top placers. After the runners were awarded, *Rasheed* called up Heath, Rogue, Nate, and Cash. Each Marine was given a trophy. Six Iraqis played music on a large drum. They started the *Chobe* dance locking arms while kicking their legs in.

Heath who waited at the finish line, as promised jumped into the middle of the *Chobe* dance and ended up surrounded by the cheering crowd.

As the crowd celebrated, suddenly *Rasheed* came up and grabbed Heath and Cash with a worried look on his face.

"You must leave now," said *Rasheed*.

68

Heath calmly called for the Marines, in overwatch positions spread out covering the area, to keep alert. He called to the police chiefs to tell them to have the crowd disperse. The music stopped and the crowd slowly started to break up as Iraqis walked away from the finish line.

The company commander scanned the rooftops. No vehicles, except police vehicles, were allowed in the area. The finish line was only a hundred meters from *Sabatash*. Heath looked at the hundreds of Iraqi citizens. *The only way they will get me is by sniper fire or a suicide vest.* The Iraqi Police did a great job searching the large crowd as the people waited at the finish line.

"Cash, I'm going to head back to the base," said Heath. "Finish getting these people out of here."

A fireteam escorted the company commander back to base. Rogue and Nate left with their Marines as well and Cash was left on the celebration site with a fireteam and Rock.

* * *

"Sir, let's get out of here," said Rock. Twenty minutes passed since Heath re-entered the base.

The crowd had disbursed and there were only fifty people left milling about in the area. Cash nodded and the fireteam headed back towards *Sabatash*. Rock took point and the five Marines were spread out from *Sabatash* to the finish point. Cash took up the rear of the mini-patrol. As they walked back, an Iraqi youth trailed the small patrol. There were several other Iraqis spread out in the street and the lieutenant did not detect that the Iraqi followed them. At a distance of fifty feet, the Iraqi appeared to be mulling about.

Cash faced back to the front and looked at an empty police checkpoint. *They must have joined in the celebration.* He felt a tug on his shoulder. He turned around and saw Gonzo. The race champion pointed to a group of children still in at the finish line. In the crowd, one larger Iraqi sat motionless.

"Sir, we have to get back," said Rock.

Cash looked at the kids playing and looked at Gonzo.

"What if a carbomb comes and those kids are still out playing? Gonzo and I will run back and tell them to disperse."

The lieutenant and the Iraqi runner ran back to the finish line and yelled for the kids to leave. They all dispersed, except the larger one, who sat down as they approached. Gonzo went up and tried to pull on him.

Cash heard an Arabic voice.

"Mulazim Cashee."

He turned and saw a teenage Iraqi with Down's syndrome sitting five feet from him. He wore a puffy shirt.

BOOM.

69

The sound of an IED explosion interrupted John's sleep. His skin was cold and sweaty. He remembered being hot and sweaty on a night patrol only to be cooled after stopping for a tactical pause. The wind would blow a chill onto his sweat. He tossed and turned and fell back asleep.

Boom. Another explosion. Boom. Another.

He rolled off the bed and immediately took a low crouching stance pulling a blanket over his body. His hands went into the alert position as if he carried a weapon. He started to shake. Thud. He shuttered. *No explosion.* Thud, thud... *It's not an explosion.*

Thud, thud...

John pulled on his pants over his zigzaggy scars. He walked across the room and looked out the window. The garbage truck methodically moved through the night from trash can to trash can lifting and dumping them into the bed of the truck. Two thuds occurred; one when the can hit the truck as it dumped and another when the can was slammed back to the pavement.

John crouched next to the window breathing heavily. He lay flat under the window in his jeans with the blanket wrapped around him.

The next morning he woke up under the window with a realization. That morning, it occurred to John the country should not be in Iraq. He felt mixed emotions on it before. *It does not make sense for Marines to be over there.* That morning he justified to himself why the country should pull out. *It's the right thing to do for Flynn's sake.* He no longer felt guilt about his position.

He sat down and wrote two letters, one to his brother lieutenants in Iraq and one to his Virginian senator. The one to his senator gave the policymaker a detailed experience of what had happened to him and why he believed the country should pull out. At the post office he dropped the first letter addressed to an FPO address in Iraq into the slot. He stood looking at the letter addressed to his senator.

Up to that point, in his heart, he felt right. Looking at the letter he wavered. At that moment he had a second guessing of himself. *I can't do it.* He ripped up the letter.

John grabbed his walker and hobbled out of the post office. *I'll wait till Cash and Bama get back and talk with them before I send the letter.*

70

Two Marine officers drove a dark-blue Ford Taurus with government plates. The vehicle pulled up and parked outside of a house in Twentynine Palms, California.

"Is this the right address?" asked a captain.

"I hate this," replied a major.

The two men looked at each other. They heard the situation and could not bear what they were about to do. The major sighed.

"Okay, let's do this."

He got out of the car and pulled his dress-blue jacket tight with his left hand. In his right hand he held a letter. He leaned over and looked at his reflection in the driver's side window and straightened his cover.

* * *

Jill looked at the letter she recently received from Cash a few days ago. It usually took four days for a letter to get from Iraq to the states. She read it the night before, but wanted to read it again. She rubbed her eight and half month belly. She sung to her stomach, "He'll be home in three weeks, right in time for your birth."

She sat down in the chair holding the letter which read:

Dear Jill,

It's only a month till I get to see you! There are no words to describe how much I love you and miss you. I will be home...
I have a wife and a new baby to take care of, and you both are my world.

Love, Courtney

She heard a knock at the door and set the letter down.

* * *

Three weeks later, a wide-eyed second lieutenant and a salty sergeant stared back at the southern lieutenant in disbelief.

"You've got to focus on them people," explained Bama to the new Ramadi Marines.

The new unit had come to replace Golf.

"And the district council meetings, they're important. I'm telling ya'll that's how to win! Focus on the people; get in with the Iraqi Police and treat them like people. The guns on the post won't keep you safe, your relationships will. I'm telling you— all this kissing babies and hugging Iraqis is the way to win! With that being said, stay alert and keep your Marines focused."

The green lieutenant wrote in his book, "Focus on the people." The sergeant wrote in his book, "Golf lieutenant is off his rocker."

* * *

"I'll take two them there Guinness's."

The bartender handed him two drinks and he walked down stairs in the Shannon Ireland Airport to the smoking area and handed Rogue a cold beer. Rogue handed him a Dunhill. They lit up the British imported cigarettes and alternated a drag off a smoke with a drink of their beer. The two sat in silence. They nodded at each other and their faces agreed it was the best beer either of them had ever tasted.

The chartered 747 hovered thousands of feet over the Atlantic heading west towards Maine. All of the Golf Company staff sat in the first class section of the plane. There were two seats on each side of the aisle. Next to Bama sat Rogue and across the aisle Heath slept.

"That's the first time he's slept for more than about three hours in nine months," said Bama.

Behind them Nate and Rock slept, as well as the rest of the Golf staff. The two lieutenants were the only ones still awake.

Bama looked out the window into the dark night. He saw the moonlight's reflection off of the ocean far below the plane. He was restless. Something bothered him.

"Rogue, you sleeping?"

He nudged the maverick lieutenant who was also restless.

"No, what's on your mind?"

"I can't sleep, dude. Every time I start to dose off, I see his face."

Rogue looked at Bama.

"When my grandparents died I felt sad, but they'd lived a full life," said Bama. "When a young man dies it's a— well you know a tragedy. I can't shake it."

"I know how you feel."

"I want to know," said Bama pausing, "I want to know if their deaths were meaningless?"

Rogue wondered the same thing.

"I've thought about this a lot," said Rogue.

Bama listened intently to his friend.

"I've thought that they could have been killed in a car wreck or they could have drowned in a freak accident. Or they could have lived a non-eventful life, never standing up for anything they believed in and died of old age."

Rogue looked up at Bama and the two men locked eyes.

"Then their deaths would have been meaningless."

They did not say another word.

Senator William Whiting, the IV, known only to his closest of friends as Bama, lit up a cigarette in the cold morning air. He deeply inhaled the smoke and stared at the tombstone.

It had been twenty-two years since his first wife had died of cancer and eighteen years since he had married Jill Cash. In his second term as a senator he had lost the accent.

Their relationship was a connection of companionship. He had, after all, taken care of her for forty years. Over the decades he fixed broken sinks, replaced dead car batteries, and been a surrogate father to Courtney, Jr. He pinned lieutenant's bars on the young man when he was commissioned.

He stared at his best friend's and Courtney, Jr.'s father's tombstone. The simple eloquent white stone contained an imprinted cross and read in carved letters-

COURTNEY L. CASH
2ND LT
US MARINE CORPS
IRAQ
DEC 28, 1981
APRIL 16, 2007

Behind the single white marker, thousands of other tombstones stood tall like men in formation preparing for battle. He sighed and took another drag of the cigarette.

He had slept three hours and needed a change of scenery. Early that morning he drove to the Arlington Cemetery. He touched the tombstone of his friend one last time tracing the name and then pushed himself up.

As he drove away, he could not help but look back at the Iwo Jima Memorial. He continued to drive across the Arlington Memorial Bridge and looked down at the Potomac River. He drove around Lincoln Memorial and turned onto Constitution Avenue. He looked back towards Tidal Basin and through the bursting cherry blossoms; he caught a glimpse of the Jefferson Memorial.

That morning the story broke about the Malaysian nudge and the radio shows were all a buzz about the senator's sole decision. Someone had leaked the story to the press about Courtney Cash, Jr. being the Battalion Landing Team Commander. Across the radio-

"You know for the senator, this is a real litmus te—"

He turned the radio off and parked at the Russell building.

He pushed through the double doors and walked into the chamber of the United States Senate. When he entered the colonnaded room, the entire floor became quieted down.

He always thought the room looked like a cavern and today it was especially imposing, packed tight with every voting member. The upper gallery was also over-flowing with journalists. Camera flashes ignited as he walked down the aisle but the air remained silent.

Normally the southern senator would have slapped his fellows on the back as he walked by. He was often seen talking gregariously or grabbing someone and pulling them in to tell them a secret. Today he walked very seriously, almost in a military march, and spoke to no one. His face looked solemn and everyone in the room stopped and turned to watch him walk by. They all knew the weight of his decision. He stepped down the aisle looking at the other senators who had all decided their vote. They sat behind their desks in each of the four slightly raised tiers.

He sat down at his wooden desk and the silence in the room was broken. Chatter began to rise as the other occupants turned back to their own business. He rubbed his hand on the wooden counter of the desk that had been carved in 1819 and thought about all the decisions and votes that had been cast in its proximity. He looked up to the gallery and could barely see the white marble busts of the first twenty presidents behind all of the people crammed into the upper deck. He looked to the front of the room and studied the American flag framed by two marble columns.

The chatter ceased as the majority leader suddenly announced to take the roll. After the announcement of the joint resolution, the clerk called for the yeas and the nays. There was only a single undecided who would not reveal his position until he uttered either yea or nay. The Senate of the United States would soon make its position known, whether it was willing to transform the world for better or worse.

He was confident in his decision. He pushed up with his left hand to stand erect. His hand remained on the desk steady and sound. He looked down at his firm hand pressing against the wood. He took a deep breath. He exhaled slowly sure of his choice. In a commanding voice he cast his vote.

~ THE END ~

GLOSSARY OF MARINE & IRAQI TERMS

Al Anbar: The largest province in Iraq geographically. Encompassing much of the country's western territory, it shares borders with Syria, Jordan, and Saudi Arabia. Al Anbar is overwhelmingly Sunni Muslim Arab. Important cities in the province include Ramadi, Fallujah and Haditha.

As-Salāmm `Alaykum: An Arabic spoken greeting used by Muslims. The greeting may also be transliterated as Asalam 'Alaykum which means "peace be upon you."

Azzizziyah: Neighborhood in Ramadi.

Cammies: Slang for camouflage uniform.

CASEVAC: Casualty Evacuation.

CAAT: Combined Anti-Armor Team: infantry Marines who train to fight on vehicles using heavy machine guns.

Chai: A thick, sweet Arabic tea popular in Iraq.

Chobe: An Iraqi line dance.

CIED Ambush: Counter IED Ambush.

Crossfit: A strength and conditioning fitness methodology adopted by several Marines specifically those of Lima 3rd Battalion Seventh Marines in 2007 per their company commander. www.crossfit.com

COIN: Acronym for counterinsurgency. A military term for the armed conflict against an insurgency by forces aligned with the recognized government of the territory in which the conflict takes place.

CP: Command post.

Dishdasha: One piece garment worn by men; made with wool commonly dark for winter and white for summer. Also known by Marines as mandress.

ETA: Estimated Time of Arrival.

Fireteam: A small military unit of infantry usually consisting of four Marines led by a fireteam leader.

Flak Jacket: A form of protective clothing designed to provide protection from shrapnel and other indirect low velocity projectiles.

Higher: A general term to identify the next layer of leadership in the larger organization of the Marine Corps. If they are not located at the same location as you higher generally seems to have a diabolical plan to make your life painful. An example would be by keeping all of the sweet cereal, such as Fruit Loops, on the big bases.

Hookah: A water pipe used in the Middle East for smoking tobacco, also called *narghile*. Men often sit in a circle and smoke it communally.

IED: Improvised Explosive Device: a homemade bomb often built using artillery shells, mortar, or rockets.

In šā Allāh: Arabic term used by Muslim's that can be translated as "God willing" or "If it is God's will."

Intel: Short for intelligence, a Marine Occupational Specialty dedicated to collecting information on the battlefield in order to analyze the data for commanders.

Irhabin: Iraqi Arabic for Insurgents.

IOC: Infantry Officer Course: The Man School where Marine Lieutenants are trained in infantry tactics.

Jumuya: A neighborhood in Ramadi.

Jundi: Arabic for solider.

KIA: Killed in Action.

LOO: Logical Line of Operation

Mara'J'on: Arabic term for marathon or any race no matter what the length.

MAM: Military Age Male.

MRE: Meal Ready to Eat. Vacuum- packed meals served in tan-colored plastic pouches.

*Mukadem***:** Arabic term for Lieutenant Colonel.

*Mulazim***:** Arabic term for Lieutenant.

Overwatch: The state of one small unit or military vehicle supporting another unit, while they are executing fire and movement tactics. An *overwatching*, or *supporting* unit has taken a position where it can observe the terrain ahead, especially likely enemy positions. This allows it to provide effective covering fire for advancing friendly units.

*Oguf***:** Arabic for stop.

PTSD: Post Traumatic Stress Disorder: A type of anxiety disorder. It can occur after you've seen or experienced a traumatic event that involved the threat of injury or death.

*Qatana***:** A neighborhood in Ramadi.

Ramadi: Short for *Ar Ramadi*: The provincial capital of *Al Anbar* province. Sits in between *Euphrates* River and *Habiniyah* Canal. Has a population of over 400,000 and sits roughly 70 miles west of Baghdad.

RPG: Rocket Propelled Grenade: A hand-held, shoulder-launched anti-vehicle weapon capable of firing an unguided rocket.

*Sabatash***:** A neighborhood in Ramadi as well as an Arabic word for seventeen.

*Shiek***:** A word or honorific term in the Arabic language that literally means "elder." It is commonly used to designate an elder of a tribe, a revered wise man, or an Islamic scholar.

*Shoukran***:** Arabic for thank you.

*Shurta***:** Arabic for police.

Terp: Short for interpreter.

*Thaylet***:** A neighborhood in Ramadi.

Ville: The area outside of the firmbases where Marines patrolled and interacted with the locals.

***Warar*:** A neighborhood in Ramadi.

***Wasta*:** Iraqi social capital. Having the ability to survive and prosper based on an expansive web of interpersonal relationships and network connections.

WIA: Wounded in action.

XO: Executive Officer. Second in command of a unit.

***Zien*:** Arabic for good.

Author's Note

And

Acknowledgements

There are those among us, men who will rise to the occasion and carry the rest. I'll tell you there is no one brilliant flash of inspiration that defines these men. I would argue millions of small seemingly insignificant events routinely done the right way define them (cleaning your weapon every day, keeping your men engaged by checking on them and letting them know you give a shit about them, walking the lines at night– dark, cold and hungry). If you are a leader you have a choice to be one of these few. I challenge you to be one– make a difference.

While this story is written as fiction it is based on facts. Every story or vignette in this novel in essence happened to some Marine or soldier in Iraq or Afghanistan. The hope is that some lieutenant or sergeant can pull at least one lesson from these pages and expedite their own learning cycle giving them the knowledge to avoid unnecessary costs.

Above all, I would like thank my wife Kristen who endured not only two tours to Iraq as a military wife but also supported this book which is a testament to her patience, endurance and love. The rest of my family also gave undying support and encouragement. A special thanks goes to my sister, Sarah Decker, for her phenomenal drawing which brings the cover to life. I'm also forever indebted to my father who told me at a young age, leading Marines is the greatest privilege an American can have.

I received equal support from my Marine family and a few Army soldiers, which if I were to list them all it would fill the pages of another novel. So to my brothers– all of them– much thanks and Semper Fidelis.

ABOUT THE AUTHOR

Luke S. Larson was born and raised in Washington State and grew up on the Olympic Peninsula with his four siblings. He attended University of Arizona on an NROTC scholarship and graduated with honors with a degree in Journalism. He served as a Marine infantry officer and saw action in two tours to Ramadi, Iraq in 2005 and then again in 2007. He was awarded the Bronze Star with V for valor on his first tour. He studied non-lethal weapons, policies and procedures at Penn State's continuing education program and is currently pursuing an MBA at the Thunderbird School of Global Management. He lives in Phoenix with his wife and daughter.

HONOR THEM BY REMEMBERING...

A portion of this book's proceeds will go to the Eternal Valor Foundation dedicated specifically to the Shaun Blue Memorial Scholarship and the James Cathey Jr. College Fund.

www.eternalvalorfoundation.org

The Eternal Valor Foundation's mission is to facilitate and assist in the creation and management of scholarships, charities and events in order to honor the memory of deceased veterans.

The foundation is a 501 (c) (3) non-profit organization.

4956019R0

Made in the USA
Lexington, KY
20 March 2010